GW00503671

Katie Ward always knew that she wanted to write for a living. After completing a degree in Journalism at the University for the Creative Arts in Farnham, she moved to Dublin. While there, she had a short story published in an anthology titled *Do the Write Thing* which was part of a competition being run by Irish TV show *Seoige and O'Shea*. This story was originally written when Katie was fourteen after she was inspired by an article in her favourite teen magazine. The anthology reached the Irish Bestsellers List. Katie was also shortlisted for a competition judged by Man Booker Prize-winning author Roddy Doyle a few months later. Katie's first novel, *The Pretender*, was awarded a prestigious BRAG Medallion Award in April 2019.

Red Roses is her second novel but is in fact the first book she started writing and is the one that developed her writing skills.

Katie currently lives in Devon where she enjoys singing in a choir, archery and dancing.

Red Roses

RED ROSES

Katie Ward

Red Roses

A CIP catalogue for this book is available from the British Library

ISBN e-book 978-1-9164300-2-0
ISBN paperback 978-1-9164300-3-7

Typeset by Move Design
Printed and bound in Great Britain by
Amazon

Red Roses

This book is dedicated to my aunt Susan Ward
who we sadly lost to cancer in
July 2020.
Also, to all who lost loved ones in 2020/21.

Red Roses

Prologue

Tap, tap, tap goes the roulette ball, each bounce making the same distinctive sound, becoming slower and softer as its velocity gently reduces. The little ball appears almost thoughtful, as if cautiously deciding where to settle. Who will it bestow its favour and fortune upon this time? One innocuous little white ball with the power to make a winner of someone whilst simultaneously making a loser of another.

Never could I have been described as a gambler in life. The fear of losing everything I held dear would far outweigh the thrill of a win. So, the realisation I made shortly after my death seemed odd. You see, life is a roulette table and every one of us is a gambler. Our choices are the chips we place on the table. Each day we hedge our bets, waiting for that little ball to dance across the wheel and reveal whether we win or lose. These tiny incidental decisions silently build to shape and mould our future bringing about the major changes we just can't help but notice.

Now, my death may have happened in a moment but it came about because of one decision I made almost three years previously. Stuck in a rut, I'd been desperate to escape the fears that bound me so I decided to take a gamble and place my bet. Did I lose? Well, time will tell. Invariably, life is a game we all lose in the end.

But does anyone ever truly die? Doesn't every person leave an imprint of their time here? Even the shortest lives can leave the biggest legacies on the hearts of those who loved them. A single memory acts like a solitary spark, keeping the embers of love burning through the most painful of separations. It's these memories that bring warmth to my heart; these are now my priceless possessions.

It is often said that everything must come to an end and whilst that's true, everything must also have a beginning. This story starts at the beginning of my end.

Chapter 1

Seaton Beach, Devon – February 2017

The wind whips past my ears as I sit alone on the cold stone shore, frost coated pebbles shining brightly under the winter sun. Reflected beams dance upon the boisterous waves like magical fairies, captivating me with their beauty.

The serenity of the ocean acts like a magnet to me in times of turmoil and today I sit here in fear of my own future, so scared I'll make the wrong decision; subconsciously, I've stopped making any at all. Unsurprisingly, my life has ground to a halt and I know this has to change.

In the distance, I see the silhouette of a lone figure standing by the shore, a lady who appears to be throwing petals into the ocean. The colour red boldly streaks the sky as the breeze violently whips them out across the ocean. The swirling petals against the crystal blue sky catch my eye. The wind holds them in precarious suspension, causing them to almost sparkle.

After the last of the petals are thrown, I return to my quiet contemplation, casually noting as the lady leaves the shore. How can I make my life as serene as this view? How am I going to take that first step? Where do I even begin to try to break this cycle I feel trapped in? Suddenly, a voice behind me, speaking softly, interrupts my thoughts, momentarily making me wonder if I'd imagined it.

"There's nothing more beautiful than the beach on a bright winter's day, is there?"

I turn my head to see an elegant lady, perhaps mid- to late-sixties, holding an empty basket stood behind me and speaking a little louder this time.

"I'm glad I'm not the only one who thinks that, I always thought maybe it was weird to prefer the beach in winter," I say.

"Well, if it's weird, you're in good company. On a day like this, it's hard to believe anything bad can happen in this world. It's just so perfect, almost magical," the lady adds whimsically.

I smile as I watch her look out to the horizon before closing her eyes for a moment.

"Do you mind if I ask why you were throwing petals into the ocean? It was beautiful." My curiosity piques as I wait for her response.

She raises her head towards the shoreline for a moment as she sits down next to me. "I do it every year on my birthday. You see, my husband passed away a few years ago. We'd been married for forty-two years. Each year since we first met, he would buy me a dozen red roses on my birthday. In the beginning of our courtship, he would have to save up for weeks to buy them." She smiles warmly at the memory.

"He sounds like a wonderful man," I say.

"Oh, he really was and we had so much fun together. But I don't think I ever realised what those roses meant until I woke up on my first birthday without him and saw the empty vase. It made me feel like I'd lost him all over again." The pain visibly etches itself over her face as she speaks.

"So how come you have roses now to throw into the sea?" I ask inquisitively.

"Well, I decided to change my perspective. I buy him the roses instead, as a thank you for all the happy years we spent together. Now, each birthday, I wake up to roses in my vase and the day after, I scatter them across the ocean. It's become my new tradition."

"What a great way to remember him. I bet he'd love that." I pause for a moment to look at the horizon before continuing. "I hope I get to meet someone as special to me as he was to you." I feel a pang of sadness as I remember my ex and the way I had naively felt that we would be together forever.

"My mother always said to me that your heart is your map to love. Do you ever have an impulse to do something but don't know why?" The lady looks at me expectantly.

"Yes, sometimes," I respond quickly.

"That's your heart guiding you to where you need to be. True, it's not just love that applies to but since that's what you desire, I know you'll find it. The quest for love is a lot like shopping for a pair of shoes, you have to keep going until you find the right fit." She chuckles softly as she picks up a smooth cold stone from beside her and presses it gently in her hand.

"You're right!" I exclaim in surprise before continuing. "The trouble I've had over the years trying to find a pair that look great but don't have me in tears at the end of the night." My sombre mood lifts as we talk.

"It's an age-old problem, dear, I remember my mother saying the exact same."

"Was she talking about shoes or men?" I ask with

amusement.

"Both! She knew a good pair of shoes and a good man when she saw them. So, what brings you here by yourself on such a cold day?" Her eyes search my face as if she's trying to figure me out.

"I'm contemplating my life and whether I should stay here or move to Dublin. It's the craziest idea but I can't stop thinking about it." I pull my hair away from my eyes and sigh deeply.

"It's simple, dear, you say bon voyage and go. You're too young to be stuck in God's waiting room. Life is short and you need to fill it with the best experiences life has to offer. I think Dublin would be great for you."

Her enthusiasm is catching but I have a problem. "Well, there's just one thing, I'm actually £30 over my overdraft and I don't have a job. It's just impossible. What I need is a sign of where I'm meant to be and then I can take it from there."

"You could always start preparing for it today even if you don't actually go until later, dear. That way, at least you'd know you were working towards something," she says helpfully.

"That's it; I don't know why I didn't I think of it before. A sign is coming up!" I quickly retrieve my phone from my pocket and tap furiously on it before typing and continuing to tap. The lady watches me, a bemused smile crossing her lips.

"Remember I said I had no money right now?" I say as the lady leans in closer to see my screen.

"Well, here's an aeroplane ticket to Dublin and whether I go or stay depends on what happens when I press the pay button." A pang forms in my stomach. The lady's eyes widen in astonishment.

"Since you're already overdrawn, it's not likely to go through," she says kindly.

"As my witness, my destiny will be decided by what happens when I press this button. If it goes through, then I go to Dublin, no ifs and no buts." I smile mischievously at the lady who beams back at me.

"That would definitely be a sign, there's no denying that," she agrees.

"Exactly, now for the moment of truth." I press the button and we both watch the circle twirl in contemplation, neither of us taking our eyes off the screen as it flashes up its decision.

"Oh my God, it's gone through. What am I going to do?" I gasp as I quickly recheck that I've read it right, a sudden fear gripping me.

"When did you book it for?" She looks at me in stunned anticipation.

"For next week," I admit, which causes her eyes to widen before she looks back at the screen.

"Couldn't your parents help you?" she encourages.

"They might, I mean once they get over the shock of it all. I could always pay them back when I'm settled." A tingling wave of panic envelops me as my breathing begins to quicken.

"See, there's your plan and right here is your answer. Off to Dublin you go." The lady smiles warmly at me with the most positive attitude I've come across in a long while.

A blast of cold air forces me to wrap my coat tighter around me. Glancing down, I notice a single blood red rose petal resting gently by my foot before it's carried swiftly away by the wind. We watch it depart in silence.

"It looks like my husband thinks Dublin is a good choice for you too. So, will you go?"

"Yes, I will," I say decisively. "I don't want to disappoint your husband now, do I? What's your name, by the way? I'm Autumn." I hold out my hand to shake hers.

"I'm Maggie, it's been lovely to meet you, Autumn, and I hope one day our paths will cross again so you can update me on how these exciting plans all go," Maggie says sincerely.

"I have no doubt they will, Maggie. Keep me in your thoughts next week as I start my new adventure in Dublin." As I speak, a wave of fear fills me as I think of what I'm about to undertake.

"Good luck, Autumn, I'm sure it'll be the making of you." Maggie pats my arm gently as she rises to her feet, wishing me goodbye before she leaves with her basket.

To the side of me, I notice the rose petal further down the beach being gently carried away by the wind and for a moment I watch it bounce and tumble across the icy stones, out over the sea in honour of its rightful owner.

Leaving the beach behind, I feel a sense of contentment that I finally have a direction with which to move my life forward, so all that is left is to see how my parents react to my request for their help.

"What the hell are you moving to Dublin for?" is my father's reaction. He isn't pleased, especially when I tell him that I'm going in less than a week.

"Things have to change, Dad. If I stay here, it means giving up all my dreams and I'm just not ready to do that,"

I plead as I feel tears start to well up inside me.

"Autumn, do you need to go next week? Can't you at least take some time to plan a move? What's the rush?" Dad looks at me with concern, folding his arms tightly across his chest.

"Because if I don't go now, I never will, Dad, so please can you help me and whatever you spend, I'll pay you back. I promise." I nervously await their response, catching a glance between Mum and Dad as if they are trying to gauge each other's thoughts without speaking them.

"We don't have a problem helping you, Autumn, but my only concern is why it has to all happen right now? You can't go through life thinking everything happens in an instant," my mum says before adding, "It's up to your dad, Autumn, I'll do what he thinks." She throws her hands up and walks to the sink to continue peeling potatoes for dinner.

"We'll help you, Autumn, but only for two months. If you can't support yourself by then, you're coming home. We'll cover your costs for those first two months. It's the best we can do. Do you agree with that, Brenda?" Dad waits for a response from Mum.

"That seems sensible to me, I'm happy with that. If you can't make it work in two months, you come home. There's your chance to try," my mum says, her voice softening slightly as she dries her hands and re-joins us with a smile.

"Thank you so much, Mum and Dad, you're the best. I will make you so proud, I promise," I say, excited, as I wrap my arms around them both.

"We just want you to be happy and live the life you want to," my mum says wistfully as she releases me from her embrace.

"You'd better get packing since you'll be going in a few days," my dad says. He winks at me before I rush off to my room.

I sit on my bed and replay the day's events; a creeping fear envelops me but I refuse to succumb to it. That time is coming to an end and I finally have the chance to live the life I want to. Now it's up to me to make it happen.

Chapter 2

Five days later . . .

The warming glow of daybreak streaks across the sky. Each minute of our descent into Dublin seems to flood the plane with light as orange gently gives way to blue. While the ground hurtles towards us, I cast my eye over the city below me, wondering which corner of it I'll call home. I know this city holds many surprises for me, but as we touch down with a gentle bump, an unbridled excitement fills me. My friends are out there, my opportunities are waiting for me and if fortune favours the brave, then I can't fail.

Sauntering through the airport, I soak up the new sights and sounds with no idea where I'm actually going. It doesn't take long until I spot the massive queue for the buses which I duly join, sighing and causing the woman in front of me turn around. She gently smiles at me which I return before retrieving the map from my bag to search for where I need to go when I finally get into the city centre.

"Excuse me."

I lower my map and look back up to see the woman in front still smiling at me.

"Are you heading into the city centre? If so, do you fancy sharing a taxi? It might be quicker than waiting in this queue?" The woman asks politely. Her dark brown hair is scraped back into a ponytail and despite her dressed down traveller appearance she still manages to look stylish. She has a cheeky smile that lights up her pretty face.

"Absolutely; I really don't fancy standing in this queue all day. I just want to get into town and start exploring. I'm Autumn, by the way," I say as I hold out my hand to the stranger. She extends hers to shake mine.

"That's exactly how I feel, I'm itching to get rid of my bag and explore as well. I'm Amelia, it's really nice to meet you too," she says.

We make our way into the first waiting taxi. Amelia gives the address where she's staying, while I awkwardly try to retrieve the details of the hostel I've booked from my bag.

Finally, retrieving it, I quickly search for the address to give the driver. "You won't believe it, Amelia, we're staying at the same place. Look, I'm at the same hostel," I exclaim as I show her my confirmation.

"That's so freaky, when does that ever happen? We're hostel buddies," Amelia says, excited as she compares our documents before handing back my confirmation.

"I'm so grateful about that too as I don't know anyone here." I finish tying up my bag before placing it on the floor beside my feet.

"So, what's your story, Autumn? What brings you to Dublin?" Amelia asks.

"I'm moving over here, it's a bit of a spur of the moment thing as I only decided a few days ago," I confess. My cheeks redden under the weight of her stare.

"That's interesting, not at all sensible but definitely interesting," Amelia says. She continues to eye me curiously.

"In fairness, I wouldn't consider myself a sensible person,

I'll admit to that," I say with a wide smile.

"I'm guessing you're not a patient person, either?" Amelia raises her eyebrows towards me with a knowing glance.

"Oh, don't you start; you're not allowed to get all judgemental on me until you've known me for at least a day." I look over at her playfully as I check my phone and see that my parents have sent me a text asking if I've arrived.

"Note taken, I'll reserve all opinions until tomorrow then," Amelia says as she pretends to slap the back of her own hand and we both start laughing.

The taxi pulls up outside our hostel and we both make our way to the reception desk where I arrange for Amelia to share the private room I have booked. Upon entering, it's a clean and comfortable room with twin beds as well as being nice and airy. It has two cute art deco type bedside lamps, albeit made of plastic and a good-sized wardrobe and one chest of drawers.

"Wow, this is actually quite a sweet room. It's not going to win any awards but they've matched the curtains with the bedding. They even have a colour scheme. That's fancy for a hostel." Amelia surveys the room, nodding silently in approval as she places her bag on the bed next to the window.

"I don't normally do hostels but I think this is going to be just fine, I quite like it and to be honest, you can't fault the location. It's right in the heart of everything," I add.

"Do you fancy an early lunch, Autumn? We could have a mooch around the city and I believe Temple Bar is directly opposite us." Amelia lays her map out on the bed to check.

"Ok, I might as well confess it now; Temple Bar is my favourite place. There's a whole street of bars, it's like a funfair for adults!" I say happily as I start to unpack my suitcase and hang up my clothes in the wardrobe.

"Where the hell are you from?" Amelia asks in mock disdain as she kicks her suitcase against the wall by her bed, moves her map and lays down.

"Devon, my village doesn't even have a pub," I say. I put the rest of my clothes in some of the drawers and slide my suitcase into the back of the wardrobe. Finally, I place my phone, wallet and card key into my shoulder bag, which I place on the floor by my bed.

"Ok, fine, I'll let you have that one. But can the country girl cope with city life? Or will I need to carry you home tonight?" Amelia smiles at me mischievously.

I pause for a moment to consider my answer. "Hmm, as yet I'm undecided but it's good to know I have the option." I usher Amelia out of the door and we make our way down the hall and out onto the city street.

Sauntering through Temple Bar, we fall silent as we absorb the sights and sounds. Despite the cold temperatures, people still sit outside, wrapped up warmly, to enjoy their coffee with a cigarette. Amelia comes to a stop outside Temple Bar's most famous pub, the traditional red and black paint blends in to the myriad of colours found in this street. A mysterious look falls across Amelia's face as she silently cocks her head towards the door and I dutifully follow her in.

"Good afternoon there, ladies, now what can I get you?" the barman says.

I instantly notice his radiating smile as he rests his arms upon the bar, his dark fringe stopping just above his green eyes. He looks effortlessly handsome and he clearly knows it.

"I'll just have an orange juice, thanks," I say as I take

a seat at the bar. When I look up again a few moments later, I notice that no one has moved and the barman and Amelia are staring at me, bewildered.

"Would you like some vodka to go with your orange, perhaps?"

The barman awaits my response but before I can reply Amelia jumps in, "Sure, make it a double, my treat." The barman quickly scurries off to make the order before I can utter a word in protest. Amelia smiles widely as she passes me the drink, with the barman still grinning as he finishes making Amelia's drink.

"That's how it's going to be, eh? Looks like you will be carrying me home tonight after all then," I say to Amelia as I reach over to take a straw from the bar dispenser, before swirling the liquid and taking my first sip of the potent drink.

"Ahh, don't you worry about that, I'll make sure you get home ok. Where are you lovely ladies staying?" The barman focuses his eyes on me with a big smile.

"At the hostel across the road, I can't remember its name, can you, Autumn?" I shake my head at Amelia's question as I take another sip of my drink.

"You mean the one directly opposite, the other side of the river? Sure, that's O'Connell's Hostel, your man that owns it went to school with my brother. He's a bit of a gobshite mind but loaded all the same. I'm James, by the way. So, what brings you both to Dublin?" He leans closer, resting his muscular arms on the bar.

"Well, James, I'm moving over here, I'd say permanently but that really depends on a few factors right now. So, consider it TBC. Amelia here is on her travels and we met at the airport quite randomly a couple of hours ago and have become firm friends already." I look over to Amelia with a smile.

"Nice to meet you, Amelia." I watch as James shakes hands with her before turning back to me. "And who might you be? You haven't told me your name yet and I'm not leaving here until I know it." He gives another winning smile.

"I'm Autumn, it's nice to meet you too, James." I reach out my hand to him across the bar. He gently cups it in his own before lowering his lips to kiss the back of my hand.

"It's a pleasure to meet you, Autumn, it's a very pretty name." He gently releases my hand, then adds, "It's my favourite, by the way."

"What's your favourite?" I ask with a suspicious smile as I look over at a smirking Amelia.

"Autumn, it's my favourite season. Always has been and always will be." He nods his head toward some new customers and leaves us to go serve them their drinks.

"Someone has a not-so-secret admirer, he's so smitten. It's cute," Amelia says and I feel my cheeks begin to burn.

"Oh, don't be ridiculous, that guy's the biggest player in the bar. I'm not buying the smitten kitten routine for a second." I've barely finished speaking when two guys interrupt our conversation.

"Hello, ladies, do you mind if we join you for a drink?" they ask politely with a strong Australian twang and as I look over at Amelia, she has the biggest smile on her face as one of the guys pulls up a stool next to her.

"I'm Autumn and this is my friend Amelia." I move to make room for the second guy next to me.

"I'm Noah and this is my friend Ethan," the stranger next to me says and I note that they are both very handsome, with blonde floppy hair and healthy tans making it clear they have not been in Dublin long. Amelia shakes hands with Noah as I shake hands with Ethan.

"We've just arrived from Melbourne for a business trip. We didn't realise it would be so cold, so we're both in need of a drink to warm us up," Noah says, rubbing his hands together to warm them up and flashing a wide grin.

Amelia immediately strikes up conversation with Noah as James wanders over to our side of the bar to serve Ethan. He has a sullen look, narrowing his eyes at Ethan before pulling a strained smile as he takes his order.

"Two Jamesons on the rocks and whatever these two lovely ladies are having as well." I see Ethan smile back at me as James quickly looks away, moving to the other side of the bar. Amelia gives me a knowing look.

"Here you go, Autumn," Ethan says, handing me another drink before continuing. "Cute name, by the way. So, what brings you to Dublin?" He slides two drinks over to Noah and Amelia who are both still engrossed in conversation with each other and fail to notice at first.

"I'm moving out here. It was a spontaneous decision and not exactly well thought out but sometimes you just have to go with your gut and mine was saying move, so I did. Now, I just need to see how it all pans out."

Ethan looks at me in astonishment, taking a sip of his drink before responding. "Crikey, that's brave of you. I can't imagine I'd have the guts to do that. I'm definitely a planner. Don't get me wrong, I can be spontaneous too but not to that degree. I really admire you."

"What brings you over to Dublin then, Ethan? What business do you do?" I enquire, curiously, as I place my drink back on the bar.

"We work in the pharmaceutical industry; we're heading up a big international project so we're here for a month. We've a couple of days before we start so wanted to see some of Dublin as otherwise you just end up going from office to hotel," Ethan says.

As the daylight gives way to night, the drinks flow liberally between us all and the quick drink soon turns into a river of alcohol that takes us into the next day. Stumbling out of the bar together, my hands intertwined with Ethan's and Amelia's with Noah's, we walk side by side towards our hostel.

Stopping for a moment on the centre of the Ha'penny Bridge, I survey the view of lights, reflected up and down the water as if there's a parallel water universe beneath its murkiness. Ethan wraps his arms around my waist and gently rests his head on my shoulder. I turn around to face him, gently pushing his hair off his face as our lips meet.

"Come on, you guys." Our perfect kiss is rudely interrupted by Noah's bellowing. Breaking away with a smile, we once again link fingers and make our way to re-join Amelia and Noah, who drop us off at our hostel before heading to their own hotel.

Lying down on our beds, exhausted from such a long day, the room gently begins to spin in circular motions, making me feel quite ill.

"Autumn, guess who I'm going to meet up with when I go to Australia?" Amelia says with an undeniable excitement in her voice.

"I'm thinking Noah?" I reply with mock uncertainty in my voice, smiling to myself in the dark.

"Of course, he said he can't wait to see me again. We swapped numbers and are keeping in touch. He's so cute. I really like him," she says.

My eyelids are beginning to feel heavy. "That's great, Amelia, he seemed really nice, they both do. Who knew we would end up snogging hot guys on our first day. You should definitely meet him again."

"James looked gutted though when he saw you with Ethan. I know you think he's a player but I'm not sure, I think he genuinely likes you," Amelia says thoughtfully.

"Hmm, I'm not sure, he's got so much patter, I'm just not sure it's genuine. He's cute, don't get me wrong, but I'm not convinced," I say honestly.

I smile to myself as I recall how our first day in Dublin has turned out to be one of the most eventful and fun nights of my life. If this is a flavour of what is yet to come, then I definitely made the right decision in moving here.

Chapter 3

Valentine's Day 2017

The muffled hum from the wakened city outside our window rouses me from my sleep. A searing pain darts across my head as I open my eyes, the brightness causes me to scrunch my eyes and place my palm across my forehead to soothe it.

"Amelia, are you awake?" I utter in a near whisper to the unresponsive figure in the bed across the room from me. There was no reply so peeling myself out of bed, I walk over to her.

"Amelia, we need to get up," I say as I gently shake her, resulting in a groan of protest at this rude awakening.

I make my way over to the sink and see the remnants of last night's makeup still plastered across my face. Walking over to the chest of drawers, I retrieve my makeup remover and cotton pads from the top and clean my face.

"What time is it, Autumn?" I turn around at Amelia's muted question.

"It's 9.30 a.m., how are you feeling?" I watch as she pulls her pillow over her face before taking it back off and placing it on the floor beside her bed.

"Not good, Autumn, we started drinking way too early. I think I'm going to be sick." Amelia rolls onto her side and dangles her feet off the bed.

"Yes, and whose fault was that? You're not going to be sick, you're just hungry. Get yourself up and we can go for a big greasy breakfast and then we'll be just fine. We need to get some paracetamol though; my head is pounding." I soothe my head again before I start to brush my teeth.

"OK, I'm up. Let's leave in five as I need those painkillers as soon as possible," Amelia says quietly as she rummages through her suitcase, unaware that her hair is two times its usual volume and sticking out all over the place.

Within five minutes, we leave our hostel and walk to the end of the street, beckoned by the reassuring green light of the pharmacy on the corner of O'Connell Street. After picking up some painkillers, we find a nearby café, give our breakfast order and take our tablets the second our drinks arrive.

"Take my word, Autumn, I'll never drink again after this and I'm not even sure I'll survive," Amelia says dramatically, taking a sip of her hot chocolate followed by a sip of water as her pale face and dark eyes attest to her hangover.

"You'll be fine, once you've had your breakfast. Oh my God, Amelia, today is Valentine's Day. I'd totally forgotten." I show Amelia the Valentine's menu that's wedged in behind the ordinary one.

"We could have done with meeting those guys tonight really, then we could have both had a sweet Valentine," Amelia says as she takes another sip of her water.

"Well, we don't have to miss out just because we don't have a guy. We can be each other's Valentine. Who says it has to be about love?" Before Amelia can answer, the waiter brings our food.

"I think traditionally it is all about love and couples

though but sure we can do Palentine's Day and it's all about friendship," Amelia says as we take a bite of our breakfasts.

"Happy Palentine's Day, Amelia," I say. I raise my arm to clink our water glasses against each other before continuing to eat our breakfasts.

Leaving the café, the painkillers have finally begun to ease our sore heads; the morning sun shines brightly in perfect contrast to the cold temperatures.

"Since it's such a nice day. I've got the perfect place for us." We walk purposefully across the city and up Grafton Street where we're surrounded by ardent shoppers bustling in and out of the many shops that line the street.

Strolling slowly up the street, we peer into the windows of the shops that interest us. From clothes to trinkets and jewellery, we peruse the wares on offer as we continue to the top of the street where we cross the road towards the entrance of St Stephen's Green. Despite the frantic city life happening on all sides of this park, inside there's an oasis of calm and tranquillity that has to be seen to be believed.

"Wow, this is amazing and the perfect day for it. Good choice, Autumn," Amelia says. Her eyes are drawn to a line of ducks that pass by hopping one by one into the stream in front of us.

Turning left from the entrance, we walk towards the band stand that sits beside the gentle flowing stream meandering serenely through the park.

"Good morning, ladies." We turn to see an elderly man on the path behind us with pigeons perched delicately on his head and shoulders while others feed from his hands.

"Why do all these birds' perch on you like this? Are they your pigeons?" I ask, captivated by the scene.

"No, these are wild birds but I come here every day to

care for them. They trust me implicitly and know I won't hurt them. Here, hold out your hand," he says with a smile. I extend my hand as I see Amelia's eyes widen in anticipation of what is about to happen. The man puts bird seed in my hand and places his hand next to mine. The pigeon that's perched on his hand jumps onto mine and begins to gently feed from my hand.

"Aww, they're so cute and really gentle. I can't feel a thing. I expected their claws to scratch me. I feel I've got a whole new insight into pigeons now," I say, excited. I turn to Amelia with a big smile to show her while she gets her phone to take a picture.

"They are choosy little animals, he wouldn't have taken to you if he didn't want to. But he's very contented in your hand there so he must like you. Did you want to try?" He looks over to Amelia who steps forward and holds out her hand as a bird happily jumps into her hand to feed as well.

After handing back the pigeons, we bid farewell to the man and after cleaning our hands with alcohol gel, we sit beside the most spectacular tree with a ring of daffodils standing protectively around its trunk. Coupled with a great view of the band stand and stream, this just has to be the best spot in the park.

"So, as this is your second day in Dublin, Autumn, have you given some serious thought about your next steps?" Amelia enquires gently.

"It's a simple plan to be honest, Amelia. Firstly, I have to find somewhere to live, which is followed closely by getting a job. I have two months with which to be up and running or I have to go home." I contemplate the situation quietly as I twiddle a nearby stick between my fingers before I gently run it across the ground in front of me, scoring a line in the soil.

"OK, so the first thing you do is get somewhere affordable, just a room in a house and the further out of town you are willing to go, the cheaper. Tomorrow we'll start contacting places and get the ball rolling. Take a leaf out of my book; keep your costs as low as possible so you can enjoy yourself too. What do you want to do?"

"I'm an actress so I'm wanting to get in to that eventually but right now, I'll just take anything to get the money coming in. Then once I can sustain myself, I can start to look for acting roles." I feel a rise of determination as I say this, which I haven't felt for a long while.

"Absolutely, that's the perfect approach. Do you know what, Autumn? You're the first actress I've ever met so when you become big and famous, I can be that smug friend who knew you before you were famous."

"It might be a while before you can say that but hey, let's keep it positive and say that's exactly what's on the cards for me. I promise I won't let my fame change me. Come on, I've got an idea," I say as I get up and reach out my hand towards Amelia to help her up as we walk out of St Stephen's Green and back towards Grafton Street.

"Don't worry; I'll always be here to bring you back down to earth, with a mighty bump if you need it," Amelia says.

After finding the shop, I turn to Amelia with a smile. "When we walked past earlier, I noticed this pretty little bracelet." Amelia pushes her nose close against the window and peers at the delicate silver bracelet with a row of small stones coloured yellow, blue, green, red and clear in a crystal setting.

"It's gorgeous and made from local silver too, what a lovely memento. It's not something everyone will have,"

Amelia says, continuing to peer through the window.

"My thoughts exactly, it's the perfect memento of both our time together in Dublin and of our friendship and since you are only here for a short while and given we are Palentines, I thought we should buy them as a friendship bracelet." I await Amelia's response.

"Yes, I love it. You buy mine and I'll buy yours and let's never take them off. They are perfect, so bright and colourful," Amelia gushes as she opens the shop door and we walk in together.

After paying for each other's bracelets, the store clerk helpfully fastens them onto both our wrists as we happily take a photo of our new bracelets and leave the shop with our empty boxes in a bag.

"This was such a brilliant idea, Autumn, wherever I go in the world I know you'll always be with me. I love it. Now, I did spy a lovely little Italian restaurant last night in Temple Bar. We could go to for dinner if you liked?" Amelia beams as she pulls her phone out of her bag.

"That sounds like the perfect way to end the day. Oh, there is just one thing I need to see before we head back, the Molly Malone statue," I say

Amelia retrieves her phone from her bag. "You lead the way, Autumn, and I'll book us a table. Given it's Valentine's Day, I don't think we'll be in luck otherwise." Amelia taps her phone's keyboard, looking up every so often to follow where I lead, while she finds the correct number to call. Turning just off Grafton Street, I follow the steady stream of people gravitating to Dublin's most famous lady.

"Great to see you, Molly. Here she is," I announce proudly as Amelia clicks off the call before motioning me to stand closer so she can take a photo.

"Just one thing, Autumn, who the hell is Molly and why has she got a statue?" Amelia looks puzzled.

"They were playing the song last night; did you not hear it? It's a traditional folk song depicting Molly's life. But when coming from me there are two versions. You see as a child, I thought it depicted the story of a little girl taking part in a wheelbarrow race who got lost in the woods and died as she wasn't found in time." I start to laugh as I reminisce the memory.

"Well I suppose this cart could be a wheelbarrow but she doesn't look like a kid. So, what's the other version?" Amelia asks as she looks closer at the statue as if trying to accurately gauge her age.

"Erm...that she was a fishmonger by day, selling her goods from this trolley but at night she was a prostitute who contracted syphilis and died." I cover my face with my hands as Amelia bursts out laughing.

"That might be the funniest thing I've ever heard, so innocent in your interpretation but so, so wrong." Amelia continues to laugh as she inspects Molly further.

"The awkward part is that I only found out when I confidently shared that meaning and found out how wrong I was. It was like my whole childhood was a lie." I turn to see Amelia bent over double, hands over her face as she tries to stop herself laughing.

"I had no idea how hilarious you could be, Autumn. I thought I'd heard the most ridiculous part of this story then you just knocked it out of the park with that final bit." Amelia straightens herself up and we carry on walking back towards Temple Bar.

"Did you manage to book a table for us?" I ask as we cross the road and head into a side street leading to Temple

Bar.

"Yes, 8.00 p.m. was the only slot they had because of a cancellation." Amelia's lips curl gently into a smile as if she is trying to stop herself from laughing.

Walking through Temple Bar as the sunlight begins to dim, it seems busy with people already milling outside the pub we were in last night. A rose seller stands on the corner selling roses to passers-by and I consider that this must be a great day for business.

"A beautiful rose for a beautiful lady?" the flower seller says with a smile as she extends her arm out towards me, holding a rose.

"Thank you! But I have no strict no buying myself roses on Valentine's Day rule. Sorry." I smile back at the flower seller and as we prepare to carry on towards our hostel, an unexpected voice from behind makes me, Amelia and the flower seller all halt.

"I'll buy a beautiful rose for a beautiful lady on Valentine's Day." Curiously, we all turn to see who this voice belongs to while passers-by also stop to watch with interest. Turning, we see James in the doorway of the pub, smiling before coming to join me and the flower seller.

"Don't be silly, James, you don't need to buy me a rose." My cheeks redden as he picks out a beautiful red rose; he turns and hands it to me with a smile.

"Be my valentine, Autumn? Let me take you out on a date at some point?" James asks, placing the rose in my hand.

I look towards Amelia whose face is smiling broadly at this sudden display of affection.

"You can be my Valentine, James, but let's not get hasty with a date. I've only ever spoken to you once and I need to be sure you're not a psycho first." I smile mischievously back at him. Amelia drops her head to her hands.

"Well, then you'd better make sure you come in to the pub more often so I can show you why I'd make a great date." James reaches for my hand and places a gentle kiss on the back of it as the amassed crowd cheer in support.

"Fine, I'll come into the pub again but no bullying me into doubles this time. I was totally wasted last night," I say. I smile back at James as he nods in agreement. I wave him goodbye and return to Amelia to carry on back to the hostel.

"You've no game, Autumn, literally zero. You need to check he wasn't a psycho? The fact he took that so well is testament to how much he likes you. Oh, I just love to be right." Amelia has a look of smug satisfaction on her face as I roll my eyes and smile back, shaking my head in denial.

Arriving back at the hostel, we get ourselves ready for dinner at a leisurely pace and as I sit on my bed, looking down at my new bracelet. I realise just how lucky I am to have made such a special friend in Amelia. While she will be leaving in less than two weeks, I know that we will always be friends and can't help but feel that right now, I am living one of the best moments of my life.

Chapter 4

Four days later

The piercing shrill of the alarm reverberates around the room, shaking us violently from our sleep. Amelia shuts it off and crouches over her suitcase to find an outfit to wear.

"Come on, Autumn, we have a viewing this morning and we can't be late. I'm leaving in a few days for my tour of Ireland and I'm determined to see you with a place by then." Amelia picks up her clothes and makeup bag and heads towards the door.

"I wish I was able to come with you as just think of all the fun we'd have." I throw the covers off and finally get out of bed.

"Absolutely, every day I spend with you is so much fun," Amelia says sincerely.

We walk towards the bus station, stopping briefly to get something to eat before we join the queue to board the bus.

"Two returns to the Carpenter pub, please?" Amelia asks politely as she hands over the money and takes our tickets. "Do you know if it's easy to spot as we've not been there before?"

"Sure, I'll give you a shout when it's the right stop so you don't miss it," the driver reassures us. We thank him and take our seats.

"Ok, so I'll give Cian a quick call to say we are on the bus as he said he'll come meet us at the pub and drive us to the house," Amelia says.

"Do you think it is a good idea to get in a car with a stranger?"

"Usually no, but he is lovely and he said it can be a bit of a maze so I think on this one occasion, we'll be fine. Besides, we have each other."

I look out of the window at the changing landscape as we leave the city. The houses seem bigger with more space between them and pretty parks and tree-lined streets become the norm.

After twenty minutes, the bus driver calls out our stop and we disembark with a thank you before taking a seat at the pub entrance while we wait for Cian's arrival.

"It seems a nice area and already a lot better than some of the ones we've seen before. You get a bit more for your money if you are willing to go a bit further out," Amelia says while we survey the immediate surroundings.

"It's an easy distance to the centre, so if the house is decent then it could be the one," I say.

Amelia's phone rings and she answers. "Hello Cian, yes, we are by the entrance. Ok, see you in a minute." Before Amelia has even put the phone down, a blue Mercedes pulls up next to us. The window rolls down and we are both shocked to see a young handsome man with dark brown hair styled casually and a broad smile with cute dimples.

"Heya girls, I'm Cian, it's nice to meet you," he says, motioning for us to get in the car.

There is a slight pause before I reply, "Hi Cian, it's lovely to meet you too. I'm Autumn and this is Amelia." I watch as Cian's eyes hold Amelia's gaze for a second too long and a slight blush appears on her cheeks.

"Ok, let's get to the house, shall we? Amelia, you go up front as don't want your travel sickness kicking in," I say with a knowing glance to Amelia.

"So, Amelia, are you moving to Dublin too?" Cian asks casually as he drives out of the pub car park.

"No, I'm only here for a couple of weeks as I'm off travelling. I suppose after my travels, I will need to actually get a job and join the rat race."

"I went travelling a few years ago myself and loved it, so I'm very jealous. Would love to go back to Australia as just so much to see there, couldn't fit it all in."

Amelia's face lights up.

"I'll be going there towards the end of my trip and I'm really excited about it. You'll have to give me some tips on where's good to go," she says.

"Sure thing, I've got your number so will send over some suggestions. Well, here we are, this is the house," he says as he parks outside.

It's a smart house with a tidy front lawn. On first impressions, it seems quite nice and somewhere I could really see myself living.

A tall lady with gorgeous auburn hair and a big smile on her face opens the door. "Hi guys, come on in, we've been looking forward to meeting you. Nice to see you again, Cian." She holds the door for us all as we walk in.

"Great to see you again too, Kiera. Hey Connor, long time, no see." Cian takes a seat at the kitchen table.

"Did you know each other before or have you met through the house?" I ask Kiera as she fills the kettle up with water.

"Oh, I've known Cian since school. His fiancé is my

cousin so we go way back." She smiles as I feel my heart sink and I see the disappointment etch itself across Amelia's face.

"So, Autumn, what brings you over to Dublin?" Kiera asks, passing me a drink and ushering Amelia and me to a seat at the table with the others.

"I just wanted a change and the chance to pursue my dreams and I wouldn't have had the chance at home, so I thought why not?" I say a little self-consciously. I feel the weight of their eyes upon me.

"So, what's the dream, Autumn?" Cian asks kindly.

"I want to be an actress and I just felt that I wasn't ready to give up on that dream just yet."

"You are very brave, Autumn, and when you get your big acting break, we'll all come to see you, won't we?" Kiera says and everyone around the table agrees.

As we finish our drinks, Cian shows me around the rest of the house. We say our goodbyes to Kiera and Connor before making our way back to the car.

"So, what do you think, Autumn? Do you like it?" Cian asks hopefully.

"I love it, Cian, and Keira and Connor are both so lovely too," I say.

"Great, so let me know tomorrow if you want to take it and we'll get the ball rolling. Would love to have you as a tenant," Cian says.

We say our goodbyes and board the bus that will take us back to the city centre. As we take our seats, Cian gives Amelia a little wave.

"I think he seems to really like you, Amelia, don't you think?" I ask.

"Yes, the signs were all there but he has a fiancé. So, I'm

confused, surely it can't have been a flirtation at all," she says.

"Take it from me, Amelia, it was definitely flirtation on both sides. Yes, he isn't available and it can't go anywhere but the interest is clearly there. Do you want to go to town and talk it over?"

"Now you're speaking my language, I'd love to." She lets out a heavy sigh and drops her head onto my shoulder.

Chapter 5

Three days later

The rain rattling against my window feels strangely soothing. As the downpour intensifies, a crescendo of sound fills my ears. I lay peacefully in bed. Finally, I have my own little space in this land of strangers. My only sadness comes from knowing that Amelia will be leaving in less than a week. I already feel her absence as she is currently backpacking around Ireland but at least I know I will see her in a few days, unlike next week when she leaves for good.

The past few days has given me the space to put my focus into finding a job that allows me to cover my costs but that also challenges me. As I scroll through the endless job vacancies that are out of my reach, I suddenly see an advert for a company recruiting Business Development Managers. Initially, I'm hesitant because I don't have experience in this area but then I see that they provide all training and the essential criteria is only that candidates have good communication skills and enthusiasm. I clearly have both of those in abundance.

So, before I can change my mind I reach for my phone and quickly tap in the number before waiting nervously for an answer.

"Good afternoon, Cross Communication, how may I help you?" There is a pause as I nervously find my voice.

"Oh hi, I'm calling in relation to the advert you have for Business Development Managers."

"Yes, what's your name?" The person on the phone asks in a very officious tone, which makes me feel more nervous.

"Umm, it's Autumn Sutherland." I kick myself for managing to sound unsure of my own name. I feel my face flush red.

"Are you available to come in for an interview tomorrow at 11 a.m.?" The lady on the phone asks politely before pausing for my reply.

"Ah yes, that's fine," I say as she then begins to tap into her computer. The ease in which I get this interview seems a little odd, given I thought they'd want to at least see my CV but maybe it's just a sign my luck is changing. If I doubt it, then it'll only breed negativity and I don't want to go back there.

"Can you make sure you bring your CV with you, Autumn, and we'll email over a confirmation with all the details you'll need. We'll look forward to meeting you tomorrow," the lady says as we end the call.

As soon as I hang up the phone, I immediately call Amelia to tell her; my pulse racing in anticipation that this could finally be the start of something truly fantastic.

"Autumn that's perfect, you've loads of enthusiasm and communication is definitely not a problem for you. I bet you'll be their star employee and all their clients will just love you," Amelia says positively.

"Thanks, Amelia, you're always on hand to make me feel awesome. So, where in Ireland are you today?" I ask enviously.

"I'm in Dingle right now, it's just gorgeous but I really wish you could have been here, it's been so much fun. I'm back in a couple of days so we will need to arrange a catch up as soon as I'm back. I can't wait to see you," Amelia says warmly.

"That sounds great; I can't wait to see you and hear all about your trip," I say happily.

As soon as I finish the call, I saunter down to the shopping centre in Blanchardstown to pick up a new outfit to wear to my interview tomorrow.

The Next Day

Waking up early the next morning, I feel surprisingly relaxed and confident. I check the clock and see that I have plenty of time so make my way down to the kitchen, where Kiera and Connor sit at the table having their breakfast.

"Ooh you look very glam, Autumn, are you going somewhere nice?" Keira says with a smile as she looks up from her cereal.

"Does a job interview class as nice? I'm not sure it does but thought it best to start making some money," I say to Keira as I walk to the fridge to fill up my water bottle.

"Good luck, Autumn, we'll keep our fingers crossed for you as we don't want you home all day using up all the electricity while we're working." Keira winks playfully before moving to the sink to wash up.

"You'll do great, Autumn, no doubt about that," Connor encourages, passing his dishes to Keira who sidles over quickly while the bowl is filling with water.

"Thanks guys, how come you are both off work today?"

I tighten the top of my bottle and place the jug back in the fridge.

Kiera looks to Connor with a smile before replying, "It's our five-year anniversary so we are going away for a few days but our first treat was a lie in. So, we'll be out of your hair for the weekend. The place is all yours." Keira begins washing up their dirty dishes.

"Happy anniversary, guys, hope you have a great time," I say before waving goodbye and making my way out of the front door.

On the walk to the train station, my nerves give way to a hope that this interview will signal the start of easier times for me. A flutter of nerves envelops me as I pay for my ticket and board the train before making my way into town. As I sit down, I consult my phone to find the route I need to take once I'm there. It looks like it's around a fifteen-minute walk towards the other side of the city. I check the time from the station and it looks like I'll have time to spare which is a relief.

Disembarking the train, I plug in my headphones and follow the instructions walking what feels like miles up the Quay until I finally arrive at the office with a sigh of relief and a smile on my face.

I enter the building and ascend the stairs, quickly noticing that the offices seem a bit on the drab side. Continuing up a second staircase to the reception area, a chorus of chatter and a room full to the brim with people greets me. A wall of sound surrounds me as people talk amongst themselves while others are diligently scribbling on clipboards. I feel myself falter. Surely, I must be in the wrong place? I continue towards the reception desk in the hope that they will be able to point me in the right direction.

"Hi, I'm not sure I'm in the right place but I'm Autumn Sutherland and I'm here for an interview," I say hesitantly.

The receptionist silently scrolls her pen down the names in front of her before replying. "If you could please fill in one of these and take a seat, someone will be with you in a minute. Please take these with you when you are called." The fog of confusion that has surrounded me since the moment I walked into the building continues as I perch on a bay window, trying to understand why this interview is being done in bulk.

"Autumn Sutherland and Tom Smith." A suited man standing at the top of the stairs studies a clipboard before looking up to find us. Tom rises, walk towards him and shakes his hand. I join them and follow them both into an office on the lower floor.

"Hi Autumn, Tom, my name is Kevin, please take a seat," he says politely as he motions to the seats.

I take a seat opposite.

He turns to me first with his question.

"So, Autumn, do you think you are someone who can influence people?" he asks with a smile.

"Yes, I believe I'm someone who can influence people and I am also someone who is able to offer support and guidance when required," I reply confidently.

I finish my sentence but continue to keep eye contact. He doesn't look away immediately and I notice patches of crimson appear on the top of his cheeks. He smiles and turns to Tom.

"What would you describe as your best quality?" I notice that the crimson in his cheeks are getting bigger, in fact, as Tom answers the question I notice it creeping all the way down his neck.

As he continues to ask alternating questions to both me and Tom, I find my confidence growing and answer each question fully. When the questions stop, I feel happy with my efforts.

"Well, I would like to thank you both for coming in today. Do either of you have any questions?" Kevin looks at us both waiting for a response.

Since I've managed to go through the whole interview and still not manage to ascertain what it is that they actually do, I decide to ask.

"Would you mind explaining a bit about your company and what it is that you do?" I say as I wait patiently for a response.

"We're a direct advertising agency. We're hired by companies who want to raise their profile with the public. The difference we make to their business is phenomenal. We're able to make our clients market leaders in their field," Kevin says.

Despite this explanation, I still feel perplexed as to what it is they actually do, what the hell is direct advertising? I've never heard of it in my life.

"What does direct advertising consist of exactly?" I ask politely as the confusion I feel crosses my face.

"Direct advertising is when we go out into the field and promote our client's business interests and try to actively drum up business for them." Kevin's smile falters slightly as he purses his lips and looks down at his notes once more.

Suddenly a sickening realisation hits me. "Do you mean like door-to-door sales?"

"Yes, you could call it door-to-door sales but we refer to ourselves as direct advertisers," Kevin says with notable irritation as he nervously scratches his head before closing his notebook.

"So, do you have a salary or is it based on commission?" I fix my eyes on Kevin, noticing how fidgety he has become since my questions begun.

"We do work off commission but it's really very generous and you have the capacity to earn a lot of money very quickly. I would be the perfect example of that, it wasn't long ago I was sat where you are." He happily points towards my chair before lowering his eyes to his desk.

He stands up from his seat and begins to gather up his papers. I notice the crimson in his face is now covering his whole face and beginning to turn purple.

"Well, if you both wanted to return tomorrow afternoon, we'll put you both on trial and see if you've got what it takes. Are you up for that, Autumn?" Kevin focuses on me as his smile twists ever so slightly.

"Sure, why not?" I say, faking a smile despite wanting to tell him to stick it. I feel almost duty bound to come back tomorrow but I figure if I do really badly on the trial then clearly, I won't have what it takes.

The next afternoon, I go in with dread of what lies ahead, knowing that I have no intention of wanting to do this job a second longer.

"Hi Autumn, Debbie, my name is Declan and I'll be showing you both the ropes. We're going out into the field today so you'll be able to see first-hand just what we do. Have either of you had any experience in direct advertising before?" Declan asks with an enthusiasm I find slightly irritating.

I shake my head to confirm I've not, not even bothering to speak. However, Debbie takes this moment to shine.

"Oh yes I've done door-to-door before, so this is second nature to me," she says with a wide grin.

"You'll be a dab hand at this then, Debbie," Declan says.

"How about you, Autumn, have you ever gone door-to-door before?" Declan fixes a glowing smile on me.

"Nope, this is the first time." My answer is glib. I throw my eyes towards the floor.

The clouds thicken above in a threatening manner and it looks like it might be the start of an absolute downpour. I begin to wonder if it's just waiting for the minute we walk out the door.

"It looks like the weather might not be on our side today, but that's usually a good thing as it means people feel sorry for you and you get more sign-ups, so it has its advantages." Declan is emphatic as he gathers up his stuff and herds us out of the door.

While I admire his enthusiasm for the most pointless job in the world, it's likely to wear thin very quickly while I'm being drenched in monsoon conditions. I'm beginning to feel like a petulant child with an attitude problem as we wait for the bus, my mood exacerbated by Debbie who seems just as pointlessly enthusiastic as Declan.

My mood sours even more when we reach the suburbs of Dublin at 4 p.m. The rain that's been looming starts to fall heavily as we disembark the bus. I sigh loudly, causing Declan to turn back towards me before frogmarching us to our first house.

"Come on, girls, time is money, time is money. Sometimes when it's raining hard like this, people will invite you into their homes to shelter but you shouldn't go. If you do, it'll take away from other potential sign ups and you need to capitalise on the sympathy," Declan says confidently with no idea how bad that sounds.

"I know what you mean, Declan, we always go out come wind, rain or shine and it gives you a lot of satisfaction," Debbie says cheerily as she struggles to keep pace with Declan.

"I can think of better ways to spend a Sunday, in bed for instance," I say as I smile back at Declan and Debbie who both look disappointed in me.

"Well, Autumn, you'll be pleased to know that we only work six days a week, but that is only because Irish law doesn't allow charity work on a Sunday." Declan smiles weakly back at me as we continue on our march through the now torrential rain.

What the hell, I'm not working six days a week when all I'm doing is pestering people in their own homes; you've got to be joking.

"Declan, can you tell me your normal working hours?" A fear suddenly grips me that this is effective exploitation.

"Well, from 11 a.m.-2 p.m., we train and practice our presentations then we head out to the field signing up from 2-9 p.m. After that we head back to the office to submit our sales and for the bells ceremony so we usually finish around 11.30 p.m." He speaks nonchalantly as if it would be ridiculous to actually get paid for near thirteen hours of work.

"What're the bells?" I ask in an attempt to hide exactly how I feel about this situation.

"It's to acknowledge the best sellers of the day. Anyone who signs up more than four people in a day are all applauded in the bells ceremony. Everyone has their own unique bells song that we all sing, it's great fun. Sure, you'll see tonight," he chirps as if he thinks I'm finally coming onside.

"I think I might have to see it to believe it?" This just gets weirder by the second and I'm still reeling from the thirteen-hour day and the six-day week. This has to be a joke, right?

"You certainly will tonight, then you'll meet Kevin again and he'll decide which one of you gets the job. I don't mean to make it feel like a competition but it is," Declan says as we approach our first house.

I hate to break his bubble but it's only a competition when both sides want to win and I want nothing more than to lose.

After six hours walking the suburbs of Dublin in the pouring rain, we finally make it back to the office. By now it's 11 p.m., I haven't eaten all day, I'm soaking wet and I can barely think straight. Finally, I'm called into Kevin's office. Taking a seat opposite him once again, I see his smile is very bright given the dark and wet day we've all endured.

"Congratulations, Autumn, you've got what it takes to join us and we're proud to give you this amazing opportunity to build yourself a bright future alongside us," Kevin says as he smiles back at me awaiting my response.

I pause, looking around briefly before I respond. "What about Debbie?" I am genuinely shocked by this turn of events, my stomach sinking.

"Unfortunately, Debbie isn't the right fit for us so you'll need to come back tomorrow for 11 a.m. and we can start your induction," Kevin says brightly as he holds his hand out to mine to shake which I glibly do.

"Sorry, Kevin, but I'm really not the right person for this

role. In short, I just don't want to do it. I gave it a chance but I'm not coming back tomorrow." Kevin's face hardens as I stand up and walk out of his office and down the stairs to the bus stop.

As I wait for the bus, I retrieve my phone to call Amelia. "Hey, just checking when you're back from your trip?" The exhaustion of the day is catching up with me.

"I'm back tomorrow, Autumn, did you want to catch up?" Amelia's sunny voice makes me feel so much better.

"I've an even better idea, my flatmates are away for the weekend so come and stay at my place." She squeals in excitement. As I text Amelia my address, I feel grateful that I don't have to go back to that hell hole again tomorrow.

Chapter 6

Five days later

Sitting on my bed with a hot cup of tea firmly pressed into my hands, I gaze out the window at the crisp and bright morning. The sudden shrill of my phone jolts me, almost causing me to spill my drink. Looking down at the number, it's one that I don't recognise but after placing my drink on the table, I answer it tentatively.

"Morning, Autumn, it's Jacqui calling from Top Temps. So, I've had a job come in that I think will suit you. It's only for a day but it's a start. Are you familiar with a switch?" Jacqui enquires brightly.

"Oh yes, absolutely," I say, my heart quickening with the excitement. After two weeks, I finally have a potential job coming in. The fact that I've never actually used a switch doesn't worry me. I'm a fast learner. Besides, it's only a day so if I'm terrible, there really isn't going to be a lot they can do about it. I'll be getting paid either way.

"That's great, how many lines did it have?" Jacqui asks with a pause for my response.

I rapidly think on my feet; how many lines does a switch usually have? I've no idea but go with a big number to show confidence. "About twenty," I say happily.

"Well, this one has 250 lines; do you think you could

manage that many?" Jacqui asks tentatively.

Oh my God! How is it even possible to have that many lines for one organisation? I try to keep the note of surprise from my voice as I reply. "Of course, I don't think it'll be a problem at all. They'll show me the ropes, right?" I try to keep the shock from my voice. The point is, right now I don't have much choice, I need a job more than anything so there is no way I'm letting this opportunity slip away.

"Yes, they'll show you how it all works and there's another girl there who works the switch full time, they just need you to cover lunch for her."

"Great, it sounds perfect," I say, feeling relieved to know that there will be someone else there as well.

"It's based in the IFSC, are you familiar with that area of town?" Jacqui asks.

Luckily, I've seen the building from the train so I know exactly where it is. I give her my reassurance her that I do. A huge sense of relief envelops me. While this job may only be for today, it's a start and I feel like I'm finally taking a step in the direction I need to go in.

I walk over to my wardrobe and look at the limited options before picking out a simple black shift dress. I pair it with a stylish pair of patterned court shoes with a cute little red flower on each side.

Leaving the house, I easily make the train and before I know it, I'm in the city centre and have easily found the office I need. Walking through the doors with a smile and a sense of confidence, the entrance lobby is elegant and minimalistic with a fabulous display of white lilies. The warmth surrounds me as I leave the cold winter day outside. Removing my coat, I walk up to the desk to announce my arrival to the receptionist.

"Hi, I'm Autumn Sutherland and I'm temping here today," I say warmly to the receptionist. Her expression remains blank while she seems to spend an age surveying my face with great scrutiny before replying.

"You do realise the IFSC is a whole area and not just one building, don't you?" she says curtly.

It takes a few seconds for the realisation to sink in. I feel a wave of crimson flood my cheeks and the pride I felt just seconds ago is replaced with awkwardness, causing my confidence to plummet.

"Oh no really? I didn't know that, I've only been here for two weeks," I reply, trying to claw back any dignity I can while avoiding direct eye contact and sweeping my eyes over the wider lobby.

Her face softens slightly as she produces a map and asks me where I need to go; she diligently marks my path out on the map. I leave through the back entrance as instructed, finding myself in an urban maze of buildings dotted around the river and following the map to find the correct office.

Approaching the reception desk with more reservation this time, I feel a huge sense of relief to hear they are expecting me.

"Hi, Autumn, my name's Belinda. If you'd like to come around and sit here, I'll talk you through the system," she says with a big smile as she pats the chair next to her.

I'm shown the ropes and luckily, despite 1,000 buttons, I only need to remember three –

the pick-up, transfer and hold buttons.

"How are you getting on, Autumn?" Belinda asks kindly.

I look up from nearly cutting the person on the phone off and Belinda again shows me the button I need to press to put them on hold.

"Yeah fine, I think I have the hang of it. Quite easy actually," I say as I successfully transfer the person and end the call with a sense of relief.

"It looks a lot harder than it is; I think it's the buttons that put people off," Belinda says as she turns to me with a smile.

"They're a bit intense; I mean, why do they have so many buttons if you only have to use three?" I ask while I make a mental note again of which buttons those are.

"Beats me, but it does make you look like you know what you're doing," Belinda says as she passes me some letters to put into envelopes as we talk.

"I suppose you're right, no one really notices that you'll only use the same buttons over and over," I say as I fold the letter before realising I've done it wrong and the address doesn't show in the window at the front.

"Exactly and I won't be telling them either. So where are you from, Autumn?" Belinda asks inquisitively.

"I'm from Devon in South West England," I say as I watch Belinda seamlessly do a letter and copy what she does and inspect my perfect fold before sealing it in place.

"Really, you don't have an accent at all, I'd never have guessed. My sister lives in Somerset and the accents down that way are really strong, she can understand them now but I don't have a clue what they're saying half the time," Belinda says honestly.

"Well, I grew up down that way and even I struggle sometimes," I say with a smile as I add a letter to the pile and reach over to grab another letter and envelope.

"How long have you been over in Ireland?" Belinda asks as she checks the time before grabbing another letter.

"Two weeks now. This is my first temp assignment, it

took the agency a while to come back to me and I really began to think that they weren't going to," I say as I recall the panic I had begun to feel at the slow progress on the work front.

"They do take a while sometimes. Sure, I'll give you the name of my agency if you like, it's always best to have more than one agency in case one doesn't have much work on their books," Belinda says kindly.

"That'd be great if you could, every bit of help is really appreciated while I get settled," I say gratefully.

"Hang in there, Autumn, you'll find something soon I'm sure. Are you ok on your own? I'm going to head out for some lunch, I shan't be long," Belinda says as she packs up her bag and gives me a wave goodbye.

I feel a wave of panic as it suddenly feels as if I've only been here five minutes, what if ten calls come in at once? I try to hide my fear and project an air of confidence, perhaps then I'll convince myself too.

"Of course, that's fine. I've got everything under control here. Have a great lunch, it's a lovely day despite the chill," I say. I watch Belinda leave and my smile dissipates as I look at the clock wondering how long she'll be gone. I resume folding the letters.

However, after the first call comes in, I quickly realise that how to work a switch is the least of my worries right now.

"Hello, could you please put me through to Cathal?" The caller asks as I put them on hold and realise that I don't know if the person is a male or female. My instinct tells me it's a female name as it sounds a bit like Catherine but honestly, it's just a guess. Noticing that they have a female PA enables me to circumnavigate that awkward conversation.

It isn't long until the next call comes in and again I'm flummoxed by the caller's accent as I can't understand a word she says.

"Can I book a meeting room please, for an err," the lady says curtly.

"Sorry, a meeting room for what?" I reply politely.

"An err," the lady says with a slight frustration in her voice.

"Sorry," I say awkwardly as there is a slight pause before she responds.

"An err," she says forcefully, irritation evident in her voice.

But I just cannot fathom what she is saying. Sensing her growing frustration, I decide to change tact.

"Sorry, could you spell that for me?" I ask politely. The firm silence my request is met with makes me wonder if she has put the phone down. I cautiously ask again, feeling slightly unnerved by the pronounced silence that has fallen between us.

"From 12 p.m. to 1 p.m." She sighs heavily, annoyed at my inability to understand her the first time.

"Oh, an hour, yes, that's fine." I'm mortified as I realise that I've just asked her to spell the simplest word in the dictionary. I take her name and jot down her booking in the electronic diary and say goodbye, happy to hang up the phone and not speak to that lady ever again.

Belinda returns from lunch shortly afterwards and the rest of the day passes quickly and without any more misunderstandings.

Before long, it's time to leave and as I say goodbye to Belinda and make my way up the Quay to meet Amelia at our favourite pub in Temple Bar, a pang of upset hits me as I realise this time tomorrow she'll be leaving to continue her travels and I'll lose the one friend I've come to rely on these past two weeks.

"I just don't know what I'll do without you, Amelia," I tell her.

"You'll be fine, I've a lot of faith in you." Reassuring, Amelia brushes her hand on my arm.

"Do you think that you'll ever come back to Ireland at all?" My throat constricts and tears prick my eyes.

"I don't know. I've had a great time but there comes a time when you have to stop travelling and settle down. Even I can't avoid that one all my life, although I've done a good job up till now." Amelia smiles ruefully as she says this.

"You get a job and settle down? Don't you think that we're a bit too young for that?" I tease playfully.

"Well I do think that but apparently we're the only ones, it seems twenty-five isn't considered that young anymore." She's playful as she says this.

"Speak for yourself, Amelia, I'm twenty-four. I don't know if I'll ever feel fully adult but I suppose we all have our weaknesses," I say wistfully.

"I'm exactly the same, perhaps that's why we get on so well," Amelia says.

Finding a table away from the bar, we chat fervently but the atmosphere between us is more subdued because deep down we both know that this might be the last time we see each other.

As the evening ends, we leave the pub and I wave goodbye to James as Amelia walks with me to my bus stop. We prepare to say goodbye to each other, a wave of unspoken sadness hanging between us that's really only evident in our moistened eyes.

"You take care of yourself, Autumn," Amelia says.

"You'll stay in touch, won't you?" I ask sadly, gutted to be losing the person who has come to mean so much to me, the tears welling up of their own accord as I fight them back.

"Of course, just try and stop me. You know I've always thought true love and true friendship are similar. It's rare to come across but when you do, you need to grab it with both hands. We'll always be great friends, Autumn, call it a hunch." Amelia wraps me in a big hug and as we break away, I catch a glimpse of my wrist, which puts a smile on my face.

"Absolutely and we have our bracelets, so wherever we are in this world, we are always together," I remind her optimistically as we cross our wrists over the other's just as my bus pulls up to the stop.

With one final hug, I board the bus but continue to wave at her through the window as the bus pulls away and she disappears from sight. The tears that have been threatening to come spill down my face as I realise that Amelia will no longer be here to share my journey. The only thing I can be sure of right now is that I'm about to find out just what I'm made of.

Chapter 7

In the week since Amelia left, we've stayed in regular contact but not knowing when we'll next see each other plays heavy on my mind. I've not worked since my last temp role and I'm beginning to feel nervous about my dwindling funds as I'd hoped to make my own rent this month and not need my parents' help.

My reverie is broken as my phone jumps into life, buzzing against the bedside table. Expecting it to be Amelia, I feel a pang of disappointment when I see the Irish number flash across the screen.

"Morning, Autumn, it's Jackie from Top Temps," she says way too brightly for this time of the morning.

"Hey Jackie." My disappointment quickly subsides as I eagerly await to find out the purpose of her call.

"Are you still available for work? I've a job come in for three weeks, if you're interested? It's a lovely role in a small design firm, I think you'll really like it." She is enthusiastic.

I let her continue the hard sell on me even though there really is no need as I'd take anything right now.

"That sounds perfect, Jackie. When do you want me to start?" I say happily as I write down the pay rate and circle it absent-mindedly.

"Well, it starts tomorrow but they'd like you to go in this afternoon so that the person you'll be covering can show you the ropes before she leaves. Is that ok?" Jacqui asks with a slight trepidation.

"Of course, I'm happy to drop in this afternoon." I feel my heart accelerate with excitement that I will have three full weeks of work.

As we wrap up the call, I work out my weekly pay and feel a huge sense of relief. I'll make more than I need for my rent in just one week which means I can pay for it myself as I'd hoped to be able to.

As I arrive at the correct place, I gaze down the long street of houses, noting how much they remind me of the period properties you'd find in London. I silently count down the numbers of the houses. The further I wander down the road, I notice they begin to look slightly less plush and as I find the house I need, it's far more weather beaten and haggard then the houses at the top of the street.

Pressing the doorbell, I'm quickly buzzed through. I see a pretty blonde-haired girl, her heart-shaped face breaking into a smile to reveal immaculate teeth, hair cascading in dramatic curls past her shoulders. Her bronzed skin makes her look like she's been sunning herself on an exotic beach. She sits behind the desk, tapping loudly into a computer and as I enter, she looks up.

"Hello, Autumn, is it? I'm pleased to meet you." She is cheerful.

"You too, Megan," I reply.

I pull up a chair and sit down beside her as she finishes writing her email.

"So, you found it OK then?" she asks with a warm smile.

"Yes, I thought it would be harder to find so I'm a bit

early," I say a little sheepishly.

"No worries, I did exactly the same for my interview," she says as she smiles at the memory.

"So, how long have you worked here, Megan?"

"Not that long, I've been here about eight months now." She moves a pile of papers from one side of her desk to the other side.

"How come they need a temp? Are you going somewhere nice?"

"I wish. No, my sister has just had a baby, so I'm going to stay with her and help her out for the first few weeks. Her partner is in the forces and only has leave for the birth. So, I'm swapping work for more work." She raises her eyebrows as she motions for me to sit down next to her.

"Well, it'll still be nice to have a break from the office," I say in consolation.

"I'm looking forward to the break but I'm wondering if I might come back more in need of a holiday than I do now. Sure, if the baby likes to sleep as much as it cries, we'll get on grand."

I pull the chair next to her out and sit down, placing my bag by my feet.

I find myself instantly at ease with Megan, due to her friendly manner coupled with an obvious good sense of humour. She seems like someone I could easily get on with.

"Ok, so let's show you the ropes. To be honest, there isn't that much as most of it can wait until after I get back but sure, I'll give you an overview." She hands me a little guidebook she made herself.

As Megan goes through what I need to do, I write a few notes on the back of the guide but to be honest it mostly goes in one ear and out the other as I try not to glaze over.

"I'm sure you'll be fine tomorrow when you're on your own. You can get into your own routine then."

My ears suddenly prick up as my eyes widen when I realise what she's just said. "Are you not here tomorrow?" I ask.

"No, my holiday starts tomorrow," she replies.

Suddenly, I'm gripped by a sinking feeling that all I have are these few hours to get a sense of everything I will have to do in Megan's absence.

"Oh, I thought that you were here tomorrow as well. Oh shit, talk about the deep end," I say ruefully.

"Tell me about it, I asked them to bring you in yesterday or at least for the full day today so I could show you what I did but as you can see, I was overruled by those who know my job better than me," Megan says with evident frustration.

"Don't worry, every job I've ever had has thrown me into the deep end so I'm used to it, really." I try to sound confident but a sense of dread wells up in the pit of my stomach.

"Well, that'll certainly go down well here then, if there is a deep end they will have you in it for sure. Don't worry though, they'll probably go easy on you because you're a temp so you shouldn't have any bother." She smiles and locks her computer, taking her bag from under the desk.

"Right then, I'll take you over to the post office and show you where it is; you'll have to go there every morning to get the papers and biscuits. I don't mind really as it gives us a bit of fresh air and gets me away from this bloody phone, I swear I can't even go for a piss without permission, it drives me crazy," she says with a laugh.

With that we make our way at a slow pace down the

road to the post office, stopping for a few minutes on a wall away from the office so that Megan can have a cigarette. We chat about ourselves as we soak up the spring sunshine for just a few stolen minutes.

"So where are you from, Autumn?" Megan asks before she takes a deep drag on her cigarette.

"Have you ever heard of Devon?" I ask as I watch her puff out a cloud of smoke.

"Sure, never been but they have the rice pudding, right?" Megan flicks ash onto the floor in front of her.

"Yeah we do, that's the place," I say with a smile

"So, what brings you to Dublin?" Megan relights her extinguished cigarette.

"I'm an actress and so I want to get into that, so I thought why not give it a go," I say a little self-consciously, waiting for her reaction.

"Why not, eh? An actress, have you had any roles?" Megan finishes her cigarette before stepping on it and twisting her foot over the butt end to ensure it is properly out.

"I've done a few commercials but nothing much, it was all minor stuff really," I admit as we move to an area on the wall with more sun.

"How come you decided to move to Dublin, instead of London?"

"I was living in London and didn't really like it. It was always too big and busy but Dublin felt more manageable and not a million miles from where I'm from so I thought I'd see what happens." My reply is confident to cover up that I don't feel it.

"Good for you, Autumn, I wish you all the best with that. So, in a few months I'll be seeing you on the TV, will I? Don't forget that you have to be hooking me up with some gorgeous actors and take me to those red-carpet events?" A playful smile crosses Megan's face.

"Sure, why not, I'll be wanting to find a nice guy for myself too. As for the red-carpet stuff, that may be a while off yet but rest assured, when it does, I'll be sure to give you a call," I reply.

"You better do, I love all that glam and glitzy life style, and in my next life, I'm going to be so famous. I can just feel it," Megan says with a little laugh.

"Why not in this life?" I find myself wondering why she would be so quick to write off the life she's already living.

"I left it all too late, spent too much time pissing about instead of working hard. Bet you didn't do that, did you?"

We leave the wall and make our way to the end of the road towards the Post Office.

"No, but I went to a small school and all the teachers knew you and your family, so there was nowhere to run," I explain.

"Dear God, that sounds like prison, I'm glad I didn't go to your school," Megan says.

We reach the traffic lights at the bottom of the road where she points out the post office before we casually make our way back to the office where Megan continues to show me through what I've got to do. But in reality, most of the time, we're just chatting in reception and looking like we're busy when people walk past. We have so much fun, I barely notice the day flying right by us.

"Right, well, I'd better introduce you to everybody or tomorrow you'll come in and not have a clue who anyone is," Megan says as we leave her desk and make our way to the stairs.

"Honestly, I probably won't anyway but at least I'll know their faces if nothing else," I reassure Megan as she takes me from room to room, introducing me to the myriad of faces in the office. Everyone smiles cordially back and some ask a few questions about how I ended up moving to Dublin.

We make our way up the never-ending staircase to the next floor and realise that this office has so many rooms, each one with more people hiding behind their desks. From the exterior, I'd never have realised how many people actually worked inside.

"Hello, everyone, this is Autumn and she is temping for me while I'm away, so make sure you're nice to her, won't you?" Megan says with mock sternness to the room of strangers.

Random faces momentarily bob up from behind their computer to smile at me. Suddenly a lone voice cries, "Of course we'll be nice, we're always nice." A blonde lady around my age pops out from behind her desk as she gets up to join us.

Megan laughs before saying, "Autumn, look out for Stella. She's not to be trusted but I'm sure she'll be nice to you."

"Of course, I will, I'll take you to lunch one day if you like?" Stella offers kindly.

I accept her offer and thank her, feeling pleased that I'm starting a new job tomorrow where everyone seems to be so nice and friendly. To have a job that will enable me to get some money behind me properly and give me a bit of stability is more than I could have imagined so to have so many lovely people around is a welcome bonus. As we leave the office, I say goodbye to Megan and wish her the best and as we go our separate ways, I feel a pang of sadness that I won't get to know her well or the chance to see if we could have been friends.

Chapter 8

Three weeks later…

My alarm energetically buzzes beside me as I reach to turn it off before pulling myself out of bed on what is the last day of my assignment. Never could I have expected to have been welcomed with such open arms; not one day has passed where I've not had an invite for lunch and being this far from home, that really means a lot.

I busy myself with getting ready, holding up a sunny yellow wrap dress with a diamante detail at the side to the mirror. It pairs perfectly with the new off-white pair Mary Jane shoes that I got for Christmas. I scrape my dark brown hair into a half ponytail. Glancing at the time, I rush out of the house to catch the train.

Walking through the door, I cross Stella making her way out of the kitchen with her breakfast. Her blonde hair scraped back into a messy bun and her casual attire is in perfect contrast to most other employees in this office. Her individualism stands out in the best of ways.

"Oh, wow, Autumn, you look amazing. What's with the glam look, do you have a date?" Stella raises her eyebrows at me before taking a bite of her toast.

"I wish. No, it's my leaving drinks tonight, remember? Are you still coming?" I hold my warm coffee cup close to me as I turn towards Stella, suddenly aware that I better not spill it on my dress.

"Absolutely, you try to stop me. So, what's the plan, Mrs?"

"I've booked a little Italian restaurant in Temple Bar for 6.00 p.m. and then we'll head for some drinks. Now, I only know Temple Bar so I might need some help on where to go after."

"Ah here, Mrs, it costs the earth in Temple Bar if you're off drinking for the night but just across the road, there's a great place. They do the best cocktails and it's trendy not to mention the fellas are off the richter," Stella says emphatically as she awaits my response.

"That sounds like a plan, let's go there after for drinks then. I can't wait, I'm so excited." I bid my farewell to Stella and head to my desk to set up for the day.

As the clock ticks down, I finish the last of my work and print out the handover notes for Megan on Monday. I pass the phones through to Stella as I nip to the toilet to redo my makeup so I'm all set for my leaving drinks tonight.

I've not been back at my desk long when the door buzzer bleats unexpectedly, making me jump. Clicking the buzzer, I await the visitor's arrival in reception. Glancing at the clock, I realise this will be my last chore before I finish.

"So, you survived without me, I see?" Megan stands in the doorway looking glam and exceptionally pretty, her blonde curls cascading down her back and her tiny frame looking sensational in a white dress matched with bright pink shoes.

"Oh my God, Megan, I wasn't expecting to see you until later. What a lovely surprise. You look fantastic, by the way," I gush.

"Thanks, Autumn, I got my nails done especially for tonight." She thrusts her hand in front of me where I see her glittery pink nails glisten in the way only fresh polished nails can.

"So, what brings you here, it's so nice to see you. I've just printed off your handover for Monday."

Megan grimaces at the thought of returning to work. "Well, Autumn, I was going to meet you in town but I found out the most exciting thing today and I had to tell you straight away. My brother works with a fella whose sister works for The Gate Theatre and they are holding auditions for a new production, so I've got you the details. You have to go." Megan hands over a piece of paper with a handwritten date and time on it.

"But you need to be invited to attend these; it's not an open audition." I fold the piece of paper up and hold it in my hand.

"Says who, Autumn?" Megan looks at me quizzically.

"It's the rules, it's the way it's always been." I smile back at her as I shut down my computer.

"Screw the rules, Autumn, you need to find a way, even if you have to bluff it. These things are never robust anyway," Megan says sternly.

"Ok, well, I'll have a think about it but thank you, that's really sweet of you. We'd better be going; I'll just call Stella to let her know we're leaving."

I pick up the phone and tap in Stella's extension number. Megan and I lock up the office and go to leave as Stella skips down the stairs to join us.

"Autumn, can I have a minute?" I turn to see my manager, Linda, red faced from running down the stairs.

"Did you girls want to go on ahead and I'll meet you at the restaurant?" I watch as Stella and Megan leave as planned and I walk back up the stairs to speak to Linda.

"Sorry to stop you when you're leaving, Autumn, but we've had another role come up here that's in need of a temp and wondered if you'd be interested. It's a PA role so a bit different but we think you'll be fab at it and it's got the potential to go permanent," Linda says, voice soft.

"Are you serious, Linda? That would be fantastic. I've really enjoyed my time here with you all."

"Right so, we'll see you back here on Monday then and don't forget to enjoy your leaving drinks tonight. I'll see you later for a few, I'm sure."

I skip down the stairs and out the door, meeting the girls in the restaurant. When I arrive, there are balloons and table confetti to wish me all the best of luck and a big bag of gifts waiting on the chair that they have assigned to me.

"Here she is, the girl of the moment. We are going to miss you so much." Megan rises from her chair and gives me a big hug.

I smile awkwardly.

"Thank you so much, guys, but there is something I need to tell you. I feel a bit bad now but as I was leaving, Linda asked to speak to me and wants me to come back on Monday in a different role. So, I'm not technically leaving anymore," I say with a wry smile.

There's a brief silence while the others process what I've just said before the smiles start to appear on each person's face.

"So, we're not getting rid of you at all now? That's great,

Autumn, it's been lovely having you in the office." Stella beams back at me.

"That's great news, Autumn, we can plan some lunch dates. With me being gone for three weeks, I've missed all the fun. Besides, I might need you to help me remember what I'm meant to do," Megan jokes.

The rest of the evening passes in a blur of alcohol and dancing and for the first time since Amelia left, I feel like I finally have some friends who will make my time in Dublin that bit more exciting.

Chapter 9

Two weeks later...

I carefully apply my makeup, being sure to pay particular attention to my eyes so that I pull out the blue and make them sparkle. The nerves bubble up in my stomach as I realise that this is the closest I've ever got to a hustle. However, Megan is right, if the opportunity isn't coming to me, then why shouldn't I make my own?

Reaching for my hairbrush, I carefully style my hair into my signature braided half-ponytail, flicking my straighteners through the loose hair, curling and tousling it into place. The ring of the doorbell makes me jump. I race down to answer the door and find Megan pushing back her sunglasses onto her head with a smile as she surveys my outfit.

"Swit swoo, look at you. Autumn, you look absolutely gorgeous, you really do have such a pretty face and the rest of you looks scorching hot in that outfit too. Are you ready to con your way into the hottest audition in town?"

"Shh! Megan, my neighbours will think I'm a crook. I'm glad you like the outfit though; I wanted to be casual but also stylish. Wait until you see the boots."

I quickly pull on bright red ankle boots with delicate gold embroidery around the laces, which sets off my black skinny jeans and the off-the-shoulder black top I'm wearing.

"Oh my God, Autumn, it's the perfect outfit. Those boots are gorgeous and look quite period but in a modern way, if that makes sense. Trust me; you have this in the bag. Just be confident and you'll walk it."

I appreciate Megan's note of support. As I finish getting ready, she makes me some breakfast even though I feel too nervous to eat. Sitting at the kitchen table, distracted, I nibble at some toast Megan.

"Right, Autumn, it's time for us to go. My car is out front, are you ready for this?" Megan beams.

The sun shines through window as we hurtle towards the venue, nerves swilling around chaotically in my stomach. The traffic is light. Before I know it, we are there and it's too late to back out now. I have to see this through.

Walking in to the room, I see a queue of people around a table and quickly join the back with Megan at my side. A woman joins behind me, her long black hair styled perfectly and her flawless make up makes her look like a film star. We share a smile before I turn back to Megan. I take a deep breath before I approach the table, smiling widely at the lady who sits behind the table with a list of all auditionees which I already know doesn't include me.

"Can I please have your equity card and can you confirm your name?" she asks politely.

"Of course, my name is Autumn Sutherland." I hand over my card and despite the pounding of my heart, I act as if I really expect my name to be on that list.

I watch, daring not to look at Megan as the lady scans the list several times, the confusion etching itself on her face.

"I'm so sorry, you don't appear to be on my list. Who was the agent that put you forward and I'll see can I find you that way?"

I keep the smile on my face but hesitate slightly unsure of how to proceed.

"If I'm not mistaken, Autumn, don't we have the same agent? Aren't you also with Colm Brennan at Top Talent Agency? I'm pretty sure we met at the last social?"

I turn to see the glamourous stranger who was behind me with a knowing smile as she holds up her equity card as she subtly points to her name, for me to take notice.

"Oh my God, Eleanor, of course I thought I recognised you, wasn't that a great night having to call a taxi for Colm as he'd got rather carried away with the tequila slammers. It's happened to us all." I smile back at the lady confidently with no idea why she chose to help me in my hustle but feeling so grateful.

"This is Colm's newest signing and the rising star of our agency so if she isn't on that list now you had better make sure she is or he'll be tearing shreds off you," Eleanor adds with an intimidating smile.

The lady asks no more questions and scribbles my name to the bottom of her list and ushers me into the waiting room while Megan stays in the foyer.

Sitting quietly in the corner, I listen to the excited chatter of the hopefuls around me when my eye is caught by one woman sat a little ahead of me. She is effortlessly beautiful, her face angled perfectly and her cat-like eyes smouldering under her heavy eyeliner but contrasted beautifully with her pale pink lips, which softens the look. She flicks her long honey-blonde hair carelessly to the other side of her head as she surveys the room to check if anyone has noticed her and when she sees they haven't, she raises her voice slightly.

"Oh my God, girls, did I ever tell you about who I met on Grafton Street before he was famous? Can you guess who it is?" She waits until her gaggle give enough wrong answers before again raising her voice to make sure all the room hear.

"Jessie Phillips, he was outside smoking and I asked for a light so he handed me his cigarette to share. It was kind of cute and then he asked me to join him, so I did and we had the best night. He told me I was the only girl who would ever have his heart," she says in a dramatic and over-exaggerated way.

"No way, Mia, didn't he have that song out, 'My Irish Heart?' Oh my God, he totally wrote it after you, didn't he?" One of her friends says with a big smile.

"Well, he'd be hard pushed to deny it but I'm raging he cast someone so plain to play me in the video, I mean why bother with the imitations when he could just get me to be myself," she adds, irritated, as she slowly caresses her hair before letting it fall down her back.

"Wow, he's so famous, Mia, you're so lucky, did he take your number?" her friend asks.

"Obviously, and he texted a good few times about meeting up but he isn't established enough in the US to be a serious contender for me. I mean, how hard is it to find a rich, handsome, successful guy with an international profile that can open doors for me there? If I can't find one, then what hope have any of you got?" Mia sighs, disappointed.

"I think the problem is that they are all in the US and

you are not, but this play will be your stepping stone to Broadway and international stardom. You're such a talented actress, Mia," the friend gushes emphatically.

"I suppose you're right there, I am indeed both exceptionally talented and extraordinarily beautiful, that I can't deny. Perhaps I can invite Jessie to opening night, I mean if we're seen leaving together, that's bound to get into the papers, isn't it? I'd be happy to help raise his US profile when I'm established there," Mia adds thoughtfully.

"Wasn't he was recently married though?" another friend adds.

"Oh Francesca, my beauty is the kind that makes men want to be single and I can't help that. Besides, did I say I was going to sleep with him?" Mia reprimands.

I smile to myself as I inwardly cringe at the vanity of this group of girls and think they would be far more suited to reality TV than theatre.

"Hey, Autumn, can I sit here?" I look up to see Eleanor smiling at me.

"Yes, of course, thank you for your help back there. I really appreciate it." I smile as I turn to her.

"Well, I thought it was pretty ballsy to bamboozle your way in like that, so what part are you going for?" Eleanor asks.

"I figure go for gold, so I'm going to go for Desdemona," I reply.

"Absolutely, my agent would be snapping you up for real then. I'm going for Emilia, the lady-in-waiting so we'll have lots of scenes together. Just take some of that ballsy attitude in with you and you'll be fine," Eleanor says kindly.

"Autumn Sutherland." I feel the hairs on my arms prick up at the sound of my name and the churning in the pit of my stomach resumes, I feel the palms of my hands begin to sweat. Taking a deep breath, I leave the safety of my seat.

After a brief introduction to the panel, I'm asked to read through the script with the actor who has been cast as Othello. I smile as he enters the room and stands opposite me. He has short spikey hair, deep set dark eyes and brown skin that contrasts perfectly against his jumper, showing off his muscular body.

As we read through the script, I'm trying not to focus on how attractive he is.

"Thank you, Josh, that'll be all. Autumn we'll be in touch on Thursday with a decision and thank you for taking the time to audition today," one of the panel members says sincerely.

Despite everything, I feel quietly confident that I did a good audition and if nothing else, at least I can be proud of that. As I go to re-join Megan in the foyer, I feel the weight of someone's stare on me but from this distance, I can't see who it is. As they walk towards me, I realise it's Josh, the actor from the audition, and he's smiling at me. I smile nervously back. Suddenly he stops in front of me. "Hey, I just wanted say how well I thought you did in there. You owned that part, it's clear you have a passion for Shakespeare," he says kindly.

"Thanks, Josh, I do love Shakespeare, *Othello* is one of my favourites and always has been so that's well observed," I reply with a smile.

"Whatever the outcome, just know you did an amazing

job."

I thank him again and we say our goodbyes. As we part, I see Megan in reception. Her face tells me she has seen the exchange with Josh and as my face flushes, I know I'm not hiding anything.

"Autumn, do you know who that was just talking to you?" Megan asks, excited.

"Yes, a fellow actor, I had to read some of my lines with him," I reply.

"That's not a fellow actor, Autumn, that's Jack from *Phoenix Lives*."

"Who? What's *Phoenix Lives*?" I ask, slightly confused.

"It's an Irish soap, consider it the Irish version of *EastEnders* and before you ask, yes, everyone does also seem to have gangster tendencies. I suppose it makes a good story line in any country," she says.

"Dublin has a soap, I never knew, is it good?"

"Well…it has a…cult viewing, shall we say. Most people will say that they don't like it but they still secretly watch it. So, what was he saying to you?"

"He was just saying that he thought I had done really well and wishing me luck," I say with a lot less enthusiasm than Megan.

"Oh my, Jack from *Phoenix Lives* was flirting with you. Autumn, you've been in the country no time at all and one of the most eligible bachelors in Ireland is falling over himself to speak to you," Megan gushes.

"How is that flirting? He's just being nice and supportive of his fellow actors. It doesn't make me special," I reply.

"Well, it's clear to see why you're still single. I hate to break it to you, sunshine, when a guy likes you, he doesn't wear a neon sign. You need to read between the lines and look for the subtle clues." Megan has a look of bemusement on her face.

"Well…he was probably just being kind because he knew I was nervous. Besides, if a guy likes you, he should be upfront about it and stop messing around with subtle clues, I'm not good at deciphering clues; I'm not bloody Sherlock Holmes."

"Bless you, Virgin Mary, but when it comes to guys, there are very few who will be kind for no reason. I mean, in the sense that they'll go out of their way for someone. If they don't care, they won't and he went out of his way to speak to you and that wasn't because of kindness and I know you are not really so dumb as to think it was," she says as we reach her car and I get in to the passenger side.

While there was no reason for Josh to come to speak to me, I'm not yet confident enough to believe that he likes me. The real proof comes in whether he makes any further effort and that remains to be seen. But I feel a pang of excitement at this new possibility.

Chapter 10

Two weeks later...

Two days after my audition, I get the call I've been waiting for, the one that proves my insane decision to move to Dublin wasn't such a crazy idea after all but the leap of faith I'd hoped it would be.

"Hi Autumn, it's Trisha from The Gate. I'm just calling to let you know that we thought you did so well in the audition and really made the part your own. Therefore, if you are interested, we would like to cast you in the lead role of Desdemona?" Trish says cheerfully.

"Are you serious? I'd absolutely love to. Thank you so much," I say as I try to choke back happy tears.

"Brilliant. Well, rehearsals start next Wednesday at 10.00 a.m. sharp. We look forward to seeing you then and congratulations." Trish says her goodbye and we hang up the phone.

A surge of emotions hits me as it sinks in that I've landed my first major part; sadness at the fact I'll have to leave my job but happy that all the doubts have been vindicated in this one moment. I grab my laptop to send an email to Amelia and update her on my news because wherever she is in the world right now, I know she'll be delighted for me. Picking up my phone, I let Megan know the fantastic news as well. Without her, none of this would've been possible.

"No way, Autumn, I'm so proud of you. What an amazing opportunity for you. We'll be hitting those red carpets before we know it," Megan enthuses, almost as excited as me.

"Thanks, Megan, for everything, you gave me the kick I needed to take that chance and see how it all worked out. I can't believe it. You'll definitely be my red-carpet date but it'll be a while off yet, I'm sure."

"Well, if I'd told you a month ago that you were going to take the lead role in a play doing a run in the Gate Theatre, I don't think you would have believed that either, would you?" Megan says.

"You've a point there, I'd never have seen that coming," I admit.

"Good, so we're off celebrating tonight then?" Megan asks expectantly.

"Do you really need to ask? Of course, we are," I say brightly as I couldn't think of a better way to celebrate

"Great, then get yourself round mine for 6.00 p.m. and we can get ready together too," Megan exclaims.

Finishing my call, I feel relieved to know I have the day to myself and make my way to the kitchen to make some lunch.

"Hey, Autumn, are you not at work today?" Keira asks brightly.

"Hi Keira, no, I took the day off today. I've been waiting on some news and just couldn't miss this call," I say with a broad smile.

"Ooh, what news is that? Do you have a permanent job?" Keira enquires.

"No, it's even better than that. I've just been cast as the lead for *Othello* at the Gate Theatre, alongside Josh Bailey from *Phoenix Lives*," I say, excited.

I watch as Keira's eyes widen and her mouth drops to the floor. She looks at me for what seems like an eternity as what I've just said sinks in. "Oh my God, Autumn, that's fantastic news. Congratulations! I'm so happy, what an opportunity that is. You'll have to let us know when it's on as we did promise to come see you."

"Thanks, it would be great to have you there. Rehearsals start on Wednesday so I'll let you know as soon as I know the performance date," I say.

I continue to make my lunch as Keira pats me encouragingly on the arm before she leaves the kitchen.

After lunch, I call my manager Linda to tell her the news and that I will need to finish up my assignment next week but to my surprise she offers to hold my role open. I feel such a sense of relief knowing I will have a job to go back to after this. I call my parents to tell them the news and speak to my mum who is thrilled for me but doesn't fully understand how big this is for me.

"Well done, Autumn, your father and I are so proud of you. We've not seen you in a play since school but we always enjoyed them," my mum assures kindly.

"Thanks, Mum, this is a professional production at the Gate Theatre. Have you ever heard of that?" I ask softly.

"Yes, of course I've heard of the Tate, love, I wasn't born in the middle ages."

"No, not the Tate, Mum, The Gate." I try to sound the "g" to make sure she hears it this time.

"Oh, The Gate, no, I can't say I have, love, but I'm sure it's just as nice. I hope the seats are comfier than the school ones as they do your back in after ten minutes."

"I don't think they will be like the seats from my school days, Mum. So as soon as I know the dates, we'll book you and Dad to come over for opening night."

"That sounds great, love, I'll look forward to a little holiday and you can show us all the Dublin sights," my mum says happily.

"Well, you can tick The Gate Theatre off your list for one," I joke.

I go downstairs to wash up my lunch dishes and put them away before running a nice bubble bath. Upon leaving the warm water, I wrap myself with a soft and fluffy towel and make my way back to my room, picking out a fitted body con dress in port red to the knee, that I haven't worn yet. It looks nothing special but once on, it is such a flattering fit for me and really accentuates my curves in the best way for my diminutive frame. I fold it neatly into my bag along with my makeup, ready for tonight.

Arriving at Megan's, I hastily ring her intercom. She takes a while to answer but she buzzes me in and I make my way up to her apartment. She had been in the shower, and opens the door dressed in a fetching towel ensemble.

"Hey, Autumn, I tell you it wasn't the same without you at work today. Did you have a nice day?" She asks.

"It was so lovely and relaxing. Glad to hear you missed me though. I'm looking forward to tonight." I put my bag down on the sofa.

"Absolutely, got to love midweek drinks, it's like the adult version of misbehaving, isn't it? I thought we could go to your favourite place, Temple Bar? It'll be the liveliest place at this time of the week." Megan tips her head over to towel dry her hair before letting her long blonde hair fall down her shoulders.

"That sounds like a great plan to me." I grab a drink of water from her kitchen and take a seat on the chair.

"Well, we'd better start as we mean to go on. Fancy a gin?" Megan asks despite already pouring me a generous glass.

"Of course, I have to be getting myself into the drinking habit for tonight, don't I?"

As we finish up the last of our drinks and give our makeup the finishing touches, we end by surveying ourselves in the mirror and taking the obligatory selfie to liven up our social media profiles.

"Autumn, would you ever just put those breasts away? I can't stop looking at them; they'll knock you out if you're not careful," Megan says playfully.

"Well Megan, you got the legs and I got the boobs, seems we can't have it all," I say as we leave the apartment and make our way down the stairs and out onto the street.

"I wish my boobs were like that instead of these pancakes," Megan complains as we make our way down the hill towards a busier street.

Hailing a taxi, we make our way into town. The constant rain has thankfully stopped just enough for us to get to the pub without getting soaked. Despite it being a Thursday, it's still jammed when we get there but we manage to prise ourselves to the bar.

"Evening, stranger, you're looking lovely tonight, now what can I get you to drink?" James smiles enthusiastically at me.

"Well, fancy seeing you here! Can I have pink gin and

lemonade and a vodka and coke please, James?" I reply.

James gives me a wink before disappearing to get our order; I feel Megan's eyes boring in to me for an explanation.

"Autumn, do you know him? He made a beeline to serve you the minute you walked into this bar despite it being absolutely heaving, which is pretty handy actually." She smiles at me as he returns.

"Here you are ladies, I put yours in the cutest glass we have. That'll be €14.35." James takes the money from me with a smile.

"Oh my God, Autumn, the guy is practically salivating like a puppy dog around you. He's got it bad." Megan laughs.

"That's €5.65 change, sweetheart." He hands me back the change with a killer smile and I smile back shyly as I take the money and put it back into my purse.

"Autumn, what was that?" Megan scolds me as James goes to the other side of the bar to serve the other customers.

"What do you mean? I ordered a drink?" I sip my drink, waiting for Megan to explain.

"What I mean is why didn't you flirt back with him when he was so clearly flirting with you. This guy would clearly take you out on a date in a heartbeat and you don't even need to try." Megan shakes her head, disappointed.

"Well I know that, he's already asked me out for a date but I told him to hold his horses, I need to make sure he isn't a psychopath first," I say logically as I notice Megan's face drop to the floor.

"Please tell me you didn't really say that? You're being funny, right?" Amused, Megan waits for my response.

"Why does everyone keep saying that? It's funny," I say defensively as a smile creeps across my face.

"Oh, dear lord, you've got a lot to learn. You're the worst flirt I've ever met." Megan shakes her head in disapproval.

As the drinks flow throughout the night, I feel excited that I seem to have so many romantic options opening up for me and I resolve to try and put myself out there and not hold myself back in the way I've been so used to.

Chapter 11

Six days later

Reaching the ornate door of the theatre, a fog of nerves suddenly grips me. Today is the first rehearsal for *Othello*, my first major acting role. I momentarily catch my breath as my steps slow to a complete stop. What if I can't actually do this? The foyer of the theatre is illuminated by the morning sunshine, the deserted space seems to echo my every move as I try to find where I'm supposed to be. Finally, I find another person who is looking intently at a notice on the wall.

"Excuse me; you don't happen to know where today's rehearsal is, do you?" I ask politely.

"Oh hi Autumn, I was hoping that I'd see you here. What part did you get in the end?" Eleanor smiles as she turns to face me.

"Hi Eleanor, it is so nice to see you again. My gamble paid off, I got the part of Desdemona. Did you get Emilia?" I ask her.

"Brilliant, I'm so thrilled for you. Yes, I got the part of Emilia which I was so happy about. Did I mention my colleague is playing *Othello*? I think you'll get on well with him," Eleanor enthuses.

"Is that Josh? We read together at my audition and he

did seem nice," I say, diverting my eyes to the ground.

"He is and a great actor too, you should take it as a massive compliment to be cast beside him. The competition for your role was so fierce. In fact, the girl who plays his on-screen girlfriend also auditioned for that part. She took the rejection badly, but it's hard not to find it amusing so thank you for that." Eleanor chuckles.

"I feel a bit bad now. Did she get another part in the play?" I ask.

"Oh no, if she didn't get the lead, she wasn't going to have anything to do with it. She's not exactly Ireland's brightest star, let's put it that way, but she certainly thinks she is. You have to see it to believe it." Eleanor motions me to follow her.

"I'm thinking I'm lucky to not meet her, she sounds fierce and not in a good way," I add.

"I've often wondered if she's actually a bit unwell as she does seem to have a very distorted sense of herself. We're all used to her delusions by now." Eleanor says honestly.

"So, do you work at *Phoenix Lives* too?" I ask Eleanor.

"Yes, have you seen it? I do enjoy it; such a blast and I get paid for it." Eleanor's smile is broad.

"No, the friend who came to my audition recognised Josh but I've never seen it," I admit.

"Well, it is kind of an Irish version of *EastEnders*," Eleanor explains.

"So, all doom, gloom and gangster then?" I add.

"You've hit the nail on the head right there, all the best elements for any soap."

As we find our rehearsal room, I take a deep breath, walking in behind her. I feel the sudden weight of every face turn towards me, which is a bit unsettling.

"Hi Autumn, it's so good to meet you again, how have you been?" David, the director, shakes my hand.

"I'm fine, thank you, a little nervous," I admit.

"That's only natural but I know you'll be fabulous! I see that you met Eleanor already but let me introduce you again to your co-star, Josh Bailey." David motions for Josh to join him from across the room.

"Autumn, I'd like to introduce you properly to Josh Bailey who is playing *Othello* and Josh, this is Autumn Sutherland who is playing Desdemona. I know you both met briefly before but I'll leave you both to get properly acquainted." David smiles at us both as he departs.

I slowly run my hand through my hair and smile back at Josh, extending my hand towards him confidently before speaking. "Hi Josh, it's nice to meet you again."

He takes a firm hold of my offered hand and smiles back at me. "Hi, Autumn, it's nice to see you again too. Seems we are going to be spending a lot of time together from now on, what with the rehearsals and all." A cheeky smile lights up Josh's face as he gives a little suggestive wink. I feel my cheeks redden but make sure to hold his gaze.

"Well, I hope you'll be gentle with me being new to Dublin." I notice that he is still shaking my hand. It's as if he's read my thoughts. He gently releases my hand and takes a step back. I notice a slight pinkness appear on his cheeks.

"Right, people, can I have your attention?" As David rallies everybody together, Josh stands next to me, a little closer than I'm expecting or is necessary. I look at Eleanor who raises her eyebrows slightly before looking at Josh and then back to me.

"I think he likes you," she whispers before also turning her attention back to David.

As David begins his briefing, I hear nothing, my mind occupied with thoughts of Josh. A flurry of excitement at the prospect of "us" hits me but I rally myself with the reminder that this is my big break and I can't let anyone, not even Josh, throw me off my game. This may be the only chance I get to really prove myself.

"OK, people," David continues. "I want you to get into pairs. *Othello* and Desdemona, you two have to pair up. Here, take these scripts. I want you to read through your lines with each other, get that chemistry flowing, I want to feel the passion," David says emphatically.

Suddenly there's a tap on my shoulder; turning around, I see Josh standing behind me. I hand him his script as a coy smile crosses his mouth.

"So, Autumn, are you ready to feel the passion?" He smiles broadly as I flick through my script.

I feel every ounce of blood in my body rush all at once to my cheeks as if my body is holding a marathon.

"Well, that'll depend on how good you are, Josh. Let's hope you're not setting yourself up for a fall now. Shall we take it from Act 4? There's a lot of dialogue there," I say with a slightly bossy tone.

As he speaks, his voice booms with scathing as if he really does suspect his true love and beloved wife of cheating.

"What is your pleasure?" I gaze up at Josh, I watch him as he speaks, I notice everything – the way his brow furrows in the middle when he scowls, how the dimples etch themselves at the side of his mouth when he smiles.

"Autumn, it's your line now." He smiles kindly at me.

"Oh God, sorry, I was just…sorry," I stutter.

"Upon my knees, what doth your speech import? I understand a fury in your words. But not the words," I say defiantly because Desdemona is not about to lose her ground, even if she's meant to.

"Why, what art thou?" Josh scolds his eye narrowing on me.

"You're wife, my lord; your true and loyal wife," I sweetly reply.

"Come, swear it, damn thyself. Lest, being like one of heaven, the devils themselves." Josh's scathing Shakespearean prose cuts straight through Desdemona's sweetness.

"Fantastic, I can really feel the chemistry, you're the perfect match."

I dart my eyes to the floor to hide how much I wish those words to be true.

"We seem to have already impressed David; you know this kind of role really suits you. You truly are a leading lady," Josh says.

My eyes widen in surprise at this comment and it takes me a few seconds to know what to say in return.

"Thanks, Josh, I'm happy you think that as I didn't just move all this way to fail," I admit.

"Where did you move from? I love your accent by the way." A slight redness appears on his cheeks as he says this.

"Have you heard of Devon?" I query.

"Ahh, rice pudding land, I love it, what would my childhood have been without it. But do you really know how they make it so creamy?" he jokes.

"Of course, but it's top secret. If I tell you, I'd have to

kill you. That's the rule, I'm afraid."

"It's a price I'm willing to pay." He smiles again and I notice how nice his eyes are and how they really sparkle. "So, what made you move over here?"

"Well, truthfully I didn't have enough money to move to a sunny country like Australia and I didn't want to save up, or more to the point, I have never been able to save anything in my life."

He bursts out laughing, puts his hand to his head and looks at me with a stunned expression before exclaiming, "Are you serious?"

"Well not entirely, I'm not very good at saving but I liked Dublin and wanted to go somewhere different and pursue my dreams. That's it really.

"I didn't have you down as being so spontaneous but I like it because it takes guts and here you are doing what you set out to do."

"I'm definitely spontaneous but not usually that much. Perhaps it was fate that brought me here, so maybe it wasn't my choice at all," I say confidently.

"Well, I can safely say that I have never met anyone as interesting as you before. I don't think I would be able to do it now," Josh says frankly.

"Anyone can do it, if they want to. But I honestly I didn't think too much about it, I just did it," I explain.

"Well, for what it's worth, I think you'll do really well. I mean, you already have the lead role in this play. My co-star Mia is one of the most popular characters on the show and she didn't even get shortlisted. It should really pave the way for something fantastic for you," Josh encourages.

"I really hope so, Josh. It means a lot for you to say

that. I say as we continue with our lines.

The day seems to pass in a moment and before I know it David is wrapping up our first rehearsal as he confidently commands the attention of the room before speaking.

"Right, people, it's been a great first rehearsal. This is now a full-time commitment, this is your job, it's not some am-dram hobby," David says sternly. "We haven't got long to pull this all together but we have a first-class team here and I know we can do it. Now off you go and see you tomorrow."

As I pack up my bag and grab my script, I notice Eleanor waiting for me and I smile as I anticipate her questions on how I got on with Josh but before I can reach her, Josh catches me on my way out.

"Well, Autumn, I'll see you tomorrow. You did really well today and I am so pleased to have you as my co-star and I am a tough cookie to please." He raises his eyebrows at me and pats me gently on the arm as he goes.

I thank him for his kind words. Eleanor has sidled up to me and is also saying goodbye to him. We stand in silence until he is a good distance away.

"So, you both clearly got on well. You were both flirting up a storm." Eleanor is gleeful.

"I wasn't flirting. Besides, I think he's probably like that with all the girls." I say coolly.

"He's never been like that with me and I've worked with him for years. No, he definitely likes you. I have bad news for you though, Autumn," Eleanor says with gravity.

My face drops as I turn to face her. "What?" I await her response too eagerly.

Eleanor pauses as if she is enjoying this, before saying,

mischievously, "Well, my co-star who wanted your role will be even more jealous now then she was before. You see, she likes to keep him hanging on a string for her but now it looks like you have cut her cord and she isn't going to like that at all."

"Is that Mia?"

"Yes, that's the one, we're all waiting for the day she actually leaves for her Hollywood fail but despite her announcing all her big and wonderful options on a daily basis, they are yet to emerge," Eleanor mocks.

"Well, lucky for me, I doubt I'll ever have to meet her but if I ever have the misfortune, I'll give her a wide berth," I say happily.

"She's like your one from Mean Girls, she has her little posse and thinks she is queen of the castle. I don't know how anyone can stand her," Eleanor exclaims.

"Josh did? He's a guy, after all," I add.

"He did used to really like her. They dated a few years back but that ended when he caught her in the toilets at an awards ceremony with a well-known Irish actor who shall remain nameless. I think she was seeing him for about a week before he hooked back up with his ex and got engaged but that ended just as dreadfully as you'd expect."

"That's terrible. Josh must have been so upset by that," I say sympathetically.

"Oh, he's no angel himself. He hasn't had a serious girlfriend since, just a succession of girls to pass the time while Mia keeps him where she wants him. She torments the poor guy, but I think he's seeing her for what she is as he just ignores her now. And then today, he was definitely making his interest in you known."

"No, he wasn't, he may have been flirtatious in a cheeky way but that was probably just to get the chemistry between us," I say as my cheeks flush.

"Oh, there was chemistry between you two alright but it didn't need any stoking. You two are both a gas. The only people that don't realise you fancy each other is you. But promise me, as soon as you do, make sure the first person you tell is me and we can scheme to snare him for you."

"What do you mean, snare him?" I ask.

"Honey, if you wait for him to take the initiative, you'll be here until next century. You'll need some insider knowledge to help engineer a meeting outside of work and I'm your woman, I am excellent at these types of things. I love it actually." Eleanor sounds excited to make her point.

"So, you're going to be my fairy godmother, are you?" I ask sarcastically.

"I suppose I am, I've never thought about it like that before but given the performance between you two today, I won't need my magic," Eleanor adds cheekily.

I smile at Eleanor. She reminds me slightly of Amelia. It's comforting that I've found another person who I feel could be an amazing friend.

"Well, Autumn, it was great to meet you and I will see you tomorrow. You can let me know if you're ready to admit you fancy Josh?" She winks as she says this.

"It was lovely to meet you too, Eleanor, and I will see you then. Have a safe journey home," I reply.

We finish saying our goodbyes and I make my way home, feeling that my life has a whole new direction and as if anything is possible. Never could I have imagined that I would have been offered a lead role in a major play but to meet another person I get on with so well with and a gorgeous stranger who seems to like me back was way more than I ever thought possible.

Chapter 12

Four months later, August 2017

"Wakey, wakey, Autumn, breakfast in bed for the birthday girl." I open my eyes to see Eleanor placing down a cup of tea and a chocolate croissant on my bedside table along with two cards and a little present.

"Oh, Eleanor you didn't have to do that, thank you so much. I can't believe I'm twenty-five already. Where is the time going?" I reach for my tea and take a sip.

"You're still so young, Autumn, I'm thirty this year so you have nothing to worry about. Here, open this card and present first. It's from me."

I pass my tea to Eleanor and she hands me the card and present. I tear off the wrapping paper. Opening the box inside, I see a beautiful bangle sparkling back at me with delicate diamonds interspersed around it.

"Eleanor, this is beautiful, it's so elegant and dainty. Can you put it on?" I hold my wrist out as Eleanor unclasps it and wraps it around my wrist.

"There you go, doesn't it look great? I saw it in the shop and I just thought of you, which is how I knew I had to buy it for you," she says as she places the box back on the table before proceeding to sit on the bottom of my bed.

"Thank you, it's so perfect, I love it. It'll be perfect for our girly trip to Amsterdam. Megan will be here at 10.00 a.m. and we can head to the airport," I explain.

"Will she really be here at 10.00 a.m.? Or will it be 'Megan time'?" Eleanor raises her hands by her head, wiggling her two fingers on each hand like fake quotations marks as she says this.

"I hope you two will get on for this weekend? But I did set her deadline thirty minutes before we needed to leave to be safe," I add with a smile.

"Of course, we'll get on; I'm an actress, aren't I? I'm just waiting for the day she lets her true colours show and you can see her the way I do. Although I am grateful she suggested you crash the auditions, obviously," Eleanor says happily.

As I finish my breakfast and put my crockery back onto my bedside table, we both shower, dress and are ready by 10.00 a.m. when Megan is due to arrive.

"So, who is this Casey that's joining us in Amsterdam?" Eleanor queries.

"She's an old school friend of mine, I'm confident you'll like her. It's hard not to get on with her," I add.

"Unlike Megan, you mean?" Eleanor looks at me with a wry smile.

"Exactly, speaking of which she will be here soon so let's get ourselves ready to go," I suggest.

"You know full well she won't be here until she's ready. If I'm wrong, I'll happily eat my words," Eleanor says as she makes herself a cup of tea. "Do you want one?" she adds.

I shake my head no and head upstairs to get my luggage. Checking my phone, I see there's no message from Megan to say she is going to be late so head downstairs with everything to re-join Eleanor and await her arrival.

My phone suddenly flashes as I look at Eleanor, who looks at me with a slight smile. I pick up my phone and breathe a sigh of relief.

"It's from Casey to say she is at the airport and will see us soon," I explain as Eleanor waits expectantly for Megan to message me to say she is late.

The time ticks on, ten, twenty, thirty minutes pass with no word or sign of Megan. I begin to feel nervous as we need to leave now to get to the airport on time. I try to call Megan but there is no answer. I look up at Eleanor who raises her eyebrows as if to say, 'I told you so,' but doesn't utter a word.

"Don't even say it, Eleanor," I say, frustrated at Megan for letting me down again.

"Autumn, I've already said it all a million times. We should just go, text her and say for her to meet us at the airport as otherwise she'll ruin it for us all and then Casey will be left on her own in Amsterdam," Eleanor says practically.

"Ok fine." As I tap into my phone, a sudden knock at the door jolts me.

Rushing to the door, I fling it open to see Megan looking her usual glamourous self with her roller suitcase in hand and perfectly manicured nails.

"Megan, you were meant to be here forty minutes ago, I was just texting you to say to meet us at the airport as we have to leave now. Come on, we have no time." I hurry us all out of the door and into the waiting taxi and quickly lock the door behind me.

Jumping into the front of the taxi, I catch my breath as

we speed off towards the airport.

"So, Megan, what held you up this morning?" I hear Eleanor ask.

"These bad boys and me tan, no way in hell I'm going anywhere looking pasty now. But don't sweat it, girls, we've got plenty of time," Megan says, nonchalant as she showcases her new nails to Eleanor and me, oblivious to how angry we are.

I see Eleanor's eyes flame but Megan doesn't notice. We spend the rest of the journey in silence before we manage to get through the airport checks just in time to board our plane.

Amsterdam, August 2017

We make our way through the throng of tourists, smiles stretched across our faces and the hassle of a few hours ago but a distant memory. We grab our luggage awkwardly as the conveyor belts are full of people eagerly awaiting their bags.

"Autumn, I thought it was you."

I drop my bag to the floor and turn. Both Eleanor and Megan also turning to see who the voice is from.

"Casey, there was me worrying if I could find you. It's so good to see you." I wrap my childhood friend in a big hug as Eleanor and Megan join us with the luggage on a trolley.

"It's so good to see you too, Autumn, it feels ages since I last saw you. I was feeling nervous about if you missed your plane and I was here on my own." Casey smiles as she looks past me towards Eleanor and Megan.

"Casey, this is my friend Eleanor and we are starring together in *Othello* in a few months' time and this is Megan, we worked together." I step backwards to allow the three girls to shake hands.

Making our way outside, we chatter amongst ourselves as we walk over to the tram depot where I take out the map and we plot our stop.

"Right, ladies, we need to get off at Rijksmuseum and it is only a short walk from the tram. Come on," I say. I lead the way, cramming us onto the packed train, the commuters politely making way for us and our luggage.

In only a few minutes, we have disembarked the tram at our station and effortlessly find the hotel, although it is hard to miss with the size of it. The grand and imposing gothic building stands out proudly from other hotels on the street.

"So, girls, shall we drop our bags off and head out for a little exploring and we can find somewhere for dinner and a few drinks?" Casey asks, excited.

There's a chorus of agreement.

As we saunter together down the sunny streets, I feel happy to be away with my closest friends and while it didn't start off exactly as I expected, I hope now we can just look forward to a fun filled weekend.

Chapter 13

August Bank Holiday, 2017

Sitting in the back garden of my parents' house in Devon, I feel completely relaxed as I swing gently back and forward on the rocking daybed in the warm sunshine.

"Autumn, you've got a visitor," Dad shouts as he pops his head out of the back door before going back inside. The figure begins to wander down the garden path towards me.

"Casey, it's lovely to see you. Come sit here, it's so nice in the sunshine." I tap the opposite side of the day bed and pull my legs over the side to make space for her.

"Casey love, did you want a drink?" my mum yells.

"That would be lovely, Brenda." Casey sits down next to me before my mother comes bustling down the garden path with a tray.

"There you go, my loves, some freshly made iced tea with a sprig of mint and some biscuits I baked this morning."

"Thanks, Mum, I miss this while I'm away," I say as Mum proffers Casey a biscuit.

"Well, it's nice to be appreciated. I don't hear much of that from your father but I knew that when I married him. He's the silent type, Casey, only speaks when he has to and it's served us well all these years. If he'd been yapping in my ear all this time, he'd be under that patio right now." Mum places the biscuits back down on the table.

"Mum, you can't say that." I shake my head in disbelief as Casey chokes on her drink and quickly takes another sip to stop her coughs.

"Of course, I can, I've said it to his face many times and he knows I'm only joking. I think he quite likes it actually. Anyway, girls, I'll leave you both to it." Mum continues back up the garden path.

"Your mum is hilarious and these cookies are delicious," Casey says as she nibbles on her biscuit.

"She loves to cook and if you think these are good, you should taste her fudge. No one makes fudge better than my mum! So, tell me, what did you think of Megan when you met her?"

"She seemed nice enough but I didn't fully trust her, she's quite controlling and not what I expected." Casey places her glass back down on the table.

"You sound just like Eleanor. If it wasn't for her, I'd never have got the part in *Othello*, she was the one that pushed me to do it," I say affectionately.

"Well, maybe that's because she sees you as a ticket to the life she's always wanted or the guys she's always wanted. Don't misplace your loyalty too soon as no one can hide their intentions forever and you will see it. Anyway, I have some exciting news for you." Casey smiles broadly, pausing before the big reveal.

"The local paper wants to do an article on you about your *Othello* role in Dublin. My boss was beside himself when I suggested doing a feature on you," she says happily.

"Casey, are you serious? That's fantastic! I'm so excited," I say in astonishment.

"It's going to be great, I can't wait for the whole county to see the great things you're doing over in Dublin," Casey says.

"Well, I'll drink to that." I raise my glass and clink it with Casey's.

"Come meet me tomorrow at the office and we can go somewhere nice to do the interview," Casey enthuses.

"The beach, it'll be so nice and relaxing after the bank holiday." I smile as I think the last time I was there was when I decided to go to Dublin.

"I remember all the time growing up we'd be stripped down to our underwear to go paddling and then have to go home with no knickers on and chafing clothes," Casey says.

"Those were the best times though, weren't they? So carefree and if we tried that now we'd be arrested," I say with a chuckle.

As the sun begins to fade behind the hills and the air starts to cool, I give my oldest school friend a big hug. We say goodbye and I promise to see her tomorrow for our article.

One week later

The phone rings early on Thursday morning, rousing me from my sleep but as I hear my mum answer it, I close my eyes once more to continue my sleep.

"AUTUMN, THE PHONE!" Mum shrieks up the

stairs and I'm suddenly transported back to my teenage self.

Jumping out of bed with a start, I race down the stairs, reaching my mum slightly out of breath, both from the rush down the stairs and the fright.

"Who is it?" I ask, confused since no one has called me on my parents' phone for about ten years.

"It's *Newshour South West*," my mum whispers as she hands me over the phone.

"What? Why are they calling me?" I ask, confused.

"Well, if you speak to them, Autumn, you'll find out." Mum is distracted as she returns to her baking.

"Hello," I say tentatively with the expectation that my mum has misheard who it is on the phone.

"Hello, Autumn, it's Yvonne from *Newshour South West*. We saw the article about you in the *Devonshire Post* and would love to have you on the show to speak more about your role in Ireland. Would you be willing to do that?" Yvonne asks expectantly.

"Yes, of course, I'd love to," I say, flushing as my surprise gets the better of me.

"Perfect, so if you can come to the studio tomorrow then for 4 p.m. and that'll give us plenty of time to have a chat and get you miked and ready for the show. It starts at 7.00 p.m. and we'll get you on around 7.10 p.m. Look forward to meeting you tomorrow."

"Thank you, Yvonne, and I look forward to meeting you tomorrow too." I put down the phone, slightly shellshocked.

"Don't keep us in suspense, Autumn, what did they want to speak to you about?" My mum asks impatiently.

"They want me to go on the *Newshour South West* show

tomorrow," I say, still not quite believing it myself.

"I don't believe it, Autumn, Craig and Sophie will be interviewing you on *Newshour South West*? That's the biggest regional show for the whole South West. That's amazing," Mum gushes before rushing to get my dad in from the garden.

"Right, your daughter has some news she wants to share with you. Go on, Autumn, tell your father." Mum smiles excitedly at my father whose face drops as he looks back to me.

"Please don't tell me you're pregnant, Autumn."

"No, Dad, I'm not pregnant. I've been asked to appear on the *Newshour South West* show tomorrow to talk about my acting work in Dublin. They read Casey's article about me in the *Devonshire Post* and want me on tomorrow."

A smile creeps across my dad's face as he races to give me a big hug. "My daughter, the famous actress. I always knew that you were a special one. Didn't I say, Brenda, from the day she was born, she would be a special one?"

"We need to make sure we have a spare video so we can record it, Frank, will you sort that out today as you know I can't work the video player?" Mum adds bossily.

My dad returns to the garden and my mum to her baking. I walk back upstairs and reach for my mobile phone, gently tapping into my contacts and waiting for the familiar ringtone.

"Hey Autumn, what a lovely surprise. So sorry I've been off the radar, I've been trekking up the Andes," Amelia says.

"I'd expect nothing less, Amelia, I'm glad you're enjoying your travels though. Can you believe it's been six months now since our Dublin days?" I muse thoughtfully.

"I know, I was thinking that too, I wear my bracelet all the time and think of you just like we said we would. So, what's new with you, Autumn?" Amelia asks.

"I do have some news actually. I'm back home in Devon for a visit and I got a phone call this morning asking me to appear on our regional daily news show to discuss my acting role in Dublin. It's quite exciting." I'm still unable to believe it myself.

"Oh my God, Autumn, that is amazing news, I'm so thrilled for you. What show is it and what time? I have to try and make sure I'm somewhere I can watch it as I'm in Peru and we can only get internet in certain areas," Amelia explains.

"It's *Newshour South West* and it starts at 7.00 p.m., I'm the first item so will be on around 7.10 p.m." The line remains silent as Amelia writes it all down.

"I'm going to try so hard to watch it, Autumn, this is amazing," Amelia gushes.

"On another note, Amelia, have you met up with that guy we met in Temple Bar yet? I can't remember his name? The pharmacists on business."

"Noah? No, I don't think I will when I get to Australia as he's gone ghost, he won't respond to any of my messages anymore." Amelia says sadly.

"Are you serious? I didn't think he'd be that kind of guy. He always seemed so nice and keen," I say with real surprise in my voice.

"I know but I seem to have a knack of making even the nicest guys treat me badly. I'm trying to find the positive in that situation but I'm still looking." She says all this in an upbeat way that does nothing to hide the disappointment she feels.

"Well, Amelia, he clearly isn't all that nice but it's truly his loss as you are so lovely and he doesn't even deserve you," I say with sincerity.

"I know, I just found myself really liking him actually. Anyway, what about this actor guy you told me about? Any news there?" Amelia asks.

"Josh? Not really. There's a lot of flirtation between us but I'm not sure if it's something that could progress. He is so gorgeous though." I feel myself blush at the thought of him.

"Well, just enjoy it. I had best go, Autumn, but it's been amazing to speak to you and I'll tune try and watch tomorrow. Good luck and speak soon."

"Thank you, Amelia, have a great day and speak soon." I put down the phone and smile as I remember today's actions.

Lying back on my bed, I tap a message to Casey to see if she is around so I can tell her my big news and whether she can join me on my trip to the *Newshour South West* studios.

Opening the curtains, I see another beautifully sunny day and I can't help but recall how different my life felt just a few months ago and how things have changed beyond all recognition and in a way, I never thought possible. I suddenly realise that the doubts and fears I held only six months ago are gone and I am now living the life I always wanted to live and for that I feel so incredibly proud of myself.

Chapter 14

Three months later — The morning before the performance.

The unexpected ding of the doorbell makes me jump and my heartbeat accelerates with surprise as I race from the bathroom to see who it is.

"Surprise, Autumn, are you pleased to see us?" says my mum. As I look past her, I also see Dad and Casey with big smiles etched across their faces.

"Yeah, I wasn't expecting to see you until after the show but it's great to see you all, come on in," I say as I step back to let them in and give them all a hug.

"Well, we thought we could all go to breakfast together since it'll be such a busy day for you. What do you think?" Mum asks warmly.

"That sounds great. I need to be in town for 11 a.m. anyway for my final rehearsal, so I'll quickly get myself ready and we can head in now." I quickly check the kitchen clock to see it's 8.30 a.m. before adding, "Give me ten minutes and I'll be ready." Directing my parents and Casey to the front room to wait, I race upstairs and brush my teeth before drying and styling my hair, putting on my makeup and finally getting dressed before rushing back downstairs to check that my bag has everything I need in it for later.

"Ok, are you guys ready? Let's go."

Leaving the house, we board the next bus and make our way into town, my mum excited about riding a double decker.

"I couldn't even tell you the last time I went on a bus, let alone a double decker. Let's go upstairs," Mum bosses as she ushers Casey and I towards the very front of the bus where we can sit side by side.

"I'm so looking forward to seeing your show tonight, Autumn. My editor has told me I need to do a review for the *Devonshire Post* as so many people have been asking about it and how it is received." Casey smiles warmly at me.

"At least I can be sure of one good review then, eh? You'll be in good company tonight, Casey, as opening night is the one where all the critics attend. I've never felt so nervous in my life, to be honest," I admit. My heart quickens at the thought of what those first reviews will say. A sudden pang of fear grips me that perhaps I am out of my depth but I take a deep breath and push those thoughts from my mind. I've waited too long for this moment and nothing is going to stand in my way.

"You'll be fine, you've been waiting your whole life for this moment and I'm already proud. Even if you fell flat on your face, I'd still be proud," Casey adds supportively.

"Well said. Casey, your father and I are very proud of you too, love. You've surprised us with how well you've made this work. We both took bets on how long it would take for you to come home but I'm pleased to say we were both wrong," Mum says in a complimentary tone as Casey struggles to keep a straight face beside me.

"Thanks, Mum and Dad, I'm glad you are all here to

make this day so special and even if this is the only acting gig I do in Dublin at least I know it was a great one with such a critically acclaimed director. I'm very lucky," I say with pride.

"They must have seen a real talent in you to invite you to audition," Casey says kindly.

"Well, let's just say it was more of a spontaneous decision that led to my audition but it worked out well." I smile at the memory of how I blagged my way in with the help of Eleanor.

As my parents watch the Dublin cityscape pass them on the bus, Casey eyes me suspiciously. "Why do I get the feeling there's more to this story than you're letting on?" she whispers.

"Because you know me too well," I say with a mischievous smile.

As the bus pulls into the city centre, we make our way off the bus and onto Dame Street and down a side street into Temple Bar where my favourite café sits tucked away from the main city street but in the thick of this buzzing area.

"Good morning to you ladies and you too, sir. A table for four, is it?" The enthusiastic waiter happily ushers us to a window seat.

"So, I'm thinking breakfast is what you're after but sure, I can leave you with the brunch menu too. Do you know what drinks you want, or shall I come back to you in a bit?" The waiter stands patiently waiting a response as we quickly survey our menus before each giving our drinks order. Smiling broadly, he repeats our order back to us before leaving to go and make our drinks.

"Are you nervous about your first performance tonight,

Autumn?" Dad asks.

"Definitely but I'm also really excited but I can't seem to distinguish whether it is mostly nerves I feel or mostly excitement," I reply honestly.

The waiter returns with a beaming smile and places each of our drinks in front of us before placing the tray under his arm and retrieving his notepad from the waist band of his apron and a pencil from behind his ear.

"What can I get you to eat, guys?" he asks brightly.

"We'll go for four full Irish breakfasts, please?" I politely confirm to the waiter as he jots it down thoughtfully before placing the pencil back behind his ear and tucking his notepad in his apron. He takes our menus away and returns to the kitchen to place our order.

"You'll be just fine, my love, I know we'll just love it and with such an acclaimed director. It's going to be amazing," Mum adds comfortingly.

The sun shines brightly in perfect contrast to the cool and frosty November air outside. As we eat our breakfasts and drink our hot drinks, we chat and laugh without a care in the world until the time comes to make my way to The Gate Theatre, for my final dress rehearsal before our show tonight. A twist of nerves flutters delicately in my tummy as I bid farewell to my parents and Casey and walk the short distance through O'Connell Street to the Theatre.

Opening the now familiar heavy doors of the theatre, someone just to the side of them suddenly appears before me.

"Hey, Autumn."

The voice startles me. I step back instinctively raising my hand to my heart as I realise it is Josh.

"Sorry, I didn't mean scare you." Josh steps back slightly, realising he caught me unaware.

Catching my breath for a moment, I smile at him before regaining my composure enough to speak. "I take it you were waiting for me, or do you just happen to hang around the entrance and scare people?" I tease.

"Got to love your humour there, Autumn, one of the things I like most about you. I was waiting to show you something." Josh ushers me down the network of corridors until we come to a succession of doors, each one with different names on them.

"Here we are, our dressing rooms for tonight? And look, we have interconnecting doors so we can say hello but you can lock it too when you're getting dressed. Sure, I don't mind you coming in while I'm dressing but I don't want to be getting myself into trouble now," Josh jokes, his cheeks reddening slightly before he turns to unlocks the door from my side and we walk through into his dressing room.

"So, there's really no getting away from you now is there, Josh?" I say with a smile as I look at his handsome face, my cheeks blushing too when I realise I've lingered too long on his lips.

"Coy, are we, Autumn? Like you'd want to get away from me," he adds with a confident smile and slight raise of the eyebrows.

"Josh, Autumn, I'd thought for a minute you weren't here, stop playing with each other in the dressing room and get yourselves into your clothes and on stage in ten for a briefing," David says sternly to us as we try hard to keep a straight face like naughty school kids at his choice of words.

As soon as David leaves the room, we both burst out laughing before doing as we are told.

"Ladies and Gentleman, don't you all look fabulous. Now, thank you all for your perseverance last night for the tech rehearsal and you'll be pleased to know this is our final run through but be warned, I do not expect anything to be wrong. We've lived and breathed this for months. This needs to be tight, people. Come on, show me what you've got," David pronounces dramatically as he sweeps himself off stage with a flick of the hand to signify for us to also leave and the rehearsal to begin.

Othello Performance - Opening night

Sitting in front of the mirror, my hands tremble slightly as I put on my makeup for tonight's performance. Stopping, I pull the silky black dressing gown tighter around me, noting "*Othello 2017*" embroidered delicately in the mirror. I smile proudly as I run my finger across it gently and feel happy that I get to keep this as a memento, along with lots of other goodies the cast and leads have received. As I resume my makeup with a steadier hand, I find myself wishing Amelia could be here to see all the hard work I've been telling her about these past few months.

Suddenly a loud knock jolts me and I smear mascara across my eyelid. Sighing heavily, I reach for a cotton bud as I shout, "Come in," while I try to salvage my makeup.

"Autumn, there's a delivery that's come for you." I turn to see a runner with a large bouquet of flowers. I check for a note to see who they are from. My heart beats fast.

The card reads:

"Wish I could be there with you tonight in person but since I can't, take these flowers as a sign of my love and support for you on your big night. Love Amelia x." I smile as I take the flowers and place them prominently in my dressing room.

Finishing my makeup, my hair is curled into flowing waves and braided across the top before tumbling down past my shoulders. With the help of my costume assistant, Ella, I step into the first dress of the night, the corseted waist pulled tight as was common amongst the elite of the time. The rods pull deeper as the corset tightens and the dress is fastened laboriously at the back.

"That's it, Autumn, you're ready to go. What do you think?" Ella asks.

Taking a look in the mirror, I hardly recognise myself. I've been transformed into a Venetian noblewoman from a bygone era, the sumptuous orange and gold of my dress, the oversized sleeves that sweep down and ruffle at the wrists. My waist looks impossibly tiny, not just from the corset but the embroidery that pulls your eye in even more before ballooning out into a full skirt of many layers synonymous with the Elizabethan period.

"Wow, it's amazing. I don't even see myself when I look in the mirror," I admit.

"I'll take that as a job well done then. Come on, it's nearly time for your first scene." Ella smiles warmly at me before we leave my dressing room. Just before the stage, we part. I wait patiently for my cue to enter the wings of the stage. In the silence of this moment, I take a deep breath as Eleanor joins me and we smile broadly at each other but stay silent.

A few moments later, we are ushered up into the wings of the stage. Eleanor and I stand beside the actor playing Iago.

"When you hear the word 'witness,' I want you to all walk on together, ok?" the production assistant whispers to us before following up the point with a sweep of her hands when the word is uttered.

As we stride onto the stage, I see a sea of darkened faces and lights. Despite thinking I'd feel nervous in this moment, my fears leave me and I approach Josh in his character of Othello, the husband of Desdemona who is in fierce conversation with her father Brabantio, a Venetian Senator who has just discovered the secret marriage of his daughter to Othello. Having always assumed Desdemona was a good daughter who would always follow his rules, Brabantio concludes that Othello must have bewitched her in order to convince her to marry him as there is no other way she would disobey her beloved father.

"Come here, Desdemona. Where in all this noble company do you perceive you owe most obedience?" Brabantio looks crossly at Desdemona, awaiting her response before his eyes flick to Othello, a distinguished young soldier of wealth and African descent.

"My noble father, I perceive here a divided duty; to you I am bound for life. But here is my husband and I show him the same duty my mother showed to you, preferring you before her father." Desdemona looks to her father for understanding, a sign that he will support her marriage before stepping back from her father and taking the arm of her husband. Her choice clearly made for all to see, she stands by her husband and their marriage even against her father's wishes. Unbeknownst to Desdemona, this act seals her own tragic fate at the hands of her husband due to the coercive manipulation of Iago, a trusted confidant who harbours a seething resentment. After acquiring a handkerchief given to Desdemona by Othello, he plants it in another man's room who then gives it to Bianca.

"A likely piece of work, that you should find it in your chamber and not know who left it there. This is some minx's token," Bianca says scornfully as she tosses the handkerchief back at Cassio as Othello and Iago look on. A look of recognition flickers across Othello's face as he recognises it to be the one he gave Desdemona. As Bianca and Cassio leave, Othello's face hardens.

"How shall I murder him, Iago?" Othello says venomously as he watches them leave.

"See how he prizes your foolish wife! She gave it to him and he has given it to his whore," Iago says with feigned concern.

"Let her rot and perish, for she shall not live, no my heart has turned to stone," Othello says contemptuously.

"Don't do it with poison, strangle her in her the bed that she has contaminated," Iago adds with malice.

"Yes, the justice of that pleases me." Othello is cold.

As the play draws towards its close, the scene moves to Desdemona's bed chamber. Othello enters as she sleeps. Gently, he awakens her.

"Have you prayed tonight, Desdemona?" he asks softly as she responds that she has. "I would not kill your unprepared spirit."

"I hope you will not kill me. Yet, I fear you. Why I should fear I don't know since I'm not guilty but yet I fear you," Desdemona replies in saddened calmness as she surveys the coldness he holds for her in his eyes.

"Think on your sins," Othello says as he turns to face his wife.

"They are loves I bear to you," she pleads in the hope of making him see the love she still holds for him.

"And for that you die," Othello says as he moves off the bed where his wife stays before adding, "That handkerchief I so loved and gave you, you gave to Cassio." His voice hardens and he turns to see Desdemona's reaction.

"No, by my life and soul. Send for the man and ask him." Desdemona kneels at the end of her bed as she appeals to her husband to believe her. The gravity of the accusations catches her off-guard, her heart silently breaking within her chest.

"No, his mouth is stopped. Honest, Iago has taken an order for it," Othello says as he moves towards Desdemona in her bed menacingly.

Instinctively, she backs away. "Then he has been betrayed and I am undone," Desdemona says with heavy resignation and acceptance of her impending death, looking up into the face of her husband, his handsome features turned to stone with hatred. The memory of his loving smile and warm embrace, the fire of love that always burnt bright within him for her, has been cooled by misguided suspicion but from where is a mystery. His murderous gaze is almost harder to bear than her impending death.

"Kill me tomorrow, let me live tonight," she says pleadingly as she holds his gaze in the hope he will feel her love one last time and come to his senses.

Othello gazes at his wife, lingering on the face that

bewitched him from the moment he saw her and how even now no other woman could come close to her in his heart.

"It's too late," he says gently but with unfaltering confidence in the action he is about to take.

The pain of her infidelity cuts with excruciating agony as he steps towards her, picks up the pillow from beside her. A small smile of resignation flickers across her lips as she takes a moment to look at him one last time before lying down. Othello firmly holds the pillow over her face. Desdemona offers no resistance, no struggle, silently accepting the will of her husband to end her life.

Othello removes the pillow and sits with Desdemona until he is roused by the furious knocking of Emilia, sent by Iago to tell him of Cassio's injury after being set upon and stabbed. After observing her mistress's body, lying dead in her bed, she is horrified to discover Othello's blind acceptance of Desdemona's infidelity. Even when she tells him she never left his side, he refuses to believe her.

"Iago knows that she was with Cassio, that she gratified her love for him with the handkerchief from my mother, I saw it in his hand," Othello says venomously as Iago enters the room with two others behind him.

At the sound of her husband's name, all colour drains from Emelia's face as she turns to him, her face hardening as steps towards her.

"You fool, Othello, that handkerchief you speak of, I found by fortune and gave to my husband because he had often begged for me to steal it. She gave it to Cassio? No, I found it and gave it to Iago," Emilia says as she looks back to Desdemona's bed.

The truth takes mere seconds to sink in. The pain courses through every inch of Othello's body as Iago's betrayal unfolds before him. Turning with unbridled anger, he lunges at Iago who stabs Emilia before fleeing. Iago is quickly recaptured and brought back as Othello's position and rank is transferred to Cassio, his deputy.

Before he can be arrested, Othello falls onto Desdemona in grief. "I kissed you here, I killed you here, there is no way but to kill myself and die upon this kiss." He pulls a concealed dagger as he kisses his wife gently on her lips and plunges it into his heart, which never stopped overflowing with love for her but his pride and ego had blinded him and numbed his heart to ice.

After the performance

As the curtain closes for the final time on our first performance, we all file silently away from the stage. The hustle and bustle of the audience resounds through the theatre.

"Autumn, you were so phenomenal tonight, you really were," Josh says as he takes me to one side and lowers his voice, adding, "You'd give half my co-stars a run for their money so don't forget that." He smiles at me and for a moment we stand in silence before walking back to our dressing rooms.

"Thanks, Josh, that really means a lot. My confidence hasn't really been there for the last few years so this show has just been the making of me. I'm loving every second of it." As we reach our rooms, I give him a hug before dashing back into my room to take off my costume, the corset digging painfully and chaffing my skin.

As I await my parents, Casey, Megan, Cian and Keira to join me in my dressing room, I pull out my phone to send Amelia a quick thank you message when suddenly there is a knock at my door.

"What did you guys think?" I ask as I fling the door open but my parents, Casey, Megan, Cian and Keira are not there. It takes a second for me to realise and my face drops in shock as I let out an excited squeal and leap to hug Amelia who is standing at my door.

"What are you doing here? I thought you were travelling?" I look at the friend I haven't seen in months and the tears start to fill my eyes.

"I was but I changed my flights to come back earlier. Since I was planning to come home for Christmas, I figured a couple of weeks wouldn't make a difference and I couldn't miss your big debut." Amelia sits down in my room and we catch up on all the things we have missed since she has been gone.

My parents, Casey, Megan, Cian and Keira meet us not long after. With Josh and Eleanor, we all head together to the first night party.

Chapter 15

The chill of the November night hits us as we leave the theatre, making our way to the party taking place on the docks.

"I've never been to an after party before, love, this is all very exciting. Do you think there will be food?" Mum asks eagerly.

"You'll be in luck there, Brenda. There is the most amazing food and free drinks all night. These parties are always the highlight of the year," Josh assures her.

Mum, Dad, Josh, Casey, Cian, Keira and Megan walk ahead chatting together as Amelia and Eleanor walk at a slower pace alongside the River Liffey, which splits the city in two and causes the lights to sparkle from every angle.

"So, you know who you'll get to meet tonight, don't you?" Eleanor asks coyly.

"No, surely I've met everyone already," I say, intrigued.

"These parties are always open to the most well-known stars in Irish TV so you will finally cross paths with the illustrious Mia. Trust me when I say she'll make a beeline for you," Eleanor says.

"Who's Mia?" Amelia asks.

"She's a co-star of ours on *Phoenix Lives* but Autumn beat her to this role," Eleanor says with a flair of mock tension.

"Finally, I'll be able to put a bitch to the face," I reply and we all laugh.

"I knew there was a reason I liked you, Autumn," Eleanor says.

We all make our way into the venue. We hand our coats and bags to the cloakroom when I suddenly feel a firm grip on my shoulders.

"And here they are, the man and woman of the moment. Autumn, can I steal you and Josh away? I've got some people for you to meet." David ushers both into the main room as I leave my friends and parents in the lobby.

"Derek, I'd like you to meet Autumn Sutherland, you already know Josh. Autumn, this is Derek Kelly, he is the Executive Producer for *Phoenix Lives*." David steps aside as I step closer to shake Derek's outstretched hand.

"It's nice to meet you, Derek, I hope you enjoyed the show?" I ask politely as we break hands and I step back.

"It was wonderful and such a stunning portrayal, you made me believe that Desdemona's meek and passive nature was all your own," Derek says kindly.

My cheeks redden at the compliment. "Thank you, Derek, that means a lot. This is one of my favourite Shakespeare plays so I really wanted to do it justice."

"There's no doubt you did just that, Autumn, don't you think, Josh?" David looks to Josh for his opinion.

"Absolutely, I would go as far as saying that Autumn is by far the most talented leading lady I've ever acted alongside. There's just no comparison," Josh says.

The sound of a glass shattering across the floor fills

the air. As we all look behind us, we see the girl from my audition. Our eyes lock briefly before she turns and snaps her fingers twice to get the attention of a passing waiter. "Clean it," she demands before walking away.

"I'd asked David to speak to you as I wanted to know what you had planned next; do you have any other work on the horizon?" Derek asks.

"No, I just moved to Dublin and this role came about quite by surprise, so I don't have any future plans at present," I admit, feeling my cheeks blush as I recall the subterfuge used to land this role.

"That's exactly what I was hoping you'd say, Autumn. You see, we have this fantastic role on *Phoenix Lives* you'd be perfect for. Take my card and if you are interested, it's yours. I think you've got some real potential and there's nothing I love more than to find the next star." Derek shakes my hand once again and says goodbye as he leaves with David.

I stare at the card in my hand for a moment before putting it securely in my bag with a smile.

"So, what do you think, Autumn, are you going to do it? Josh asks eagerly.

"Absolutely, I wouldn't want you to miss me too much now?" I playfully tap Josh on the cheek as he stares into my eyes.

"Well, I think this calls for a hug. May I?" Josh opens his arms wide, a smile crossing my face as we press against each other, his arms tightly gripping around my waist. I pull my arms around the sides of his neck and rest my head upon his chest.

We join my parents, Megan, Amelia, Kiera, Cian and Eleanor when we are joined by the girl from my audition who broke her glass.

"Josh, there you are." She leans in to kiss each of his cheeks in an exaggerated manner before adding, "Aren't you going to introduce me to your adorable new friend?" She smiles intensely at him before her steely eyes fix upon me.

"Sure, Mia. This is Autumn, my talented leading lady who has made this show an absolute pleasure."

Her smile twists slightly but she quickly regains her composure. "What a thrill to meet you, Autumn, I'm Mia and apologies I wasn't able to make the show. I was in talks with a Hollywood agent. But I heard it was just fabulous so well done to you." Mia surveys my friends and family before curling her lips into an unconvincing smile.

"Hi Mia, so lovely to meet you, I'm Megan." I watch as Megan awkwardly thrusts out her hand towards Mia who surveys her before glibly shaking her hand.

"Lovely to meet you, Megan, were you in the show too?" Mia asks directly.

"Oh no, I'm not an actress. I'm a friend of Autumn, it was me that insisted she go for this role as I knew she'd ace it." Megan smiles over at me as Mia raises her eyebrows slightly.

"What a great friend you are, Megan, we should hang out some time?" Mia says.

"Are you serious? I would love that, I'm a huge fan." Megan beams as Mia pulls her into a hug.

"Well, pass me your phone and I'll give you my number. Oh, and would you be a doll and get me a refill?" Megan gives Mia her phone and runs off to get her another drink, bringing it back eagerly. "Thanks, Megan, you're such a doll, here's your phone and I look forward to hanging out together soon. Toodles everyone." Mia leaves with a dismissive wave as she goes back to join her friends.

Quickly, Megan scrolls down to find Mia's phone number and shows me with glee. "Look, Autumn, I've got Mia's number and we're going to hang out. How cool is that? Did you see how glamourous she is?" She is all in a fluster.

"She certainly is glamourous, you have to hand it to her. Does anyone want a drink?" I tally up the drinks and Eleanor joins me at the bar.

"So, what did you think of Mia? Was she as bad as I have said she is?" Eleanor asks in a hushed tone.

"She's even worse, she's the girl I saw at my audition bragging about Jesse McCarthy. What was with Megan acting like her puppy dog?" I ask angrily.

"Oh yes, that's one of her favourite stories but the truth is, she has probably never even met him. Megan is impressed by her, she's one of an army of minions that are, but thank God you're not one of them. It means we can still be friends."

"There is one other thing but keep it to yourself for now, I've been offered a job on *Phoenix Lives*. Derek asked me and said it's mine if I want it."

Eleanor gives off the quietest squeal and hugs me in delight "That's amazing, Autumn, so we'll be co-stars for ever more. I bet Josh is happy about that, isn't he?" She winks at me.

"You know, Eleanor, he didn't deny it and neither did I so watch this space."

We grab our drinks and make our way back to the

others. As the drinks flow freely and liberally throughout the night, we party the night away on the dance floor and in that moment, I feel so blessed to have everyone important to me helping celebrate the best night of my life. I look over and see Cian and Amelia engrossed in conversation and I ponder how cute they'd look together if they got the chance.

Suddenly the music stops and a slightly inebriated David takes a microphone from the DJ. "Ladies and Gentleman, thank you all for such a splendid evening and helping me and my amazing cast make our opening night one to remember. Now, I have just received here the very first review from the *Irish Times* and I wanted to share it with you all."

David takes an iPad from the DJ who holds it in front of him as he reads:

"It's a man's world, there is no question about that in the stirring and moving production of *Othello* directed by the theatre genius that is David Byrne. The darkness of the most tragic of Shakespeare's plays with a glittering cast that perfectly portrays each character in a way that even Shakespeare could not dispute. Desdemona is a believable shining beacon of virtue and loyalty, offset with the burning malice and hatred Iago holds for Othello in which she pays the ultimate price. Iago pulls Othello's strings like a master puppeteer and callously exacts his revenge on Othello by destroying the one thing he loves more than life itself...Desdemona. This performance was enthralling, beautiful and thrilling and spectacularly showcases the talents of Autumn Sutherland who is no doubt one to watch."

A rapturous applause rings out, Josh and Eleanor both

turn to hug me in turn before Casey also grabs me into a massive hug.

As the night ends I feel a huge sense of relief that I gave a performance I could be proud of. As I recall my offer at *Phoenix Lives*, I realise I've just achieved the one thing I thought I never could.

Chapter 16

Dublin, 22 December 2017

Standing in front of the mirror, I get myself ready for work for the last time. After having such a long sabbatical to be able to do *Othello*, I feel a pang of sadness that I won't be going back to this job. If it wasn't for Megan, I wouldn't have ever got to do *Othello* and I really will miss everyone so much.

Running down the stairs, I see a letter on the kitchen table with Keira looking at me expectantly.

"Are you going to open it? I think it's about *Phoenix Lives*, the postal mark is Donnybrook. That's where the studios are. Sure, if you don't open it, I will," Keira adds, impatient.

"Well I know I've got the job already, so it's probably just the HR stuff but it'll be good to know the salary I'm on as we didn't discuss that. It felt a little presumptuous to ask and it never came up. I just hope it is enough to live on," I say as I open the letter.

"Autumn, you crack me up, I think the pay will be a little more than enough to live on. Sure, have you seen the stuff the stars be wearing just going to the gym. It's more than your monthly pay right now, I'd say." Keira puts her dishes into the dishwasher and joins me.

My eyes widen as I read down the letter to the salary. "You won't believe it, Keira, it's over €100,000 a year. Surely that can't be right?" I try to read the letter again to make sure.

"What did I tell you? You're not dripping in cash going to the gym if you're on a budget and I dare say you'll get some bonuses or expenses too. I can't imagine there aren't more perks to it than the cash either. Right so, drinks are on you then, Autumn." Keira smiles and pats me on the back as she leaves to get ready.

"Oh shit, I'm late." I shove the letter in my bag and race down the road, managing to catch the train just in time.

Pulling out my phone, I look at the message to Megan I sent yesterday, asking if she wanted to join me for drinks for tonight but it is still unread despite the fact it shows she was online only moments ago. Since the *Othello* after party, Megan has been distant and whenever we do talk, her head is barely away from her phone which makes her silence even more suspicious.

Disembarking the train, I drop into a nearby shop to buy some treats for the office and a hot chocolate and make my way into the office.

"Morning, Megan," I say cheerily as I pass.

She is furiously typing and holds her hand up to me with one finger to halt me. I sigh and walk past and up to my own desk, which is laden with confetti, gifts and cards from all my work colleagues. As I give them all hugs, the phone on my desk begins to ring.

"Hello," Melissa says as she picks up the phone on my behalf, placing it on loudspeaker in anticipation of the well-wishes from the person on the other end.

"What's your problem, Autumn? Did I not make it clear for you to hold until I'd finished or did you have something better to be doing?" Megan snaps as her impatient tone rings across the room. A moment of silence ensues as everyone stares at each other in astonishment. My cheeks flush red.

"Hello, are you even going to respond to me?" Megan asks haughtily.

"Megan, this is Melissa. Autumn's busy at present. There's a room full of people here wishing her well for her new endeavour so she isn't coming to the phone." Melissa abruptly disconnects the phone and moves to give me a hug.

"Autumn, we have a special surprise for you on your last day. As you are due to become Ireland's newest celebrity in *Phoenix Lives*, there is only one lunch venue we could possibly go to. We're taking you to Fleur. We may even bump in to some of your co-stars to be." Stella beams before walking over to her desk and dialling down to reception.

"Oh, hello Megan, Stella here. Can you please order two taxis from the office leaving at 11.30 a.m., going to Fleur and returning for 2.30 p.m.? It's for Autumn's leaving lunch and it's been cleared with Rosaline. You'll be grand to man the reception desk while we're gone, won't you?" Stella puts the handset back down. "I'm not going to lie, that felt great especially after that phone call. She's on thin ice with me from now on."

I open the cards on my desk and smile at the array of messages from my co-workers but quickly realise that one is missing. Megan hasn't signed it. A pang of disappointment hits as I vow not to let her ruin my day. I think of Eleanor and how much she has always hated her and begin to see where she was coming from. Suddenly an email pings into my inbox from Megan.

From: Megan O'Leary m.leary@dcmb.ie
To: Autumn Sutherland a.sutherland@dcmb.ie
Subject: Drinks

Not sure if I'm able to make tonight, will let ya know later. Will Josh be there? I did hear he's off to a glitzy party tonight in the Shelbourne with Mia.

Enjoy your lunch and sorry I missed your card and collection, just been so busy down here!

I read Megan's email with a pang of disappointment. Of all the people, I thought she would have been happy for me but ever since she met Mia, she's had no time for me.

Suddenly my phone buzzes in my bag. Lifting it out, I see a text from Josh which I read with a smile.

"Hey Autumn, looking forward to seeing you tonight! I must admit Temple Bar has always been my guilty pleasure…ssh don't tell anyone! It'll be our little secret x."

I sign out of my computer and follow Stella downstairs past reception and into our waiting taxi without so much as a sideways glance towards Megan. As we pull off, I see her come to the window with a mobile phone stuck to her ear.

Arriving at Fleur, the doorman opens our door, where we're greeted with an impressive garland of Christmas flowers hanging over the door, complete with baubles and lights.

"Wow, this place is spectacular, it's a cross between a palace and a greenhouse," I say as I look around the impressive restaurant. The wooden panelling gives an antique feel and the impressive high-vaulted ceiling allows for trees to be strewn throughout, with impressive twisted barks and leaves made up of the most glorious flower arrangements I've ever seen.

"Did you know the décor and crockery change with the seasons to reflect the life cycle of the flowers?" Stella asks enthusiastically.

"Doesn't that mean all these flowers should be dead as we're in winter?" Melissa asks seriously.

We all start to laugh. Melissa flushes, a smile creeping across her face.

"I'm glad that they've chosen the Christmas theme instead and the winter blooming flowers instead of the dead look. These wine goblets are beautiful." I trace my finger over the bumpy embossed pattern on the blood red glass.

"Can I get anyone drinks?" The server appears with a smile as she awaits our response.

"Does anyone object to a bottle of red wine?" Stella asks. We all nod in agreement and the server smiles and goes off to get our drinks, returning with an ornate red decanter that matches the glassware on the table. We watch as she shows the bottle to Stella, opens it and pours a small amount for Stella to try before decanting it into the bottle for us.

"Now Autumn, it is a very sad day for us at DCMB, as you have been such an asset to us in the short time you've been here. We are of course pure delighted for you to be going off and becoming an actress but we wanted to give you a little gift for you to remember your time with us." Stella hands me an elegant gift bag stuffed with presents.

Excited, I open them and reveal a stylish black bag, a gorgeous silver necklace and a bottle of champagne.

"I don't know what to say, these are all gorgeous, you really shouldn't have." I offer Stella the necklace to tie around my neck.

"Sure, we wanted to set you up right in your new job now. This bag is one of those fancy overnight bags with pouches for everything, so you look the business when you need to stay overnight in those fancy hotels."

"Thank you so much, you guys, this is so thoughtful. I love it. I'll wear the necklace out tonight." I look through the bag, pulling out two inner pockets and see that one is meant for underwear and the other toiletries. There is a pouch for anything you might need to pack as well as being able to charge your phone on the go.

We finish our lunch and make our way back to the office. Before I know it, my last day is done and after saying my final farewell, I make my way downstairs.

"Autumn, wait," Megan calls and I drop my head around the door of the reception. She places a card and present on her desk and I go to retrieve it.

"Thank you, Megan, that's really kind of you. It's been lovely to work with you and I'll always be grateful for you encouraging me to go for my dreams." A pang of sadness tugs at me.

"You make it sound like it's goodbye, Autumn," Megan says softly as her eyes flick down to her desk before back at me.

"That's up to you, Megan, I've done all I can and if you

value Mia's friendship over mine then I'll let you go and be grateful for what we had. Thanks again, Megan." I raise my present and card up to her and wave goodbye.

Later that evening

I make my way into the restaurant and see a table full of familiar faces beaming back at me. A chair is saved for me next to where Josh is sitting. I note Megan's absence but recalling the conversation earlier, I feel fine with it. Both Eleanor and Amelia have raised their concerns about her. I have to accept maybe she didn't value our friendship in the same way I did.

"Thank you so much for coming everyone," I say.

Josh leaves his chair to pull mine out for me.

"Who knew you could be such a gentleman Josh?" I tease.

"Only in the presence of a true lady, which is why you've not seen it before," he retorts with a smile. A pinkness tinges his cheeks slightly.

The night wears on with everyone getting on famously. Josh and Eleanor are bombarded with a million questions about the glamour of *Phoenix Lives* by my office friends and as we prepare to leave the restaurant and make our way to our chosen late-night venue, I reflect that this may be the best night I've ever had.

"I was expecting to see Megan here, how come she isn't?" Eleanor asks with a hint of suspicion.

"It would seem that friendship is over. It's pretty much like you said, she has a new friend now and as I left today, I gave her my blessing. This is a whole new start for me." I say with a sense of relief.

"Good, she would only have ruined your night anyway." She nods her head over towards Josh as he talks to Melissa and Stella in front of us. "It may not just be your career we're talking about." She smirks with satisfaction.

I shake my head as a smile creeps across my face and a blush spreads across my cheeks. I see Josh turn to smile at us before joining us. "Eleanor, can I steal Autumn for a minute?"

She smiles and nods and goes to join Stella and Melissa ahead of us.

"I don't feel like I have got much time to chat to you before we start mainlining tequila and dancing like the morons I know we are. I wanted the chance to have you to myself for a bit." Josh reaches out to hold my hand in his and our eyes meet for a second as the others go out of view.

"Well, I'm all yours, Josh, what do you want to talk about?" I smile warmly but neither of us breaks the other's gaze.

A mischievous smile lights up his face as he replies, "Who said anything about talking?" He pulls me towards him and I wrap my arms around him. We share our first kiss in the illuminated streets of Temple Bar, as people hustle and bustle around us like we are invisible.

As we pull away, our hands remain clasped. There is a short pause before I ask a question that has been on my mind a while. "How come you didn't go to the awards event tonight, Josh?"

He smiles as he wraps his arms across my shoulder and we continue walking before replying, "Because there was no one I wanted to kiss there. I wanted to spend time with you. So, it was not a hard choice to make, trust me."

Walking into Indigo hand in hand, we find our friends at the bar. We wave and make our way towards them but I feel a tug on my arm from behind. It's Megan.

"You two look very cosy, what's going on here?" She turns her eyes on Josh as if she is expecting an answer. The others come to join us.

"I'm sorry, what business is it to you? If all you are going to do is come in here and cause trouble with your bitchy ways than you can just march on out of here right now." Josh glares at Megan who loses her confidence and starts to stammer for a response.

"I was only asking as Autumn's friend. Besides, if it wasn't for me, Autumn would never have even met you. She wants me here, don't you?" Megan's voice shakes as she looks at me, pleading.

"I thought you had plans with Mia? You said you couldn't make it?" I purse my lips in disappointment.

"Perhaps she's been sent here to report back to Mia. I'd find it hard to believe your presence here is to support Autumn," Eleanor retorts.

'Based on the way she was this morning at work, barking at Autumn over the phone, I'd be inclined to agree that there's an ulterior motive at work here." Melissa folds her arms menacingly as she stares at Megan.

"Oh Eleanor, you're just a sour-faced has-been full of jealously for Mia and her fame," Megan retorts.

"What fame are we talking about? The imaginary romances or her one-night stand with Darryl McNally? That girl is trying to gain her fame one dick at a time." The words are barely out of Eleanor's mouth before

Megan launches at her and sends her sprawling.

As Eleanor makes short work of Megan's attempts to overpower her, we try to split the two up but to no avail. The bouncers arrive, lifting Megan and Eleanor up before taking them outside.

"I don't want to see either of you back in here, do you understand me? Now scram and take your fight elsewhere," the bouncer shouts angrily as he gestures at them to move away from the entrance.

Storming out of Indigo, I face Megan with fury written all over my face. "Why do you hate me so much, Megan? What did I ever do to you? Why do you have to ruin everything? Go home and don't speak to me again, this friendship is over. I want nothing more to do with you or your selfish ways." I don't even wait for a reply as I re-join the rest and we move on to another pub and reunite with Eleanor to enjoy the rest of our evening.

Chapter 17

27 December 2017, Devon

Nothing makes you reflect more on your life than the end of a year. Sitting on my bed listening to my favourite music, I feel quietly contented. I think back to the day I made the decision to move to Dublin and the helplessness I felt. Glancing out of the window, I watch the icy branches of the tree swaying in the breeze. The grey clouds loom threateningly overhead.

Suddenly I realise this is the perfect way to end my year, going back to the place it all began but this time I'll be happy and excited at what my future holds instead of being in fear of it.

"Mum, Dad, I'm just heading out for a bit. See you soon," I call as I put my shoes on and pull my coat tightly around me before fastening it. Lastly, I pull on my hat before fixing it properly in the hallway mirror.

"OK, love, but make sure you are back by 5.00 p.m. as I'm making tea for then. I'm making naans by hand," Mum adds proudly.

"Sounds delicious, Mum, I'll definitely be home for that." I give my mum a quick hug and she closes the door behind me.

Walking onto the promenade and down to the stony

beach in front of me, I select my spot near the shoreline, wiggling my bottom into the stones to create a comfy seat amongst the icy cold stones. Looking around, I am totally alone with only the odd person strolling along the promenade but not daring to venture onto the beach. Selecting a stone from beside me, I run my finger over its smooth but misshapen edges, warming it in my gloved hand before I throw it into the sea with a splash.

"I was wondering if I might meet you here again on a cold winter's day," a voice calls from behind me. I turn to see the old lady I met the year previously walking towards me with a smile. This time a Dalmatian puppy pulls impatiently on a lead beside her, and as she takes a seat next to me, she unclips the dog's leash and it goes running in to the sea like a bullet.

"Maggie, it's so nice to see you again and you have a new puppy?" We both turn again to watch the puppy, who is trying to bite at each wave with excited enthusiasm.

"Yes, the house was too big with me just rattling around in it so I took the plunge and got Dottie. I always wanted a Dalmatian and she is so energetic, she keeps me active," Maggie says fondly.

"How old is she now?"

We watch Dottie frolic in the crashing waves.

"Coming up six months, she's not that small anymore. Oh, here she comes with a new stick she's found, there will be no rest now," Maggie says affectionately as Dottie places her stick at my feet and waits expectantly for me to throw it for her. "Make sure you give it a good throw, she doesn't like it too easy," Maggie adds.

I throw the stick fully into the ocean. Dottie chases

after it, diving into the waves.

"I hope I didn't throw it too far, I don't want to drown your dog," I say with concern as Dottie continues searching for her stick amongst the waves.

"No don't worry, she loves the water and this is her favourite game. I've looked out for you many times over the past year and since I never saw you, I figured you had made it to Dublin after all?" Maggie asks.

"I certainly did and you'll be pleased to know it exceeded expectations. I managed to get a lead part in a play at The Gate Theatre which lead to me being cast in an Irish soap, which I start in January," I say proudly.

"That's fantastic, Autumn, I never doubted you for a moment. Any luck on the man front?"

Dottie comes charging up to me again with her stick and drops it by my feet, her eyes fixated on me until I throw it. "There is a guy, my co-star Josh, that I like and I think he likes me too but we are not an item yet." I throw the stick into the ocean as hard as I can for Dottie.

"What a turnaround, Autumn, from when we first met and in less than a year, it all seems to have changed for the best. Can I see this soap in the UK?" Maggie asks.

"I don't think so but I'll take your address as I'm sure I can find a way to send you a copy." I swap details with Maggie and we bid each other farewell. Then she continues her walk with Dottie up the beach.

Retrieving my phone, I see a message from Casey asking what I am up to. I walk to Casey's house and knock on her front door.

"Autumn, what a lovely surprise. I am so bored, this part between Christmas and New Year is so hard. Even if you want to, there's nothing to do." Casey envelops me in a hug and ushers me through the door.

"What are you doing for New Year's? Any nice plans?" I ask as she offers me a mug of hot chocolate.

"I don't have any plans. There's a guy I work with who invited me to a party but I don't know if I want to socialise that way with him yet," Casey muses.

"Do you think he asked because he likes you?"

"Mark? No, not at all. We've always just been friends so I'd be surprised if that was true." Doubt crosses her face for a moment.

"Well, don't turn him down, offer him a more low-key opportunity to hang out and for New Year, why don't you come to Dublin with me?" I offer.

"Are you serious, Autumn? That would be amazing and I'd love a little time away. You should also invite Keira, Amelia and Eleanor and let's make a party of it," she suggests.

"That sounds like a perfect idea. Now, have you added this Mark guy on your social media?" I ask sternly.

"No, why would I?" Casey replies.

"Because it's meant for friends, which I'm not buying by the way. The tinge across your cheeks is giving you away," I tease.

"Ok, rule one of our New Year trip, you're not allowed to mention Mark, not even once," she says with a smile.

"I tell you what, you add him to your social media so he can see the amazing time we'll have and realise just how fun you are and I'll drop the subject right here and now." I'm smug, watching as she takes her phone out of her pocket.

"Fine," she says in mock annoyance. She holds the phone out to me with a curt, "See?"

"I'm even less convinced of you being just friends after seeing that picture, he is so your type. If there was a dictionary of types, this photo would be next to yours. This is so happening in 2018, Casey, this is your New Year's res, ok?"

"I refuse to confirm or deny a thing! But let's book this flight, I'm so excited!" She reaches for her laptop to check for flights.

I jot down my flight details and time for Casey to book and glance at the time, realising I don't have long left until dinner.

"Sorry, Casey, I have to get back but text me when you're booked and I'll speak to Keira, Amelia and Eleanor to see if they can make it." I give Casey a hug goodbye and make the short journey home, returning as mum is dishing up the dinner.

"Great timing, love, go wash your hands and join your father at the table. I've a treat in store for you both," Mum says happily.

My mum strides into the dining room with three plates in tow, placing them down with a flourish like she is at a restaurant.

"This smells amazing, Brenda, just when I thought I was getting sick of turkey too." My dad says in his usual brusque manner.

Sitting at the table with my parents, chatting and eating dinner, I feel the most relaxed I have for a long time. It isn't long until I return to Dublin and although I've been there for a good few months now, it feels almost like the first time all over again as I turn over a new leaf and become the actress I always wanted to be.

Chapter 18

31st December 2017, Dublin

We awaken early, full of excitement and giggling like children. Before we know it, we are making our way into town to catch the LUAS to Dundrum for a spot of shopping before we hit Temple Bar for New Year's Eve.

"I'm so glad you could make it over, Casey, it'll be so much fun but it's a shame Kiera, Amelia and Eleanor can't join us as they'd have loved to see you again." I smile as we pay for our tickets.

"Then we'll just have to make more plans for another time. It's great to be back in Dublin and this is such an exciting way to start the New Year," Casey says enthusiastically as we board the LUAS and take our seats, our conversation interrupted by the gentle chime of the bell to signal we are on the move.

"You never need a reason. You are welcome any time you like. Besides maybe you can take Mark if that goes well?" I nudge her gently.

"I can't believe you broke our deal already, it's a Mark-free zone. Ok, I do think he's very cute but I haven't been out with anyone since Greg and, well, you know why that would put anyone off." Casey rolls her eyes at the memory of her ex.

"Oh Greg, he was vile, Casey, I never know what you even saw in him. He was so creepy, you just didn't know which part of you he was going to manhandle next," I say with disgust.

"Yes, I think catching him trying to spy on my underage sister in the bathroom did open my eyes a bit to that side. The fact I didn't see it before then is what puts me off now. Can you trust anyone?" Casey asks thoughtfully.

"You know what, I don't think you ever really know with anyone. I mean we've been friends for years but you never know if we will be in ten years' time. I think you just have to try and see what happens. Besides, you are a tough cookie so don't hold yourself back," I reassure as we finally get to our stop and disembark.

"Alright, I'll try with Mark and let's see if it goes anywhere. I was always happy to have a simple life anyway. I think I'd get tired of all the glitz and glamour if I were you, Autumn," Casey teases playfully as we walk into Dundrum shopping centre and are met with an array of enticing shops with which to find our perfect outfit for tonight.

Later that evening

As we totter along the familiar cobbles of Temple Bar, we pull our coats around us. The winter evening starts to bite. Squeezing ourselves past the crowds of people inside the pub, it's almost impossible to find a space as everyone tries to cram in for the festivities. Finally, we make it to the bar, where James greets us with a big smile.

"I was hoping I'd be seeing you tonight. Who is your new friend?" James shakes Casey's hand.

"This is Casey, we've been friends since we were kids. I managed to persuade her to come over for New Year," I say as Casey smiles back.

"Well it's lovely to meet you, Casey, and welcome to the best bar in Dublin." He hands us our drinks and heads off to serve other customers in the heaving bar.

"He seems nice, Autumn, I think he likes you." Casey takes a sip of her drink.

"I know but I have always had reservations, he comes across a bit of a player and I just don't want a guy like that. It puts me off," I say.

"I don't know. He seems pretty sincere but if I'm honest, it does sound more promising with the actor guy so I'd suggest seeing where that goes first. But sure, it's good to have options and you certainly do." Casey has a mischievous glint in her eye.

As time ticks towards midnight, the anticipation of the crowd reaches fever pitch. At five minutes to twelve, James reappears with two glasses of champagne that he places down in front of us.

"On the house, ladies, here's to hoping 2018 is your best year yet." He clinks his drink to ours before we take a sip.

"Thank you, James," we both say in unison. My cheeks blush slightly under his heavy gaze.

"Five, four, three, two one…Happy New Year!" the pub roars as everyone starts hugging and clinking glasses. Auld Lang Syne rings out until it is drowned out by the chorus of voices. People begin to spill outside to use their phones and connect with the people they love the most.

As I think back to the past twelve months, I'm proud of how far I've come. I look over at Casey and feel grateful that I have one of my best friends here to celebrate this moment with me.

Chapter 19

8 January 2018 – Dublin

Throwing the covers off, I spring out of bed and straight into the shower, ready to start the day I've been anticipating since the wrap party for *Othello*. Today is my first day on set for *Phoenix Lives*. Reaching into my wardrobe, I pull out the new dress I bought for my first day. A beige woollen dress with burgundy and brown details across the neck and hemline coupled with brown tights and boots which set off perfectly my new honey brown locks.

Adding a slick of lipstick and a spritz of perfume, I take a quick photo to send to Amelia and Casey as the hoot of the car outside signals that it's time for me to leave. Rushing down the stairs, I halt as Keira calls out to me.

"Autumn, I thought you might be busy this morning so I've packed you a quick breakfast to have on your way." Keira hands me a small tub as she wraps me in a hug. "Now, good luck and have the best day, you look fab, you really do."

"Thanks so much, Keira, you're the best. I'll see you later." I wave as I shut the door behind me and make my way into the car to begin my journey to the *Phoenix Lives* studio.

A familiar face is waiting near the entrance, moving towards the car to open my door with a big smile. "Good morning to our newest cast member, I'm your designated guide for the day if you'd care to follow me," Josh says, giving his best tour guide impression.

"Thank you, Josh, although I was hoping you'd be wearing a hat and perhaps a red coat. For no other reason then I think you'd look very hot in it." I grin mischievously at Josh who blushes at my compliment.

"Now, you don't need a red coat to look very hot, those boots are better than any red coat." He smiles and motions me to follow him as we walk into a room where everyone is assembled.

"And there she is, the woman of the hour. Come here, Autumn, it's good to see you again. Those months since *Othello* have just flown by." Derek gives me a hug and motions for a chair to be pulled up beside him so I can sit down.

"Everyone, it's my very great pleasure to introduce our newest *Phoenix Lives* colleague, Autumn Sutherland. After seeing her excellent debut in *Othello*, I knew we needed her on the show. She will be taking up the role of Amber Brennan, the British moll of Mike here and every bit as deadly, if not more. I can't wait to see what you do with her, Autumn."

As Derek effuses to the room, I smile shyly. My eye surveys all the new faces in the room. Suddenly my eyes meet with a familiar face. Mia holds my stare with a cold and impenetrable gaze before turning to the lady sat next to her. Whispering in her ear, they both turn back to look at me before laughing and nodding in agreement with one another.

As soon as the meeting ends, people begin to disperse.

Derek turns to me as Josh reappears. "Ok, Autumn, so first we need to get you to makeup as we've lined up some important interviews for you and we will also need to film your promotion and title clips. Then at 2 p.m., you will meet with the scriptwriters to get an overview of the character and her signature look. After that, you'll meet your onscreen husband and sit in on the filming for Josh's scene. Does that sound ok?" Derek chirps.

"It sounds like the perfect first day, thanks for your help, Derek," I say as we wave goodbye and I follow Josh to makeup.

Rounding the corner, I see a pretty blonde lady texting on her phone with her back towards the mirror.

"Hi Autumn, it's so nice to meet you. I've heard great things about you. Take a seat. I'm Violet and I'm an absolute perfectionist which makes me a nightmare to live with but amazing at my job. I mean, who doesn't want their makeup to be perfect?" Violet ushers me to the chair and shoos Josh out as he hurriedly says goodbye.

"I've never had somebody else do my makeup for me before, this is a first," I say nervously as Violet cleans off the makeup I put on this morning.

"Ok, makeup for TV is not at all like your day-to-day look. If I put you on camera like this, you'd look dead. It needs to be heavy, so don't freak out because it'll feel as if I've caked you in it but on screen, it'll pop in all the right ways."

Violet rolls concealer under my eye in big patches before blending in with a sponge. We chatter away as she layers up my makeup. My skin begins to prickle under the weight of it but I feel a pang of excitement at how it will look once she is done. Before the big reveal, Violet calls in the hair stylist with instructions to add gentle curls to my hair then slicks on another coat of lipstick.

Violet ushers me out of the chair and over to the full-length mirror. I look at myself in awe, almost not seeing the same person.

"Wow, Violet, I look like a model! How did you make me look like that?" I get close to the mirror as if looking closer will reveal my eyes have deceived me.

"The star treatment has that effect, it is possible to manufacture beauty to an extent but sure you have to have some to begin with, which you clearly do. Now, make sure you do great in those interviews." Violet smiles as I re-join Josh who is waiting outside. He looks twice before realising it is me.

"Don't you scrub up well. With a bit of spit polish, I almost didn't recognise you. There was me thinking I was the most attractive one in this soap but seems you've stolen my crown on your first day." Josh leads me to a conference room, which is set up ready for my interviews with a green screen behind.

"Thanks Josh, suddenly my nerves feel like they might just get the better of me." I breathe deeply as he cups my hands in his and looks deep into my eyes.

"Not a chance, Autumn, this is your moment and the whole reason you came to Ireland. This is the beginning of your dream come true and who knows, maybe I'll factor in there somewhere too." He smiles broadly at me, gives me a big hug and kisses me on the head.

"That's a TBC for sure," I tease, letting our hands linger a moment longer before walking into the room, ready for my first interview

Later that day

After a busy day, I sit down alongside Derek and Eleanor with a nice cold drink ready to watch the last scenes being filmed for today. It is great to finally see Eleanor. As the scene is being set up, I check my phone and see that Amelia and Casey have both responded to my message from this morning.

"Eleanor, can we take a quick selfie, do you think we're allowed?" I whisper.

"Of course, you want to send to Amelia, huh?" She takes my phone and holds it up so we get both of us and the scene in the background.

"Both Amelia and Casey want to know how my day is going and I figured a picture is far more exciting."

"So, are you interested in finally seeing a certain person's acting repertoire?" Eleanor whispers.

"If you mean, finding out whether Mia is any good, then yes. I can't say I hold much hope." Both Eleanor laugh and I laugh as I fix my gaze squarely on Mia who quickly looks away and seems somewhat self-conscious for the first time since I've met her.

Finally, the call comes for quiet as Derek's assistant counts down to action and the scene begins.

The camera pans across a luxurious interior, showcasing the decadence you would expect from a successful premier league footballer and his partner. The chandeliers sparkle above as Crystle saunters into the kitchen in a dressing gown, then starts to get cutlery and crockery out of the cupboards.

"Babe, are you up yet? It's nearly time for breakfast?" Her shrill and exaggerated tone rings out but is met by silence. She continues to set the table, looking up as she finishes before she walks towards the door. "Babe, did you sleep in the other bedroom again?" she calls as she makes her way to a spare room to see an empty bed. A worried expression stretches across her face as she walks a bit quicker towards the home gym but that too is empty.

As she walks towards the landing, a door slams hard and Jack emerges, bleeding and walking towards the bathroom.

"Babe, what happened to you. Why are you hurt?" Crystle runs after Jack.

"What'd I tell you before, don't ask me questions, the less you know the better," Jack snaps back, slumping down upon the toilet, head in his hands as blood drips onto the floor.

Crystle grabs some cotton wool and antiseptic and starts to dab at his wounds to clean them. "Jack, you're a footballer and that is not a nocturnal sport so excuse me for wondering why you are out all night and coming home like you've been on the wrong side a boxing match," she says with concern.

Jack reaches out to touch Crystle's face, surveying her for a moment before he pulls her into a passionate kiss.

"Crystle, I love you so much and I couldn't bear to lose you." Jack drops his head down into his hands and sobs.

"Babe, you're not losing me, not now not ever, ok? Are you a pain in my backside, yes, but I'll always love you. Just give me a minute, you need a plaster." Crystle kisses the top of his head and leaves for the kitchen.

All of a sudden, a loud bang resounds as the door flies

off and masked men come in to the house with guns, dragging Crystle away but leaving a single envelope on the table in the hallway.

"Ok cut, that was great. Thanks, everybody. It's a wrap," Derek's assistant calls out across the set.

"And your verdict is?" Eleanor asks with a smile.

"She's not horrendous just a bit wooden but with a truly terrible shrill to her voice, does she really think she adds anything to the character?" I whisper.

"I think the phrase you are looking for is one dimensional," Eleanor says.

As I pack my bag and get ready to leave, Mia saunters up to me with a wry smile.

"I thought it would be good to have you sit in on my scenes so you could see the standard required. I have a Hollywood career in front of me and I don't expect a theatre minor to let my side down now." Mia folds her arms in front of her with a satisfied grin.

"Mia, you've been saying that for the past five years, yet you're still here. It's like I've said before, fucking Darryl McNally is not an actual route into Hollywood. It's just desperate." Eleanor delivers her insult with cutting precision.

Mia glowers at Eleanor before turning on her heel and storming off, shouting at the runner in the process.

"My God, Eleanor, you're so fierce. Remind me not to get on your wrong side." I laugh as we clear the set.

"She's so vile that I actually enjoy it a little bit and besides I'm not letting her ruin your day with her bull." Eleanor wraps an arm around my shoulder as we both walk out towards the car together.

Chapter 20

Valentine's Day 2018, Dublin

Sitting in silence, I watch the city skip past my window and empty my mind of all thoughts. Instead, I just enjoy this moment when I feel so happy and contented.

A piercing beep jolts me, as the car comes to a halt outside Eleanor's house. Looking down to my screen, I smile when I see Amelia's text.

"Happy Valentine's Day, Autumn. A year ago, our friendship was born and for that, I'll always be grateful. Any plans with Josh?" Amelia signs off her message with a winky face emoji.

Typing back quickly, as Eleanor makes her way to the car, I write, "Ahh, love that you messaged me. I still think Valentine's needs to be for friends too! No, plans with Josh as think that is a bit more than what we are. How about you?"

I put my phone down to see Eleanor smirking as I silently replace it in my bag. I feel a smile cross my face as I realise the implication.

"Oh, come on, Autumn, don't be coy. It's Valentine's Day, that was so Josh, wasn't it?" She turns herself in her seat to face me straight on as she searches my face for any clues.

"I hate to say it but no, we are not at Valentine's level, we're more friends than anything else right now. Besides, we are both too professional to cross that line," I say with certainty.

Eleanor crosses her arms, her brows knitting together as she considers my words.

"Do you honestly believe that bullshit, Autumn? I get that denial is kind of your thing but seriously, you both kissed on your leaving drinks. What more do you need, a skywriter?" Eleanor wipes her forehead with her hand.

"Well, how come it's never led to a date or something that shows actual progress? It just kind of went back to the friend zone after that," I say, dejected.

"Ok, Autumn, you know I love you to pieces and I want you to be happy and on occasion that requires some tough love." Eleanor's face softens.

"Why does this feel a lot like a warning? Did anyone ever tell you that you are definitely an intimidating person, Eleanor?" I ask with a smile.

"Oh God yes, since I was a child. I call it forthright but whatever! I'm going to be honest with you, Autumn, when it comes to guys, you are a little hot and cold. For all the fire you naturally have, the minute a guy you like comes along, it's like someone pisses it out." She sits back in her seat, waiting for me to respond.

"That's pretty harsh but also quite fair. I am a shit flirt but I have always flirted with him way more than any guy ever before. I ignored my ex for the first few months I knew him, completely avoided him and that included all eye contact," I confess.

As the car pulls up, Eleanor and I get out of the car and walk towards the main entrance of our production set.

"If you just give him a bit more, I think you'll be surprised by what he'll do with that. Not everything has to be talk." Eleanor lightly drapes her fingers down the side of my arm to make her point.

Walking into our production meeting, my eyes meet Josh's instantly and a smile breaks across both of our faces. Thinking for a second about what Eleanor says, I stride across towards him, my heart beating in my chest as every eye falls on us.

"Do you mind if I sit here?" I ask him with a smile.

"Not at all. To what do I owe this pleasure?" He smiles at me, his eyes sparkling as I shift my seat closer to his.

"I don't want just anyone sat next to you on Valentine's Day, now do I?" I pretend to pick an imaginary bit of fluff off his shoulder.

For a moment Josh takes my hand in his, lifts it to his lips and gently kisses my hand before placing it back down. "There, I sealed our Valentine pact with a kiss." He smiles as I feel a flush of colour rush to my cheeks. I look over at Eleanor, who is beaming. Mia sits near her with a solemn face, and rolls her eyes before intently studying us in a way that feels uncomfortable. Breaking away, she taps furiously into her phone before throwing it into her bag and crossing her arms heavily across her chest.

Later that day

The lights of the set feel warm in the enclosed space of the studio. While the designers tinker with the final details, Violet pops on stage to add some powder to my nose to stop the shine.

"Ok, Autumn, this scene is so important as so far the audience thinks Amber is a sweet and doting wife who has followed her husband to his native Ireland but this is where she starts to show her true colours. And 5, 4, 3, 2, 1…go." Derek signals with his hand for the scene to begin.

Amber is in the kitchen, preparing dinner when Mickey walks in looking flustered and sits down at the table with his head in his hands.

"Mickey, is that you? I've made your favourite." Amber walks into the dining room. Upon seeing Mickey, she immediately goes to his side.

"Amber, I'm sorry, I've made a big mistake and I've put us all in danger." Mickey turns to look into Amber's eyes.

"What's the matter? Surely, it's nothing we can't fix." She soothes, running her hand down his cheek.

"That runner I put on the Hannigan job, he got cocky and made off with the cash. Hannigan wants him dead and said since it's my mess, I have to be the one to kill him." Mickey lowers his eyes once again.

"I wouldn't have thought you needed Hannigan to suggest that to you? You're not exactly known for your patience, Mickey," Amber says with a note of surprise in her voice.

"He's setting me up, Amber. If I kill a guy on my terms, I do it to not get caught but he'll make sure I do. It's max impact, Amber, I'm exposed and all my family ruined and then once I'm inside he'll kill me anyway."

Amber ponders for a moment, remaining silent as she retreats to the kitchen to plate up his dinner. As she places it in front of him, she sits down beside him with a smile.

"Unless we take out the threat first?" she suggests coyly.

"You mean the runner? Kill him on my terms behind Hannigan's back?" Mickey toys with his food.

"No, we kill Hannigan. You've the biggest weapon sat right in front of you. He's propositioned me so many times, maybe now it's time I took him up on that offer?" Amber has a glint in her eye.

"And cut. That was superb, it's a wrap guys, thank you so much. Let's call it a day," Derek calls.

I say goodbye to my co-stars and make my way back to my dressing room.

Opening the door of my dressing room, a bunch of red roses are proudly displayed in a beautiful vase with a red ribbon and a little card sticking out. I walk and check the card, expecting that they could have been placed in to the wrong dressing room but as I turn the card over, I see my name clearly written on the envelope. My heart thunders in my chest as I open the envelope, pull out the tiny card and read the message.

"Happy Valentine's Day, Autumn, would you do me the honour of accompanying me to my friend's wedding, as my date? Josh x."

I place the card down on the table, taking a deep breath as I consider what I've just read and re-reading it once more to be sure. Quickly, I take a photo of it with the roses in the background and send to Amelia and Eleanor.

I then send a message to Josh saying, "I'd better buy a new dress since I've got a wedding to go to. Thanks for the flowers, red roses are my faves x."

As I walk in the door, struggling with the flowers, Keira helps me with a wide-eyed expression on her face.

"Wow, they're amazing. Autumn, do you have an admirer?" She looks expectant.

"I certainly do, he asked me to go to a wedding as his date." I smile happily and place the flowers on the kitchen table.

"Oh, I love this, who is it? Is he handsome? I bet he is." Keira sits down at the table, tracing her finger over the raised detailing on the vase.

"It's Josh Bailey, he's so hot and I definitely know I'm not the only one who thinks that!"

"Josh Bailey as in the actor, as in from *Phoenix Lives*, Josh Bailey as in the leading Irish playboy?" she asks in awe.

"That's the one, although he's never been anything but the perfect gentleman to me and I have no idea why people think he is such a playboy. He's lovely and I'm so excited." I make myself and Keira a drink and place it down in front of her on the table.

Her face looks concerned as she turns to me. "Autumn, I think you need to see this." Keira slides across her phone, showing a news article from a couple of hours previously with the headline, "*Phoenix Lives* Lovebirds set for Valentine day love-in." My heart sinks as the article details the romantic weekend plans set for Mia and Josh, complete with an array of photos from when they were last dating.

"I'm sorry, Autumn, but that's why they call him a playboy because this is typical Josh. He says one thing but does quite another." Keira gives me a hug as I feel the tears spill out over my eyes.

Suddenly my phone beeps. The name flashing across my screen is the last one I'm expecting to see. It reads:

"I'm sorry I hurt you, Autumn, I don't want to lose our friendship as it means the world to me. Would love to catch up soon? M x."

I feel a pang of sadness as I turn my phone screen off. I just don't want to deal with this right now.

I sit in confusion, looking at the news article and wondering how this can be true. While there is no direct quote or recent photos, it must have come from somewhere. Is Josh really deceiving me or has there been a mistake?

Chapter 21

Three weeks later

The familiar interior of my favourite Dublin pub feels welcoming as I make my way to the bar and sit down on a vacant stool. It feels as if it's been ages since I've been here, James saunters around the corner and stops in his tracks, staring at me for a moment before a big smile creeps across his face.

"Well, what do you know? It's my favourite girl come back for her man. I admit it was longer than expected but knew you couldn't keep away. Now what can I get you?" He looks around, leaning across the bar before whispering, "It's on the house."

"Can I take a gin and lemonade?" I twirl the beer mat around between my fingers.

James fixes my drink, takes the mat out of my hand as he places it down in front of me with a wink.

"So, who are you meeting? Is it a date?" he asks with an unreadable expression.

Taking a sip of my drink, I smile before I reply, "I'm not on a date, I'm meeting Megan. You know the girl I used to come in here with before. We haven't been getting on so she wants to talk." I look at my phone to see that she is already ten minutes late.

"Can I speak frankly, Autumn? I never did like that girl, she is a user and you deserve better. I'm glad it's not a date though, means I still have a chance." He winks before disappearing to serve other customers.

As I sit alone at the bar, I start to feel quite self-conscious and try to avoid eye contact with a random guy intently staring at me in a really creepy way.

"Is this chair taken?" Megan asks breezily as she sits on the stool opposite and motions to get James's attention at the bar to order. "Thank you for meeting me, Autumn, I've felt dreadful about how everything was left and I just felt like our friendship was worth fighting for." Megan's eyes dart nervously away.

"It really did feel that as soon as Mia was on the scene, you couldn't be bothered with me. A friendship is a two-way street and it takes effort from both sides," I say resolutely as James approaches with our drinks and places them in front of us both.

"Thanks, Jim, have you missed Autumn? It's been a while since we've been here," Megan teases.

"It's James to you, missy, and maybe next time you can be on time to meet my future girlfriend." He winks at me warmly a second time before leaving to serve another customer.

"How rude is he? Although got to admire his optimism eh, Autumn?" Megan smiles at me mischievously and I begin to wonder if she is going to actually broach the subject we are here to discuss.

I take a sip of my drink and see James chatting with customers across the bar, then take a breath. "So, what happens now, Megan? What did you want to say?"

I notice that Megan's eyes shift to her glass as she pauses

slightly before answering. "I wanted to apologise. I'm so sorry for how I acted and I don't even know why as I've always been so grateful to have you as my friend." Megan circles her straw in her drink as she looks away before looking back at me again.

"Look, Megan, all I wanted was for you to make a little effort. With any relationship in my life, once it's one sided, it's over. What happens between us is down to you now."

"I promise I will make all the effort you could wish for, starting with a heads up on Josh. It seems following on from their romantic Valentine's together, Mia is going to be Josh's date for an upcoming society wedding in a couple of weeks," Megan says confidently.

"I don't know where you get your sources, Megan, but Josh didn't spend Valentine's with Mia. The minute he saw that false magazine report, he video called me to prove he was alone and we spent the entire evening chatting. I even got a virtual tour of his house so I could see where I'll be staying after being his date at the wedding you've just mentioned." I smile at Megan who looks shocked. I finish what is left of my drink as James returns.

"You both back to being friends now or what? I can't be dealing with any doom and gloom in this pub. If you got sorrows to drown, this isn't the place for you." James reaches into the dishwasher, retrieving the glasses and stacking them below the bar.

Megan narrows her eyes. "Do you fancy yourself some kind of agony aunt? Read the room, Jim, your opinions not required." Megan sulks as he rolls his eyes and serves a waiting customer.

The next hour is whiled away with polite conversation but Megan seems restless and like she has somewhere to be. We bid each other goodbye and although we agree to remain friends, I can't shake the feeling that I just can't trust her. I message Eleanor as I make my way to the bus with an update on how it went. She replies with one word: "Traitor." Putting my phone away, I board the bus and feel my stomach twist with uncertainty and perhaps a little bit of fear.

Chapter 22

24 March 2018 - Dublin

Standing in front of the mirror, I finish with a slick of red lipstick to compliment the rich teal dress that I'm wearing. I trace my hand over the diamante banding around the waist that is surprisingly flattering. Slipping on my silver high heels and picking up my elegant clutch, I begin to make my way down the stairs when a loud knock makes me jump.

As Keira goes to the door, she glances up just when I descend the stairs. "Oh Autumn, you look absolutely stunning." She smiles as she continues to open the door for Josh.

"Hey, I'm here to pick up Autumn," he says.

There's a moment's pause. As I stand behind the door, I watch Keira look him up and down suspiciously.

"Be sure to be treating her right, mind. One trace of a tear on her face and you'll have me to contend with now," Keira warns sternly as she opens the door wider.

I appear behind her.

"Autumn, you look fantastic, may I?" Josh's cheeks are slightly flushed after his dressing down from Keira but he reaches his arm out to me. Tucking my arm under his, we make our way towards his car.

"Bye, Keira, don't wait up," I say as I get into the car and she waves back before closing the door behind her.

"Well, she was just a bit terrifying, I swear she was sizing me up for a coffin there," Josh says.

"She's just worried after the magazine article and you do have a rep as a playboy, how is she to know I'm different?" I put a reassuring hand on his shoulder.

"I suppose so. It's just so frustrating as half those stories were Mia leaking rubbish to the press to make herself look good so I would beg to differ about the playboy thing."

"Uh huh, although I do have it on good authority that there is some truth to it but for balance, it has been noted you hadn't been like that for a while before you met me. So, I do believe that your playboy days are behind you," I say with a smile.

Josh takes my hand and gently kisses it as he turns into a grand driveway of a beautifully imposing grey stone castle.

"I bet you didn't realise you lived on the doorstep of such an impressive castle, now did you?" We exit the car and Josh hands the keys over to the valet as he takes my hand in his and we slowly walk towards the entrance.

"No, I had no idea. It's absolutely stunning and look at how spectacular the flowers are." As we reach the door, I stop for a moment to take in the thick garland full of orange, purple, blue and pink flowers. The sweet smell wafts across as we pass under it and into the entrance hall.

We step off the red carpet and into a bright room with high ceilings and ornate cornices in white contrasting elegantly against the grey and blue hues which in turn contrast perfectly with the bold flowers strategically placed around the room. The chandeliers glisten in the sunshine, showering the room with rainbow reflections.

As we walk towards the garden where the ceremony will take place, I see Eleanor who drops back to give us a big hug.

"You look amazing, Autumn, that dress is gorgeous and the colour really suits you," Eleanor says as we take our seats on the side of the groom, flicking through the programmes we picked up from our seats.

"You don't look so bad yourself, Eleanor, you should wear dresses more often. Now, how do you two know the guy getting married?" I ask.

"He's a school friend of mine, I introduced him to the *Phoenix Lives* crew years ago." Josh's voice trails off slightly as his eyes fix on something across the way. As I follow his gaze, I see Mia walking towards the seats dressed from head to toe in ivory with Megan in tow.

"What is Mia doing here? Who in their right mind wears the same colour as the bride?" I ask crossly. Megan spots me and waves with a smile. I wave back as she turns to speak to Mia.

"I have no idea, she couldn't stand Colin or Lydia while we were together, so I'm as shocked as you are." Josh holds my hand in his and brushes his thumb over my fingers reassuringly.

"She's clearly looking to make a statement in that outfit, I dare say she will have tipped off the paps and it'll be plastered all over the mags soon enough. That one is as brazen as they come and her little lapdog is not much better." Eleanor shoots them both a venomous look as they smirk back. Mia flicks her hair to disguise the fact that she is checking whether anyone is watching her.

As the wedding music sounds, we all stand up and watch as the bridesmaids elegantly glide down the aisle in deep purple dresses, a little boy and girl leading them hand in hand. As the bride emerges, we instantly note her stunning vintage off the shoulder golden dress with a full billowing skirt and elegant embroidery. Her matching veil and glittering tiara give a nod to a bygone era. A look of irritation crosses Mia's face as she realises her attempt to upstage the bride has failed. Happily, the bride joins her future husband at the altar with only eyes for one another.

The ceremony flows seamlessly. Josh looks over towards me with a warm smile and gently brushes hair off my face. Smiling back to him, I catch a sinister stare from Mia that sends a chill running down my spine.

Chapter 23

As the wedding reception continues in full swing and the drinks begin to flow, the other people at the party seem to fall away as Josh and I sit ever closer.

Reaching out to cup my face in his hand, he draws me towards him, tantalisingly slowly, and our lips meet for a passionate kiss. My arms drape around his neck and he pulls me closer before we break away and stare at each other for what seems like an age.

"Autumn, I know we haven't really talked about what is between us and that isn't because I didn't want to but I know this business and I didn't want your moment to shine to be eclipsed by becoming involved with me. So, I hung back, took the time to get to know you but I don't think I can hold back anymore. I want to be with you properly," Josh says sincerely as he gently kisses my forehead.

"I would really like that too, Josh, I can't hide my feelings any more than you and I figure it's been the worst kept secret on set anyway. I know Eleanor has been teasing me about you since the first day at *Othello*, so I suppose it's time we made it official." I smile back before we kiss once more. Noticing that we are out of drinks, I go to the bar in the hope of finding Eleanor so I can tell her the happy news.

"Ok but don't be long, I want my girlfriend back with me as soon as possible," Josh chides, playful and kissing me before I leave.

Making my way through the crowds to the bar, I spy Eleanor across the other side, chatting with colleagues. As she spots me approaching, she smiles warmly and gives me a big hug.

"Autumn, there you are. I've missed you but sure didn't want to be interrupting as it seemed things were going well with a certain someone." Eleanor smiles and everybody around her smirks. My cheeks blush.

"I know it's been the worst kept secret ever but it's all out in the open now, we've just had the chat and we are together. I just couldn't keep it to myself, I had to tell you," I happily confide.

"Yes, you did, I've been there from the moment you clapped eyes on each other so I expect to be the first to know. I'm so thrilled for you both." Eleanor gives me another big hug as I leave her and go to the bar for drinks.

Waiting patiently for my turn at the bar, I busy myself with finding my money which has escaped the little pocket I put it in and is now awkwardly lodged in the seam of my bag.

"What can I get you?"

I look up and I'm shocked to see James staring back at me. It takes him a moment but as soon as he recognises me, a big smile crosses his face.

"Oh, hey Autumn, I didn't expect to see you here." His smile is still strong across his face.

"Likewise. They let you out of Temple Bar then?" I say

teasingly.

"Remember that rich gobshite guy I told you about who was friends with my brother? This is his wedding. He's paying a fortune to do the same job here so I thought why not. I didn't know you knew him."

"I don't know him, I just came as a plus one with the *Phoenix Lives* crew so that's why. I have never met either the bride or the groom actually."

"Of course, I caught your first episode and you were fabulous, still find it strange to see you on screen. I've never met someone famous before." James puts my drinks on the bar and I hand over the money.

"I'm not famous. You knew me before all that and I'm no different now," I say as I take back my change and put it in my bag.

"You sure aren't, Autumn, I knew you were special when I saw you and now I'm sure."

I thank James, take the drinks and head back to Josh who is now joined by Mia, Megan and Eleanor.

"Oh, hi guys, sorry I didn't get you any drinks," I say to Eleanor and Megan more than Mia. As I place our drinks on the table, I move next to Josh, motioning for Mia to move up and I squeeze in between them. I see her face flash with anger. Eleanor smirks as she sips her drink.

"We hear congratulations is in order, Autumn, you and Josh are finally official," Megan says enthusiastically while Mia remains sullen and silent.

"Thank you, Megan, we're thrilled. It was never a secret but we wanted time to get to know each other and I wouldn't change that for the world," I say as I notice Mia's jaw tighten. But Megan remains happy and supportive, which is reassuring. I find myself hopeful that she did mean what she said to me the last time we met.

"Congratulations to you both, I can't say I see the attraction but whatever floats your boat, Josh. Come on, Megan, I need a drink." Mia gets up and leaves with Megan in tow, who waves awkwardly as she leaves.

"Well, that went better than expected, never did I think she would congratulate you both so I suppose the thinly veiled insult was expected," Eleanor says as we watch Mia head towards the bar before stopping to speak fervently to Megan. They walk out of view, disappearing into the crowd at the bar.

"I'm just glad it is now all out in the open and we can just concentrate on our relationship and the Mia episode of my life is fully in the past. She has felt like a shadow over me for so long, it's a relief for it to finally end," Josh says as he reaches for his drink and we all toast our happy news.

"Oh wait, don't clink yet. I've bought us some champagne to toast properly in style. Sorry, they only had one strawberry left." Megan passes the champagne flute with the strawberry to Eleanor as we all take the remaining glasses.

"Guess who served me these drinks, Autumn?" Megan asks.

"Would it be James by any chance?" I say, already knowing the answer to this.

"Oh my God, yes, I didn't think you knew. Well, that stole my thunder a bit," Megan says.

"He served me our drinks, I didn't recognise him at first but he knows the groom. Funny how everything links up," I say.

"Who is this James fella? Anyone I should be worried

about?" Josh teases.

"He's a barman we know, he's always had a thing for Autumn though from the moment he saw her. She is quite the man magnet it would seem," Megan jokes.

"I am not! Yes, he has liked me a while but he doesn't seem the reliable type, just call it a hunch," I reply.

"You can't know that, you've never given him a chance. But that is all in the past now, so let us propose a toast to the new couple of the moment, Josh and Autumn," Megan says enthusiastically and we all raise our glasses, clink them together and take a drink.

Megan fidgets with the top of her dress but as it is so tight, it proves impossible for her to adjust by herself. "Sorry, if you can excuse me, I need to sort this dress out. Eleanor, would you mind coming to help me as I can't undo it by myself? I would ask you, Autumn, but I don't want to spoil this moment for you."

Eleanor agrees and quickly finishes the rest of her drink before they both head off together.

I smile at Josh and we resume our conversations with eyes only for each other. As time passes, I notice neither Megan nor Eleanor have returned and our drinks are once again low. I offer to go to the bar once again in the hopes of finding Eleanor. While I am enjoying this moment with Josh, I don't want to suddenly disappear on my friends either.

Leaving Josh with a kiss, I go to the bar but there is no sign of either of them. James makes a beeline towards me once he sees me there.

"Hello again, stranger, can't keep away tonight, eh?" he asks with a cheeky smile.

"James, have you seen Megan? She seems to have

disappeared," I say looking around the bar again.

"No, last time I saw she went to the toilet but I haven't seen her since."

"Autumn, there you are. Megan needs you in the toilet as soon as possible, it's Eleanor," Mia says with concern. My heart drops.

Megan is on the floor in the toilets, Eleanor's head in her lap as she lays unconscious on the floor.

"Oh my God, what the hell happened, is she ok?" I check Eleanor's breathing and her skin, which is still warm.

"It's been awful, Autumn, we came in here and she started to be really sick so I stayed with her and then she's just passed out. I couldn't leave her to come get you and only when Mia came to look for me could I get someone to get you. I've been with her the whole time to make sure she was ok." Megan's tone is worried, her dress dirtied from the bathroom floor.

"We need to get her home. Megan, can you go and get Josh, ask him to help me take her home?" I take Eleanor's head from Megan.

"I'll go and ask him. Autumn, you both stay there to make sure she is ok." Mia rushes out of the door in search of Josh. I feel better knowing he'll be here soon and able to help.

"It doesn't make any sense. She wasn't even that drunk and I know Eleanor, she doesn't get like this," I say, confused.

"You know how it is though. Sometimes, Autumn, the drink hits you all at once and that's the thing about weddings. You consistently drink throughout the day, especially an Irish one. Sure, a night out, you don't start drinking that early, except Paddy's Day, but then that's always a messy one too."

"That's true, I suppose; do you think we should get her some medical help just in case there is something wrong?" I stroke her hair.

"She sure won't thank you for that when she's landed with a massive medical bill for what's just down to her being plastered," Megan says.

Before I can answer, the door bursts open and in comes James and Mia but no Josh.

"Sorry, Autumn, I couldn't find Josh anywhere but I found your bag on the table where he was. He's always been a liability when he's had a drink and prone to wondering off," Mia says as she hands me my bag.

"Really? Maybe he's just looking for me as I haven't returned with our drinks?" I gently slide myself out of the way so James can pick Eleanor up off the ground.

"Follow me, Autumn, my car is outside and I'll take you both home. She can't be left here like this." James walks out of the toilets, carrying Eleanor.

"Megan, can you please let Josh know what has happened and why I've had to leave and that I'm sorry?" Megan nods as I rush out with my bag.

As we make our way back, a feeling of unease grows, I open my bag to message Josh but quickly realise my phone is gone. I feel the tears start to well in my eyes as I realise there is no way to contact him and a sinking feeling fills my stomach. Something about this feels so off.

Chapter 24

The pulling of the covers jolts me awake. I quickly turn to see Eleanor awakening from her sleep.

"Eleanor, how are you feeling? Are you ok?" I ask, concern flashing across my face.

Confused, Eleanor checks her surroundings and looks back again at me. "Did I miss something? Why are we sharing my bed?"

"You don't remember passing out last night at the wedding? I stayed with you to make sure you were ok," I say gently.

"I passed out? I wasn't even that drunk, I mean I paced myself throughout the whole day and the last thing I remember was toasting you and Josh. Everything after that is completely blank, like it doesn't exist." Eleanor pulls herself up and rubs her head.

"You went to help Megan with her dress and when you didn't return, I went to look for you and Mia came rushing out asking for me to help and you were lying on the floor unconscious. Josh had apparently wandered off, left my bag unattended and my phone was stolen. Luckily, Mia found James who helped get us home." The bizarre events of the night replay in my mind, still not making any real sense.

"So, Josh doesn't know what happened? You haven't been able to contact him?" Eleanor asks.

"I asked Megan to let him know, I'd find it hard to think he wouldn't understand given the circumstances especially as he left my bag unattended and disappeared. That's what has been bothering me, did he go looking for me or was he unwell? I have no idea?" A familiar feeling of fear envelops me.

"I'm so sorry, Autumn. Here, give him a call on my phone and at least then you can be reassured that everything is ok and he has heard what happened. I know you trust Megan but I never will." Eleanor gets out of bed, retrieves her bag and her phone and taps her code to unlock it before getting back into the bed and handing it to me.

"Thank you so much, Eleanor." I take the phone and search her contacts for Josh's name. I hesitate for a second before I call, my hands trembling.

"Hello Eleanor, how are you feeling today?" A female voice says brightly down the line, making me check if I've pressed the correct contact. The screen shows Josh's name. I quickly press the speakerphone icon.

"Erm, who is this? Where is Josh?" I ask, fearful of the answer.

"It's Mia. Is that you, Autumn?"

My eyes meet Eleanor's in astonishment. "Why do you have Josh's phone? Did he lose it?"

"No, Autumn, that's just you. He's in the shower, so I thought I'd be helpful and answer. Besides, I wanted to know how Eleanor was this morning," she chirps.

"Are you saying you stayed the night with him? Why

would he do that to me?" I try to keep my voice strong but the tears well up and drip down my face at this betrayal.

"Autumn, that's a conversation you'll need to have with Josh." The line cuts dead and I sit there in a stunned silence with Eleanor, the tears trickling down my cheeks.

"Oh Autumn, I'm so sorry. I feel this is my fault, if I'd been more careful then none of this would have happened. I just don't understand why he would do this to you. It makes no sense." Eleanor wraps her arms around me.

"He's just reverted to type, it would seem, the playboy he always was."

Eleanor passes me a tissue to blow my nose. "A playboy he may have been in his past but he was never cruel, that wasn't Josh at all," Eleanor fumes. "I considered him my friend and I'd never have done that if I knew he was capable of treating anyone like this. I don't think I can ever look him in the face again, that guy is dead to me."

After a quiet breakfast where I barely touch a thing, I say goodbye to Eleanor and make my way home. Every landmark I pass on the bus ride home is invisible as the events replay in my head over and over again. I try to pinpoint what I've missed and how this could happen but for the life of me, I can't figure it out.

The first thing I do when I get home is head straight to the shower. The burning beads of water prick my skin but I feel nothing except the pain of this moment. The tears roll down my face and for the first time since this morning, I let out all the pain and hurt I've been holding inside.

Getting into a clean pair of pyjamas, I sit on the bed

and pull open my laptop. I video call Amelia, hoping that she is able to answer.

"Hey Autumn, I've been thinking about you. It seems ages since we last talked. How are you?" Amelia's bright and breezy voice and seeing her face sets me off into a fit of tears once again.

"Oh God Autumn, what has happened? Is everything ok?" Amelia's face breaks into concern as she patiently waits for me to be able to talk.

"It's Josh, he betrayed me in the cruellest way. I have no idea why, it just makes no sense." I sob as I fill Amelia in on the day's promising start and disastrous ending.

"Autumn, I just can't believe it. I'm shocked. He never seemed that kind of guy. Are you sure he knows the full story? I mean it's a very odd way to behave in those circumstances," Amelia offers kindly.

"I know that Megan would've told him, she was so supportive and helpful last night, I couldn't have faulted her. Even in front of Mia, she supported us as a couple so yes, he does know and he just doesn't care. Clearly, it's out of sight, out of mind with him." I break into tears again.

"Right, that's it. I'm coming over there. Keep next weekend free, get the girls all together and let's hit town hard and I swear by the end of the night you'll not have one tear left to shed for that pathetic excuse of a guy." Amelia smiles down the camera.

"That will be awesome, I'd love that so much. I'll need to get another phone tomorrow and then I can start arranging it."

"Now Autumn, there is one thing I want you to do for me tomorrow. I want you to walk into that production meeting with your head held high, pay no heed to Josh or Mia and be the amazing actress I know you are. This is your time and I will not let two self-absorbed assholes rob you of it," Amelia encourages.

I say goodbye to Amelia, feeling better, and as I lay on my bed, my mind wanders to tomorrow when I have to face Josh at work. As much as I will go in with my head held high, I will spend every waking hour until then dreading the moment my heart is sure to break.

Chapter 25

25 March 2018 - Dublin

The dawning of the day comes early. I watch the minutes tick by until I'm forced to get ready or face being late for work.

Moving across to the mirror, I smooth down the red and blue tartan skirt which I've paired with a black long sleeve top perfect for the cool spring mornings that will invariably give way to the warmer afternoons. Pulling on my black knee-high boots and grabbing my bag, a knock at the door startles me. My heart starts to pound in my chest as I hear Keira stomping angrily to answer, loudly muttering, "If that's you, Josh, prepare to die." She wrenches open the door. Peering down the stairwell, my heart somersaults, subsiding when Keira's face quickly softens into a smile as she shouts up to me. "Autumn, Eleanor's here." She politely ushers Eleanor into the hallway.

I run down the stairs. Eleanor stands there with a smile as she hands me a gift, wrapped up in a cute little bag. She leans in to give me a big hug.

"Thanks, Eleanor, that's so sweet of you. Let's have a cup of tea before the car arrives."

Keira makes the tea as I sit down at the table and start

to unwrap my gift, intrigued as to what it could be.

"I wanted to make sure you had some moral support this morning because God knows what the hell we'll be walking in to," Eleanor says as she accepts her drink from Keira who sits down at the kitchen table with us.

"I swear to God, if that had been Josh at the door, I'd be going to jail right now. I swear to God, if I ever get my hands on him, he's a goner," Keira says angrily. She stirs her drink heavily, causing it to slosh onto the table.

"Keira, I'd help you hide the body, no questions asked," Eleanor chips in as I unwrap my gift to reveal a new phone.

"Oh, Eleanor, you didn't need to do that. I was going to get one later. Thank you, it is such a sweet gesture."

"I figured you didn't have any insurance and it's one less thing to worry about. Besides, now Josh doesn't have your new number but you can change it to your old one if you wanted. That's up to you." Eleanor takes a sip of her tea.

"Let's see how today goes, shall we? Then I can decide. On a positive note, I wrote down all my important contacts when I moved over to Dublin so I've only lost the numbers from Dublin, which you'll be pleased to know includes Megan."

I hand my phone over to Eleanor and motion for her to add in her contact number, which she does before handing it back to me with a smile. "I'm not saying a word."

"I spoke with Amelia last night and filled her in on everything, so keep this weekend free as she's coming over and wants us to all head out. Keira, are you up for that?" I ask.

"Damn right I am, I'd love a night out and we need

to make sure you forget all about Jock Strap," Keira says with a mischievous smile.

I hand her my phone to add in her number too.

"Keira, not only are you one of the funniest people I've ever met but the most spot on too," Eleanor says as we raise our mugs and chink in solidarity.

Keira hands back my phone to me, and we finish our drinks as the car pulls up outside. Taking the mugs and placing them into the dishwasher, we bid goodbye.

"Just one thing, Autumn, how about we don't invite Megan to this weekend?" Eleanor says with one eye slightly raised as we get into the car.

"You really don't trust her, do you? Even though she was really there for you at the wedding and helped to keep you safe until I could find you?" I ask gently.

Eleanor pauses for a moment as she looks out at the cityscape flicking past the window. "Nothing about the day makes any sense. I mean, why would Mia bring her to the wedding? Why not one of her male hangers-on? So, while I know she was on her best behaviour and did a lot to help, the fact she was even there is the biggest alarm bell to me."

"Any thoughts on what that reason could have been? Maybe Mia wanted to get back at me, so chose someone she knew was close to me?" I ask.

"I have no idea what gives but I know there is something fishy and all I ask is that you trust me with Megan and step it back," Eleanor says as we pull up.

"Wait, there is something that's been bothering me about all this. Remember when I called Josh from your phone and I asked Mia if he had lost his phone and she said, 'No, Autumn, that's just you?'" I ask.

"Yeah, I remember her saying that clearly." Eleanor leans a little closer to me.

"Well, I didn't check my bag for my phone until I was in the car on the way home, so there is no way for her to know I'd lost it. Also, it was Mia who gave me my bag so she clearly took it." Now my suspicions are aroused. Confirmed even.

"I knew it, you're to have nothing to do with Megan as she is clearly in on this and I have no idea what actually happened but what I do know is that it has their grubby little fingerprints all over it," Eleanor says angrily.

As we enter the studio building, my heart slumps. Amelia's words resound in my head. I take a second outside the room to take a deep breath before I enter. Holding my head high and a smile on my face, I walk into the room.

Mia meets my gaze. A slight smirk crosses her lips as she turns to Josh who is sitting next to her. "Oh honey, can we tell everyone our news now?" She plants a kiss on his lips. Not waiting for a reply, she stands up and taps her steel water bottle on the table to command the attention of the room. "Morning, everyone, I just wanted to say a few words before Derek arrives." As she says this, Derek walks in to the room but keeps quiet while she continues.

"I just wanted to announce that over the weekend, having attended a close friend's wedding, Josh and I came to realise how strong our love truly is and that nothing or anyone could ever part us, no matter how hard they might try." Mia's words sharpen as her gaze lands intently on me.

Turning back to the room with a smile, she continues,

"So feel free to congratulate us throughout on the day on our marvellous news and truly inspiring love story."

She sits down, grinning widely at the stunned room. An awkward silence descends as everyone present looks from a flushed and embarrassed-looking Josh towards me, confusion evident across their faces.

Derek walks up to the front of the room, putting a reassuring arm on my shoulder and giving me a warm smile as he passes me.

"Thank you, Mia, now back to today's meeting." Derek continues to talk but all sound fades. I take one last look at Josh, his face and body turning away from me completely as Mia fawns over him. Never once does he return her affection, his face growing redder with each dramatized display of affection. I wonder how I could mourn someone so incapable of respecting me.

Any need I had for answers is replaced by the resolve to not give Mia the satisfaction of seeing the hurt she has caused me, which she is clearly craving right now. Turning to Eleanor, I whisper, "I'll be keeping my new number, time for a complete fresh start."

Chapter 26

1st April 2018 – Dublin

A sense of déjà vu washes over me as I wait for Amelia to arrive at the airport. This is where our friendship started, outside those doors in the queue for the bus stop. I look down at my bracelet, gently twisting it around my wrist, pondering how it still feels like yesterday.

"Autumn!" rings out across the airport as Amelia bounds towards me. She lets go of her luggage and it hits the floor with a thud as she wraps me in a big hug.

"It's great to see you, Amelia, I haven't seen you since the *Othello* party. It seems ages ago now," I say as we break away from the hug.

"I know, so much has happened since then. I've joined a dating site, been on a couple of dates, but you know how it is, got to wade through the weirdos first." Amelia sighs.

"Have you ever thought you could be the weirdo?" I say in jest.

"You could have a point. Well alright, maybe I just haven't met the right kind of weirdo yet," she says as we start to walk out of the airport and towards the car park.

"I'm so glad you're here, a proper night out with the girls is exactly what I need. It has been the worst week. It seems Josh and Mia are now a couple. That I was barely out of the place before he was straight back with her." My mouth twists in anger as these words leave my mouth.

"Are you serious? I mean what you told me before was bad enough but I didn't expect this. Fuck him, if he is going to act like that he doesn't even deserve you and when we head out later you'll see that."

Keira drives the short distance back to the house, we walk in to find the table is laid out with a lovely lunch made by Connor in our absence.

"Aww, babe, thank you, that's lovely." Keira beams at her boyfriend as she gives him a big kiss and he leaves to meet his friends for a drink.

"You two are such a sweet couple, here's hoping that this time next year, Autumn and I will have both met someone lovely too," Amelia says as she gives me another hug.

"I knew he was a keeper straight away. He's always been very thoughtful and that's what I felt had been lacking in my other relationships. As hard as it is, when you find the right guy, you will know." Keira smiles broadly and we all tuck into our lunch before getting ready for our big night out.

Later that day…

The warm evening air causes the scent of the Liffey to hang heavy in the air as we walk down the Quay towards my favourite Italian restaurant at the bottom on Temple Bar.

"Autumn, it's lovely to see you again. Follow me."

Matteo shows us to our table and motions at the waiter to bring over some wine and glasses.

"A little treat from us to our favourite customer," Matteo says proudly with a thick Italian accent as the waiter arrives to set down the drinks on our table.

"Thank you so much, Matteo, I hope you're enjoying this week's episodes. As always, we are sworn to secrecy," I say as I motion to Eleanor and then pull my fingers across my lips as if I'm pulling a zip over them.

"Absolutely, I'm a big fan of you two lovely ladies. Is Josh joining you tonight too?" Matteo asks as the girls suddenly look down at their menus.

"Not tonight, I'm afraid. Mia, his girlfriend, wouldn't approve, I'm sure." I purse my lips.

"Well, you know what I say? If they didn't last before, then they won't last now. A tiger never changes its stripes. He's a fool and if he comes in here, no wine, no treat," Matteo says indignantly.

I smile back at Matteo as we start to place our orders.

"So, how are you feeling about everything now, Autumn?" Keira asks as she pours out a drink and hands it to each person before putting the bottle back in the cooler.

"Like I've dodged a bullet. As hard as it is to accept, this is who he really is and this would have always happened sooner or later. So, I need to be grateful it was sooner." I take a sip of my wine.

"I just find it all so strange. I mean when I met him at *Othello*, he just didn't seem that type and even if he changed his mind, it's very odd behaviour. It's like he's trying to punish you but for what?" Amelia asks, her voice perplexed.

"We know Mia and Megan are behind it but we just can't figure out how yet," Eleanor says thoughtfully. "I've known Josh a long time and he's never been cruel like this. If you were the one to betray him, then you could understand it but how can he act like this when he is so clearly in the wrong? It's all so strange."

"As hard as it is and will be for a while, he is in the past and I have all my favourite girls around me so I guarantee you, tonight you will not find me sad or looking backwards. I am happy and ready to move on with someone who deserves me," I say, as I motion to the waiter for another bottle of wine.

"What we need is something to look forward to," Eleanor says before adding, "Why don't we organise a girl's trip for your birthday, Autumn?"

"That's a fantastic idea. I don't think I will make it as I'll be in Australia but you should go somewhere so fun," Amelia says enthusiastically.

"Why don't we go to Vegas? I've always wanted to go," I say.

Everyone responds in unison with a resounding yes and a feeling of excitement fills me.

Leaving the restaurant, I give Matteo a big hug and totter down the cobbled street to the one bar that holds the most memories for me. The red and black paint and illuminated exterior calls like a beacon.

"Back where it all started, Amelia, remember?" I hold the door open as the girls all walk in and we make our way to the bar.

"I had a feeling I'd be seeing my favourite actress tonight," James says with a big smile across his face as he raises his eyebrows playfully.

"I'm the only actress you know, James," I say.

"You don't know that's true. Now, ladies, what can I get you?" James readies our order, oblivious to the discontented faces of customers who have been waiting longer.

"He's so clearly still in to you, why are you still so resistant?" Amelia asks sternly.

"Because he's clearly a player, I bet he says that to every woman. It's all an act," I defend myself.

"I hate to agree with Megan on this one but you've never given him the chance," Eleanor says as Keira passes over our drinks.

"Ok, no more games, Autumn. The time is now." Amelia turns away from me to James. "James, you've been outrageously flirting with my friend for over a year now. Do you think maybe the time has come to man up and ask her out?"

An awkward silence descends across the bar as every face turns to me. My face blushes red as I choke on my drink.

James' eyes dash to the side. His face blushes more crimson than mine as he struggles for how to respond.

"Erm, well, if she wanted to then I'd be happy to go on a date." His bravado suddenly failing, he keeps his head down and avoids eye contact while he fixes the next client's drinks. The customers in ear shot are all engrossed at the unfolding events.

"Well, she does want to, so name the time and the place," Amelia says, dominantly.

"Look, Amelia, I know you are trying to help but I'm not asking anyone out until they tell me themselves that they want to go," James says sternly which is quite unlike him and takes Amelia back.

My face flushes as I pause for a moment, my mind replaying the scene on Monday with Josh and Mia and the smug satisfaction of her thinking she had won.

"Yes, I'd love to go on a date with you, James," I say with a smile as I meet James' eyes and he blushes even harder than before.

"Great. So, I'm off next weekend. Keep Saturday free, pass me over your number and I'll be in touch." James winks while a round of applause rings out from the patrons waiting to be served.

I see Amelia tapping my number into James' phone, a big smile across her face, and it is clear she is feeling very proud of herself.

As the night wears on, the drinks continue to flow and we end up drinking cocktails at a dingy Temple Bar nightclub. While Amelia and Eleanor chat up a storm with guys they've met, I sit with Keira as we both nurse our last drinks of the evening.

"Thank you, Keira, for all your support since I came to Ireland, you've always looked out for me and I really appreciate it," I say with a smile.

"Oh, don't be silly, you're grand. Besides, I've always liked you and admired how you came over here and made your dreams come true. It's fantastic, not many people come to Dublin to live their dreams. Sure, that's usually why they leave," she says with a giggle.

"Autumn, Keira, fancy seeing you both here." Cian drunkenly drapes his arms around our shoulders and cuddles us both.

"You look like you are enjoying yourself, Cian?" Keira says with a smile as Cian sips his drink.

"Well, I'm celebrating. I'm a single guy these days and loving every second. Shame your friend isn't with you these days, Autumn, she was a lovely girl," Cian says.

"You mean Amelia?" A smirk crosses my face.

"That's the one, the traveller. I do think about her sometimes and what's she up to these days?" Cian finishes his drink and places it down on the table next to us.

"Well, you should go and ask her, Cian. Look, she's over there on the dance floor." I can tell from Cian's face that he thinks I'm teasing him but as he follows my pointing finger, he sees Amelia dancing, happily oblivious to anyone else. His jaw drops in shock but before we know it, he's headed off across the room towards her.

"It looks like Cian's got a big crush on Amelia there, does she like him do you think?" Keira asks. Amelia recognises him and instantly throws her arms around his neck.

"Oh yes, she was pretty taken with him when we came to view the house and was gutted when you said he had a fiancé." I notice them both slip away from the dance floor to talk.

"I'm sorry I had no idea, they had been on the rocks for years and neither of them were very happy. We all told them to split ages ago."

As the night finally draws to a close, we all make our way home in the cool chill of the evening and I take a moment to appreciate having some of the best friends I could've hoped for.

Chapter 27

Date with James, 8th April 2018

As the *Phoenix Lives* hair and makeup artists descend upon my house, you could be forgiven for thinking this was an awards ceremony rather than a low key first date.

"Eleanor, what's wrong with that outfit? It's supposed to be casual," I protest, as I sit still in my chair while the final touches to my makeup is applied.

"I've got you a VIP booth at one of the most exclusive members-only clubs in the whole of Dublin. Trust me, it's not casual," Eleanor says as she rushes upstairs and I hear my wardrobe being opened and the screeching of coat hangers as she rifles through my clothes.

"Nothing about Milieu on Grafton is casual but don't worry Autumn, once I'm finished with you they will be running rings round you. Did you know, Mia tried to get in there with Josh but they had to go to Fleur," Violet says helpfully as she slicks the last of the lipstick across my lips with a smile.

"Those vomit-inducing pap shots have burned themselves into my eyes but knowing that does make me feel a little smug," I say.

Eleanor comes down the stairs with a dress in her hand and a smile on her face. "This is absolutely perfect,

Autumn," She holds out a pleated emerald green chiffon round halter neck dress with delicate gold detailing around the neck and waist as it bleeds gently into a dusky pink colour midway down the skirt.

"Oh yes, I bought that with my first *Phoenix Lives* pay check but never had an occasion fancy enough to wear it, seemed a bit OTT for the wedding," I say as I get up from the chair and take the dress from Eleanor to change into upstairs.

Remerging into the kitchen, I feel like I'm walking down a red carpet, my accessories all in place. I feel like a true celebrity. A silence descends across the kitchen for a moment before smiles appear.

"Autumn, you look sensational. This is going to be such a perfect evening and wow, look at what Josh is missing!" Violet says, clapping her hands in front of her.

"It's perfect, Autumn, now remember whatever happens tonight is for your own good," Eleanor adds cryptically as she gives me a big hug.

At that moment, Keira walks into the house and stops in her tracks when she sees me.

"Wow, Autumn, you look beautiful. Here, let me take a picture. No offence, you always look nice but this kind of nice needs to be remembered, it's a whole new level." Keira gets in a muddle as she speaks but quickly takes a photo to show me.

"Thank you, ladies, for all your help, this is a whole lot more than I expected but let's hope James is far more worth it than Josh ever was," I say with a wry smile.

The evening traffic is light and it doesn't take long until we are snaking our way around the small streets just off Grafton Street and pulling up to the grand entrance that looks decidedly modern compared to the period architecture surrounding it.

As I leave my taxi, I see James waiting for me. Walking over, he gives me his hand and we walk into the venue together. We both stay silent for a moment, taking in the plush wooden interior, contrasting against the dark walls and teal furniture, which in turn beautifully sets off the ornate gold chandeliers and wall lights.

We're ushered into a small private room that looks more like a luxurious front room than a bar, thick dark velvet curtains hanging down to ensure absolute privacy. Our server points out the call buttons and passes us menus before disappearing and leaving us alone.

"This is all a bit intense, I thought we were off for a quiet pub drink," James says with a smile as he gazes at me for a little longer than necessary.

"I'm glad I'm not the only one, James. Eleanor wanted it to be special so she's to blame for all this but at least we have a nice area to be able to talk properly as in a pub we'd have to be shouting in each other's ears the whole time," I say.

"Right so, I can't be arguing with that, besides I'm not complaining about that outfit. You look stunning, Autumn, I feel very lucky to be the guy you're on a date with, that's for sure." He reaches for my hand, I extend mine to reach his and our fingers intertwine as he brings my hand to his lips for a gentle kiss.

The hours tick by like minutes as we forget all our surroundings and lose ourselves in the playful banter and flirtation that started from the moment we first met. My fears of his player behaviour are easily set aside and we emerge from the entrance hand in hand. Getting into the taxi to take me home, I'm stopped by a gentle tug on my arm as James pulls me towards him, placing his hand around my face. He draws me slowly in for a good night kiss. Our lips meet in the perfect stillness of the night.

A sudden burst of light jolts us out of the moment, and I turn, only to see photographers jostling for the perfect picture. The realisation of what Eleanor had planned for this date sinks in.

Turning back to James, I pull him into a passionate kiss. The flashes flicker wildly around us but we ignore it as we sink sensually into a long and lingering kiss.

"Ok, so you've passed, I'll take you on a second date but how about we ditch the paps next time," James says coyly as he wraps me in a big hug.

"Deal, let's have that quiet pub drink and you can have me all to yourself," I say as I give James a final goodbye kiss and head home in my taxi. A sudden bing alerts me to a text. It's a message from Eleanor that reads:

"I know you're too nice to play Mia and Josh at their own game but I'm not…Mia's going to get a taste of her own medicine in tomorrow's papers! Sit back and enjoy!"

I smile as I read her text, a part of me relieved that if nothing else, Josh will know I'm not dwelling on him or his betrayal.

Chapter 28

The following morning, I wander down the stairs to find Keira and Connor waiting expectantly at the table.

"Morning, sunshine, we weren't opening the paper until you were up. Eleanor messaged me to say there will be quite the story in it today. I'm thinking it's about you," Keira says.

Pouring a drink of water from the fridge, I put the jug back and join them at the table as we flick through the paper and there it is on page four and five. The headline jumps at me as I open the page. I pass the paper to Keira and Connor to take a look.

"Oh wow, well, that packs a punch, doesn't it?" Keira passes the paper back to me and I begin to read.

"*Phoenix Lives* Love Triangle: Heartbroken star moves on with new love after co-star betrayal."

A smile crosses my lips as I look down at the photos of me and James from last night and the passionate kiss we parted with. The story continues:

"Tensions have been rising between three *Phoenix Lives* cast members embroiled in a fierce love triangle. While we've all been captivated with the endless on/off romance between Josh Bailey and Mia O'Riordan, it appears there's someone new we need to add to the mix: the show's newest cast member, Autumn Sutherland. Sources close to the show spoke exclusively to *The Dublin Post* about the love triangle that led to a heart-breaking betrayal for Autumn at the hands of Josh and Mia. Yet it appears Autumn has found the strength to put her heartbreak aside after pictures emerged of her on Saturday night in a passionate clinch with a mystery man outside Milieu on Grafton. It is reported the couple spent hours getting to know each other in the secluded VIP section of the prestigious venue."

I close the newspaper, having read enough, and push it into the centre of the table. A smile crosses my lips. Retrieving my phone, I dial Eleanor and put her on speaker phone. She answers quickly, most likely expecting my call.

"So, what do you think, Autumn?" Eleanor asks coyly.

"Well, it isn't something I would have done myself but it certainly does level the playing field and given Mia is so obsessed about her public image, it will certainly hit her where it hurts," I say.

"It's brilliant, Eleanor, well done," Keira chirps in the background.

"Phew, glad that you don't mind. I didn't want to tell you as it was imperative looked natural. No one will doubt you had nothing to do with it so it'll spook them as to who it could be," Eleanor says with a hint of malice.

"As far as I can tell, no one outside Mia does this sort of thing so it's likely Mia will look at her circle rather than out of it. I don't think it'll cross her mind that anyone else will be able to play her at her own game." A smile spreads across my face and my heart feels a fraction less heavy.

I say goodbye to Eleanor and for the first time since this whole nightmare began, I don't dread seeing them tomorrow. The impending doom that had led me to dread my work day lifts and the excitement I felt once again returns.

The next day

A knot of trepidation twists in my stomach as we leave the car and make our way into the studio. While I don't care what Mia thinks or says, there is a part of me that cares what Josh thinks, which makes me angry at myself.

"Just play it cool. After all, it's your privacy that has been infringed. Let's see how the banshee reacts," Eleanor says as we walk in sharing a giggle.

As we enter, every eye turns to us.

"So, you aren't bothered about the slander from yesterday, Autumn?" Mia flings the newspaper at me from across the table, her face red with anger as Josh apathetically scribbles on his notepad.

"What can I do about it, Mia? My privacy was invaded, illicit photos taken of me without my knowledge and my personal life splashed over the news. Excuse me but of all days I need to laugh, it's today," I retort as I see the faces of my colleagues soften in sympathy.

"Well, what about me? I was made out to be a self-obsessed, spiteful and petty boyfriend stealer, which is so untrue," she whines as every eye darts down. Smiles appear on all the faces of our colleagues. "It's not my fault that Josh loves me more than anyone else and I do feel for you, Autumn, that you were never the competition you thought you were." Mia's voice drips faux sympathy but the veiled insult shines through to everyone in the room.

"Oh, don't feel sorry for me, Mia, one day he'll love you by default. When all other options have passed him by, he'll make do with you. We all know this showmance is a sham. You're a terrible actress, Mia, and Josh does little to hide his contempt for you. As for you, Josh, you are a weak, pathetic excuse for a man and I curse the day I set eyes on you." The rage builds inside me as I meet his eyes for the first time.

"Trust me, Autumn, the feeling is mutual and I'm as happy with Mia as I always was." Josh narrows his eyes.

"Great. From what you told me before, you hated every second with her so nice to know you love the prison you walked yourself straight back into," I retort.

As I storm out of the room, Eleanor close behind, Josh's eyes follow me and while his words were meant to hurt, I see a flicker of the familiar warmth he always had when he looked at me before it turns to what looks a lot like regret.

Chapter 29

August 2018, Las Vegas

The thick humid air hangs heavily in our room as Amelia goes to turn on the air conditioning. A blanket of cool air begins to circulate. I hand Amelia and Casey a drink.

"I just can't believe we're in Las Vegas. This is going to be a birthday to remember, Autumn," Casey says enthusiastically. She flicks through the wardrobe to find the day's outfit. She pulls out an oversized hat and turns to me and Amelia, pouting and posing for us.

"Check you out, Casey, looking like a movie star in that hat," Amelia says as she takes it off and with a bow, heads to the bathroom for a shower.

A loud knock at the door makes us jump. I open the door to reveal Eleanor, Keira, Stella and Melissa all waiting in the hallway.

"Are you girls not even dressed yet?" Stella says with mock disdain.

"I called it, girls, I totally called it," Eleanor says.

"Here, take our keys and use the showers in our rooms and get yourselves ready as there is only one place to go for breakfast in Vegas, The Bellagio." Melissa hands me the key for her and Stella's room while Eleanor hands hers to Amelia. Within the hour, we're all ready to go.

Making our way from the Metro, it doesn't take long to spot the impressive fountains of the Bellagio, a throng of tourists standing outside to watch this famous spectacle.

Walking past the fountains, the slight spray is refreshing in the scorching desert heat. It is early in the morning but the heat is already oppressive and heavy as we make our way through the manicured gardens and into the palatial hotel. Inside, it's instantly cool and decorated with marble and Italian-inspired statues and tall vases of flowers. Making our way past the designer shops, Eleanor stops, captivated by a red tote bag with beautifully ornate applique flowers and tiny gems in the centre.

"That is such a gorgeous bag, I'm not really one for designers but that is beautiful," Eleanor says as she presses her face up to the window to get a closer look.

"I approve as it doesn't have the name printed grossly over the top like a cheap supermarket brand. I can't stand that," I add as we carry on to the elegant restaurant where breakfast is served.

As we are ushered to a table, the waitress points out how to get to the food and drinks and it becomes clear that this place has breakfast from almost every country you can think of. "It is an all-you-can eat breakfast, so you can just go up as many times as you like," she says helpfully as she departs with a warm smile.

"I did wonder why it was so expensive but now I realise I can stuff myself silly and not need to eat again for two days, it seems much more reasonable," Keira says.

After many trips to the mass array of food on offer, we leave the Bellagio and make our way to Las Vegas Blvd in search of the shopping mall so we can find ourselves brand new outfits for our first night on the strip.

Later that evening

Leaving the hotel, our limo awaits us but before we enter, the driver takes a photo in front of the limo, of us looking our glamourous best. I send to James to keep him updated on our adventures.

"So, how are things with you and James now? They seem to be getting serious?" Melissa asks inquisitively.

"We seem to have turned a corner. I do admit in the beginning I probably went out with him more to get back at Josh but that has definitely changed now and I'm happy with the way things have turned out," I admit as I see James text me back to say how stunning I look and wishing us a great night.

"See, you need to just call me cupid, my price is maid of honour at the wedding," Amelia says with a glint in her eye.

"Hate to burst your bubble but there are no plans for marriage yet." I smile as Keira hands us all a champagne glass.

"It's great you feel that way, Autumn, and I definitely don't think that's how Josh feels. I overheard him the other day talking to his friend and he said how much he regretted the way things had gone between you." Eleanor takes a gentle sip of her champagne.

"Well, that kind of makes me feel awesome, I mean it would take the shine off how great I was feeling if he was too. Here, let's propose a toast to the exes who royally fucked everything up," I say.

We all raise our glasses, clinking them together as the limo comes to a stop. We hastily drink the contents before disembarking and making our way into the VIP section on the mezzanine. The shiny red leather sofas sparkle under the array of red and blue lights that give the place its ambience. Following our server to the table, we find a large bottle of iced vodka and an array of mixers waiting for us. Excited, we sit down and I start to pour out the drinks for us all as my friends sing out a chorus of happy birthday.

"So, who is the birthday girl tonight?" The Irish accent catches us off guard as we turn to see none other than Darryl McNally with a drink in his hand and his impish cheeky grin lighting up his face.

"That would be me, I'm Autumn Sutherland, feel free to join us." I point to a seat next to Casey who blushes bright red when he places himself down next to her, perhaps just that bit too close.

"These are my friends. This is Casey, my childhood friend from Devon; this is Eleanor, who is also my co-star; Amelia here is the first friend I made in Ireland; Keira here is my flatmate; and I worked previously with Melissa and Stella before I joined *Phoenix Lives*. I think everyone knows Darryl, right?" All my friends nod as Darryl waves his hand to the server and orders another round of drinks.

"I thought I recognised you, I caught a few episodes when I was back at me Ma's and you stand out with your accent but in a good way of course. So, you work with the psycho then?" Darryl asks, bitter as he adds, "I took the lass out on a date and wish I'd never bothered, the amount of things I've read about us, all stemming from that one date."

"She's only interested in your status and the fact she thinks you can open Hollywood to her," Eleanor says with derision.

"I banked that in the first five seconds and I don't mind that so much, kind of goes with the territory. It's the endless fake stories about our so-called relationship as that shit sticks and it's just not true. But I don't waste my time on the small fry." He winks at Casey who blushes crimson as she takes a sip of her drink.

"I'm heading to DJ Jay's set at Caesar's Palace if you want to join, I got the VIP section booked and everything will be free. It'll sure be a party to remember and I'd sure like to get to know you better, Casey." He softly bumps into her with his shoulder and a big smile.

"Sure, I'm in," Casey says without a pause as she smiles back at him before turning back to us and seeing the bemused look on our faces and gently nodding her head as she laughs at her transparency.

"It sounds perfect, Darryl, you are very generous and we'd love to. Who doesn't love DJ Jay? He's a legend," I say.

Walking into the nightclub, we are all blown away by just how big it is. A massive chandelier hangs in the centre and all around the chandelier is a swirl full of lights that creates an even bigger centre piece than the chandelier could. The dance floor is a sea of people and the air is filled with the heady smell of sweet cocktails.

"Darryl, good to see you again, we have your favourite spot all ready with plenty of room for your friends." The server ushers us into a plush VIP room, completely private with a well-placed balcony so we can see everything as well as having our own private dance floor for when DJ Jay starts to play his best hits.

I sit down next to Casey as Darryl chats to the server and orders drinks and food for the party.

"Autumn, I think he likes me, can you believe it? Darryl McNally, A-list Hollywood star rates me," Casey says all of a fluster as her cheeks burn bright once again.

"And why wouldn't he? You are such a catch but play it cool too and get to know who he actually is, I guarantee you he won't come across many women who do that," I say as I give Casey a hug and she goes to join Darryl.

"Well, well, well, what do we have here? A new couple by the end of the night perhaps? We so have to get a photo of us all together. Mia follows me so it'll be guaranteed to irritate her and obviously Josh, as you well know," Eleanor says as she tops up my drink and picks up a bite from the luxurious platter of food before us.

"That's brilliant." I walk over to the server and ask if it is possible for him to get us a club photographer. Before we know it, they have arrived.

"Darryl, you've been so generous with all of us for my birthday, we need to capture it in a photo. Would you be so kind?" I ask.

"Absolutely, I'd love to. Come on, Casey." He stretches out his arm and pulls her up from her seat, his arm gently resting around her waist, as we all line up against the balcony with a full view of the club behind us.

"Oh, would you mind taking one on my phone too?" Eleanor rushes over and hands the photographer her phone as he takes another one before handing it back to her.

"That's a great photo, you should put it up and make

sure you tag us all in it. What a lovely reminder of such an awesome night with my new friends," Darryl says as DJ Jay starts his set and we all make our way to our private dance floor to dance the night away.

Eleanor hangs back for a moment but joins us just as I hear a ping. Reaching for my phone, I see a notification that reads, "The best night, in the best venue, with the best people and DJ Jay." I smile as I put my phone back in my bag and continue to dance the night away on what may be the best birthday I've ever had.

Chapter 30

21st May 2019, Malahide, Dublin

The shrieking of my alarm forces me awake. The house feels eerily silent. Even though it's been a few weeks now since I moved into my own place, I still expect to hear the clattering of Keira and Connor as they get ready for their day.

I open my bedroom window and the calming sound of the nearby sea reminds me of home. Maggie creeps into my mind as I recall the red petals over the ocean and just how beautiful it looked.

A sudden knock at my door breaks me from my reverie as I finish brushing my teeth and open the door to see Eleanor looking at me with bemusement, adding a little headshake for good measure.

"Oh, so we're here again, are we, Autumn? You need to set your alarm fifteen minutes early so you might open the door like you expect me one of these days." Eleanor strolls in and starts to make a cup of coffee.

"Shit, I'll be ten minutes." I dash upstairs to get myself ready. Since moving out of Keira's, I've lost all track of time. I hastily do my makeup and pull on an outfit as I head back downstairs.

"Ok, I'm ready," I say breathlessly as Eleanor looks at

me up and down.

"You're not going in like that. Your face is patchy and that outfit is not happening. I can't be seen with you like that. Have you heard of the messy bun? It's perfect on a day like this." Eleanor marches me back up the stairs and pulls out another outfit as I apply my makeup better this time.

"Here, let's add in a smoky eye." Eleanor does my eye in what feels like a second and follows up with a lick of liquid liner and stands back happily to admire her work with a satisfied smile.

We go back downstairs and sit in the conservatory that overlooks the sea with our drinks, whiling away the five minutes we have left before the car arrives. We don't even get to finish our drinks when we hear the familiar toot.

Clambering in the car, Eleanor looks at me with a glint in her eye that makes me suspicious about what will come next.

"So, any news about James moving in? I mean, that is why you moved out here. Nothing shows your intention to shack up with the boyfriend more than this cosy seafront place." Eleanor sounds smug, eagerly awaiting my answer.

I smile back at her but feel a little pang in my stomach before I respond, "We've had the discussion and it's very much on the cards but it's just not possible while he's working in Temple Bar with the late nights and being so far out of town."

Eleanor's face falls. "Ok, so did you explain about this thing called a car, it moves and is solely designed as a way to get places? Sure, if we're being pedantic, let's throw in the train too." Her hand covers her mouth for a moment.

"I get where he's coming from, it'll just take some time and that's fine. I can be patient. I'm not worried there is any sinister motive," I say with a smile as we arrive at the studio to find it lively and full of excitement.

"What's going on, why all the commotion?" I ask one of the runners who appears at the door.

"The Irish Film and Television Academy and Awards have released their nominee shortlist, there's a rumour someone from *Phoenix Lives* is on there. It's going to be revealed in the meeting." Her phone bleeps and calls her away.

"Well, I can't say that I am surprised. You see Josh, talent like mine was bound to be honoured eventually. It's a little upsetting it took so long but this will be sure to put me on the map of greatness, this is my moment," Mia says dramatically as she surveys the room to see who is looking at her. Josh sighs, looking thoroughly miserable and tired.

"Autumn, can I borrow you a second?" Derek asks from behind me.

My heart jumps into my chest wondering if something is the matter. I follow him to his office. "Is everything ok? Has something happened?"

His eyes don't meet mine but stay fixed on the paper in front of him.

"You could say that, Autumn, something has definitely happened." His eyes still don't leave his desk.

"Oh my God, what is it? Am I in trouble?" My voice starts to panic as Derek finally looks at me with a bemused smirk on his face.

"Not today, Autumn, but a little part of you is always prone to finding yourself in the thick of trouble so let's not rule it out. No, today is a good day as you've been nominated for two IFTAs." He grins, handing me the paper he was just looking at.

As I scroll through the letter, I see that it's true, that I have been nominated in two categories.

"Well, I wanted to let you know first so you're not blindsided in the meeting, as obviously not everyone will be happy. But let's go and put them out of their misery, shall we?"

I follow Derek out of his office and into the meeting, taking my place next to Eleanor. Josh looks over at me, his eyes taking me in and lingering that bit too long. Breaking his gaze, I turn away as Derek commands the attention of the room.

"Ok, peeps, settle down. I know there's a lot of excitement and rumour about the IFTA nominations this year."

Mia grabs Josh's hand in excitement, her overly expressive gestures leading to all eyes in the room falling on her for what she feels will be her big moment. Beside me, Eleanor rolls her eyes with a loud tut. Mia's head whips round and she fixes her with a venomous stare.

"I can confirm that, for the first time ever, *Phoenix Lives* has received an IFTA nomination in two categories," Derek continues as the excitement builds to a crescendo.

"Josh, I've been nominated twice." Mia's excited voice cuts across the room as I lower my head into my hands that bit more.

"The two categories are for Best Actress in a Supporting Role for Drama and Best International Actress in a Drama. Congratulations to Autumn, for becoming the first ever IFTA nominated actress in the show's history."

The room breaks out in applause as anger flashes across Mia's face.

Suddenly, a shriek cuts across the room as a chair flies across the table, hitting one of the people at the end of the table. Blood begins to ooze out as people rush to help. Mia launches herself across the table, grabbing me by the throat as she pins me hard against the wall.

"You stole my nomination, that was meant for me. I've been here longer, they love me more and I will not let you stand in my way," she screeches as her fingers tighten across my throat and I find it hard to breathe. Her face cold and contorting with malice. Josh, Eleanor and Derek grab her off me and drag her out of the meeting into an adjacent room to calm down. An ambulance arrives to assess the cast member as we are ushered out for privacy.

Sitting in my dressing room, I sit in silence with Eleanor for a moment, as we both process what's just happened.

"I think you are right Eleanor, I don't think Mia is well as her reaction was so violent and her face was just so empty of any emotion. It was frightening." I say as I put my hand to my sore neck.

"A few years back she was arrested for a violent assault at an after party, no part of her is nice but the public love her so she never seems to be held accountable for her terrible behaviour. She's left a real mark on your neck too." Eleanor moves closer to look at my neck.

"I know she's always been a bitch but I think she's a lot more than that, she's unhinged too."

"Autumn, don't let her sour this moment. You have just gone into the big leagues and no-one can take any credit for this, it's all off your own back and that's amazing."

Eleanor gives me a big hug.

"It just doesn't feel real, I'm stunned and I keep thinking someone is going to tell me it was all a mistake." I grab my phone to send Amelia a text.

"Well, the awards ceremony is only a few weeks away so I guarantee you will feel excited then. I can't believe we get to go, it's like we all win. Well, except for Mia, she's totally getting sacked, which is actually another win."

"I suppose since Amelia is away travelling, I'd better take James as my date then," I say with a smirk.

"I just love that Amelia is above him in the priority list there, exactly as it should be."

My phone begins to chirp. It's Amelia. As soon as I answer, the room is filled with another shriek.

"Autumn, I'm so proud of you and I will find a way to watch it, I swear. I just can't miss this."

"Where are you again?" I ask as I hold the phone close to me and Eleanor.

"I'm back in Australia, I might be having a visit from Cian but I can't confirm or deny anything," she says with mock sass.

"That's fantastic, things really seem to be going well there. I have to go but speak soon." I say as Eleanor chimes in with a goodbye before I end the call and we make our way to the studio for the first scenes of the day.

Chapter 31

14th June 2019, IFTA Awards Ceremony, Dublin

A sharp pain shoots through my head as the hairdresser pulls firmly on my hair, teasing it into place. The concentration is etched all over her face. She's meticulous, carefully checking her work. Once happy, she sprays it in place with a cloud of hairspray.

"Perfect, I'm sure that there's nothing those bloody rag mags could ever say about you other than you look stunning." She grabs the little mirror to show me the back of the style. A stylish chignon is held in place with a delicate pearl flower detail that matches my earrings and necklace perfectly.

"I love it, it's reminiscent of the 40's but not outdated. Now for my outfit, this is so exciting," I squeal as Eleanor and my mum go to grab my dress. They carry it in carefully before unzipping the bag to remove it.

Holding the unzipped dress, I step into it, the material feeling thicker than I expected it to from sight. The dress tightens around me as it is zipped up and I can finally see the finished look in the mirror. The emerald green dress is a mermaid style which perfectly accentuates my curves, cinching in my waist to give the perfect hourglass silhouette. The top is textured with applique detail and tiny white sequins that perfectly match with my pearls, paired with a simple pair of ivory shoes that complement but don't detract from the detail of the dress and a pearl-covered dainty clutch bag.

"Oh wow, is this even me? I just love this, I feel so confident," I admit as I instinctively smooth down the material on my dress, even though it doesn't need it.

"Autumn, it's sensational. This is the perfect shape for your figure. You look amazing," Eleanor gushes as she hands her phone to my mum to take a photo of us in our outfits.

We make our way back downstairs to join the others for drinks in the kitchen. A knock at my door startles me. My heart races as I begin to wonder if it could be Amelia? Opening the door, I see a familiar face smiling back at me.

"Heya, Autumn, long time so see. We're here for your night and I have a surprise for you." I stand in astonishment as Darryl McNally looks behind him as Casey emerges from the side of the house carrying something.

"Casey, it's so great to see you. What are you both doing here and what are you carrying?" I ask as I usher them in to the house.

"So sorry that we haven't said anything to you before but we had to keep everything so quiet once we found out. We've had a baby," Casey says as she steps into the porch. Casey holds the baby closer, so I can see the little face that is soundly sleeping in its mother's arms.

"Are you both together properly as a couple?" I ask, suddenly serious and searching Darryl's face.

"We sure are, Autumn," Darryl says with a genuine

smile as he puts his arm around Casey.

"Well in that case, let's wet the baby's head and shock the others as much as you just did me." We walk into the kitchen and the same confusion crosses everyone's face as they see Darryl and Casey and realise that she is holding a baby.

"So, was this a little surprise from your hook up in Vegas or was it planned…very quickly afterwards?" Eleanor asks, awaiting their reply eagerly.

"It was certainly not planned but we are thrilled and wouldn't have it any other way now. We got on so well when we met in Vegas and whatever happened, we would have stayed in touch. I've wanted to tell you so much but obviously if it got out who the father was, I'd have no peace so I hope you all understand," Casey says awkwardly.

"Of course, we understand and we're so delighted for you and yes, when it gets out, you will be inundated so it was the right thing to do. When are you going public?" I ask as I pass everyone a glass of champagne.

"Tonight, at the IFTAs. My parents will look after the little one and we will both be there to support you and cheer you on."

"That's amazing, yes that's the perfect time and don't worry, Mia won't be there. She was banned after her antics when it was revealed I had been nominated."

"I can't believe they didn't sack her, I was sure we'd seen the back of her for sure," Eleanor says.

We finish our drinks just as the car arrives. I smile at James as he takes my hand and we all get into the limo.

"James, you are looking very handsome in your tux tonight," Mum says as Dad looks at her in disbelief.

"So, I don't then, Brenda?" he interjects with a smile.

"Oh, stop it, Frank, you've had thirty years of compliments so don't be greedy," Mum retorts back as we all laugh.

I feel my phone vibrate. I open my bag and see a call from a number I don't recognise. My heart lurches as I consider whether it could be Megan. For a moment, I watch the screen flicker in dismay as the call cuts off but as I go to put my phone away, it beeps in my bag with a message from Megan. I ignore the message and put my phone back in my bag. This is my night and Mia and Megan won't ruin it.

Stepping out of the taxi, the impressive Mansion House is before us with a red carpet rolled out to the entrance. Paparazzi are mingling close by, not able to come in to the awards but hopeful of a lucrative shot anyway. Once inside, there is an official photographer who takes every person's photo on arrival. After this, we are ushered to the *Phoenix Lives* room where Derek and Josh and the Executive Producer, Darragh, wait for us.

"Autumn, it's great to see you and don't you look gorgeous." Derek gives me a hug.

"Derek, you remember my mum and dad. This is my boyfriend James." As James leans in to shake hands with Derek and Darragh, I notice Josh looking him up and down scornfully before I catch him and he looks away with a blush. Derek introduces Josh and Darragh to the rest of the table and again I see Josh's eyes fall on me. It feels as if he wants to speak but thinks better of it and doesn't.

The room darkens as the ceremony begins. Grand crystal chandeliers hang above the room, curtains around the stage are up lit with a sumptuous orange glow and the back wall behind the stage is lit up like the night sky. It is a stunning effect and I feel my nerves tighten. I clap happily as the first winners are announced.

"One of the finest aspects of Irish television is the amazing drama we've created within this country. The talent we have across the spectrum is phenomenal and one that is being increasingly recognised on an international stage. With that in mind, can you please welcome on stage our homegrown Hollywood A-lister, Darryl McNally, to present the Best International Actress category."

The crowd erupts into rapturous applause that reaches almost deafening levels as I look around to see if I can see Casey on another of the tables. Darryl comes onto the stage with his trademark swagger and megawatt smile and speaks enthusiastically.

"Good evening, ladies and gentlemen, it is a pleasure for me to be here with you tonight and with the responsibility of awarding one of the most hotly contested categories in IFTA history. So, I won't keep you waiting. The nominees for Best International Actress 2018 are...."

A screen flicks into life and flashes across the names of the nominations. The nerves in my stomach twist delicately as I see my name flash up and it all suddenly becomes real. It feels as if time stands still, as if I'm the only person in the room waiting for Darryl to announce the winner. James takes my hand in his and gives me a smile.

"And the winner of the 2018 IFTA for Best International Actress is…Autumn Sutherland for *Phoenix Lives*!" Suddenly the table around me erupts, I am grabbed by Derek and Darragh in turn and even Josh has the biggest smile on his face as he goes to give me a hug before I make my way to the stage to collect my award.

Walking across to Darryl, his beaming smile makes me feel a lot less nervous as he gives me a hug and a kiss on the cheek before handing me the award. The gold shines brightly upon the abstract trophy as I notice three cute Celtic swirls to the right side of it.

"I would like to thank IFTA for this award and for recognising my contribution to *Phoenix Lives*. I moved to Ireland to realise my dream to be an actress and it is here in Dublin through *Phoenix Lives* that I have done that and I will be forever grateful. I want to thank Derek for taking a chance on me and making this possible. I would also like to thank my friends and family who have always supported me. Thank you and goodnight." I take a small bow towards the audience as I walk off stage with Darryl and back to my table.

It is less than an hour later when I once again make my way to the stage to receive my second award for Best Supporting Actress and as I once again thank the audience, I feel as if every decision I've made up until that point flashes across my mind and I realise that as crazy as it sounded, this is one gamble that has really paid off in ways I could never have imagined.

Chapter 32

The morning after my IFTA win, I wake up grateful to have the day off as my head feels heavy from the raucous celebrations that closed out the evening. The friends I couldn't take to the ceremony all came to the after party and we had such a great time. It was clear that James felt a little out of place. He remained quiet and subdued. It was quite an intense situation to walk into. As he has a doctor's appointment early this morning, he left early but as a thank you for his support, I decided to surprise him with breakfast on his return to his flat.

Getting out of bed, I see a flurry of text messages from people and immediately see Amelia's.

"Amazing to see you win, you've worked so hard to get there and I'm so proud."

I smile as I put down my phone, noting that I haven't heard from James and wondering if he's actually annoyed at me.

After a shower, I get dressed and put my makeup on nicely, picking out a summery red dress from my wardrobe, which I pair with wedges. I catch a bus into town, stopping off to the shop on the way to get a fabulous breakfast all ready for my surprise for James.

I think back to how things have changed over the past year, how I had initially been so adamant it was Josh that I nearly overlooked James completely. I remember back to the times his face would light up when he saw me and as harsh as it sounds, I didn't even notice. But that faded a few months in, as it always does in a relationship but I hope to continue to progress with James and hopefully we will move in together soon.

I let myself into his apartment, glancing at my watch and seeing he's due at the doctor right now, which gives me plenty of time to set up breakfast. I stop dead in my tracks, my heart pounding at the sound of voices. I smile to myself as I dispel the thought when there is an undeniable sound.

It crosses my mind perhaps it's next door but movement from the bedroom makes it clear that James's reluctance to move in together had nothing to do with distance.

Walking into James's bedroom, I open the door to find him having sex with another woman. As she sits astride him, she blocks his ability to see me standing there.

"I thought you had a doctor's appointment this morning?" I say angrily as they both jump apart with a start.

"Autumn, what are you doing here?" James asks as the woman clutches the sheet to cover herself and stares out of the window to avoid eye contact.

"Don't evade my question, James. I said I thought you had a doctor's appointment? Doing home visits, is she?" I ask.

"We met in the bar, I'm not a doctor. He said he was single," the woman says sheepishly.

"You know what? I really don't doubt that as suddenly all the excuses and all the barriers you put in front of us make so much sense. You couldn't move in with me and give up your little sex den. You are a pathetic piece of shit, James, and I hope you rot in hell."

As I turn to leave, James rushes to put on his trousers but in his hurry trips over, writhing on the floor to get his trousers on. He follows me out the door. "No, Autumn don't. I'm sorry. It was a mistake. Please, let's just talk," he pleads.

"I'm going home, James, don't contact me again," I say as the woman hastily scurries out of the door with a sheepish sorry to me as she goes.

"Let me drive you, ok? Just let me take you back and then that's it, I promise." James ushers me to sit down and turns on the tv while he gets ready.

Up flashes Entertainment Today. Expecting to see wide coverage of the IFTAs last night, I am surprised to see Josh and Mia flash up on the screen with the screaming headline across the bottom reading "*Phoenix Lives* Stars in Acrimonious Split" as the narrator reads out a joint statement put out this morning confirming the split. I turn the TV off, not wanting to see either of their faces as I wait for James to reappear.

"OK, let's go," he says.

I barge past him and out of the door and storm down the steps. He clicks to open the car. I get in and slam the door as I wait for him to get in.

"Look, I know you're angry, Autumn, but…" James says but I quickly cut him off before he can finish.

"Don't you dare 'but' me, don't you dare put the blame for this on me. This is your behaviour, James, accept this is down to you and don't try to wriggle out of it." I turn away and look out of the window. We sit in silence for a moment.

"I get this is my fault but you've always kept me at a distance and last night just showed me how much I don't belong in your world," James says.

"You knew when we got together what my world was and you pursued me and it wasn't just this once, was it? I mean, you weren't in the bar last night so how the hell did you meet her? You've been taking me for a fool for months and just haven't got the guts to admit it," I shout.

"You don't know that and yet here you are just throwing wild accusations at me and making me out to be the bad guy when you're the one so clearly hung up on Josh and the fact he ditched you for Mia and guess what, given the choice I would too," he says nastily as the car speed increases rapidly while he turns to glare at me.

Before I can respond, the car begins to slide across the lanes. As he tries to correct, he pulls too heavily. Missing the car beside us, he pulls the car into a spin across the carriageway and into the central reservation. The car behind us is unable to stop and ploughs into us, sending our car careering back across the carriage way and into the hard shoulder where we come to a stop. The car that hit us is hit by another car, the driver trapped in his vehicle.

I manage to pull myself out of the car and onto the hard shoulder, my right arm in agony. Blood flows from my nose and head but I need to help the other drivers. I spot a gap in the cars on the carriage way and run across, managing to pull open the door with the help of the driver from another car. We pull the driver out and they carry the driver onto the hard shoulder while we wait for emergency services to arrive away from the carriageway.

"Autumn, put this on your head?" I look up to see James offering me his shirt for my head to stem the bleeding as he hands me my bag.

"Thanks," I say. I hold it against my head as the bleeding shows no sign of stopping.

The wail of distant sirens is a huge relief as James sits next to me in silence. Nobody talks as the police close the carriageway to deal with the incident and we are all loaded into ambulances and taken to nearby hospitals for treatment.

While in the hospital, I text Eleanor to let her know what has happened as the doctor comes in to check on my injuries.

"Hello, Miss Sutherland, do you mind if I call you Autumn?" the cheery doctor says as I start to feel drowsy.

"Yes," I respond hazily, closing my eyes. I struggle to keep them open, my head in pain and a wave of nausea enveloping me.

"Can I just take a look into your eyes?" is the last thing I remember the doctor saying before it all goes black.

A few hours later

I awake to a rhythmic beeping. I open my eyes groggily and see I'm in a room full of beds. Someone is holding my hand, their head slumped forward onto the bed. I groan and move my hand, which snaps them awake.

"Autumn, you're awake. I have been so worried, I raced here as soon as I heard," Josh says.

"What are you doing here? Why did you come?" I ask,

my voice slightly irritated.

"I've wanted to speak to you for so long, to apologise for the way I acted but I just couldn't find the courage. You're the strong one, Autumn, not me. I didn't want to be rejected again."

"I didn't reject you the first time. I helped Eleanor home after her drink was spiked, I asked Megan to give you the message and when I come back to work, you were in a relationship with Mia. I was the one that was rejected," I say angrily.

"What did you say?" Josh says in shock.

"I said I'm the one who…."

Josh cuts me off before I can finish. "No, what did you say about Megan?"

"I asked Megan to let you know that I had to take Eleanor home because when I went to text you, I realised that my phone had been stolen. James gave us a lift home as a favour," I say curtly, not wanting to remember that dreadful night.

"Megan never gave me any message, she didn't speak to me at all. Mia told me you had left with James and when I checked with the doormen, they confirmed it. This just doesn't make any sense." His hands twist nervously around each other.

"Well, technically I did leave with him but not in the way Mia tried to make out. So, what, you got back with her to get back at me?" I ask, my eyes narrowing.

"I suppose so, I thought you'd rejected me and so, yes, I knew it would hurt you," he admits.

"Can you pass me my bag? We need some answers on this once and for all."

I retrieve my phone but a nurse stops me. "Not so

fast, Autumn, no phone calls until we've done your observations, ok? You've had a concussion so open your eyes nice and wide for me." The nurse places my bag back down on the floor, her face turning serious as she takes my obs. "Ok, it's looking better but you're staying with us tonight and once we're sure all is well then you can go home." She smiles warmly as she passes me back my bag and scratches her findings into the chart at the bottom of my bed before leaving us.

I grab my phone from my bag and find Megan's message from the night before, my heart racing as I begin to call.

"Hi Autumn, I didn't expect you to call me. How are you?" Megan asks in surprise.

"I wasn't planning on calling you, Megan, but I've been a car crash and Josh came rushing to my side. It's the first time we've talked since the night of the wedding reception and he said you never gave him the message I asked you to. So, what's going on, Megan? What are you hiding?"

Josh comes closer to hear her response and I place it on speakerphone for us both to hear.

"I tried to find him but I couldn't, I'm not hiding anything," Megan begins to protest as Josh's face hardens. A wry smile crosses his lips and he motions for me to let him speak.

"Megan, this is Josh. Mia told me the truth and if you don't tell Autumn what really happened that night in the way me and you know it happened then I will. You can kiss goodbye to any friendship with Autumn and you can kiss goodbye to your reputation as I'll go public with everything I know happened that night." Josh leans away from the phone and a silence hangs in the air while we await Megan's response.

"I didn't mean to hurt anyone, let alone Eleanor, you have to believe me. I didn't know she would take it so far, I promise, Autumn. I've felt so awful ever since, I tried to call you to come clean, to tell you the truth."

As Megan protests, tears start and the hairs stand up on my arm.

"What happened, Megan? I want to hear this from you," I say softly.

"Mia asked me to go to the wedding to help her get to Josh. I was supposed to distract you and allow Mia time with Josh. That was all I knew. But later in the evening, she asked me to get a round of drinks for you guys and she slipped a liquid into one and put the strawberry in it, saying it was for Eleanor." Megan sounds regretful as she trails off into sobs.

"You let her spike Eleanor's drink, you could've really hurt her. Why didn't you refuse?" I ask angrily.

"She knows my deepest darkest secrets, things I've never told anyone and she threatened me. I had no choice. I didn't want to do it, I didn't want to do any of it." She breaks down into more sobs.

"So what else happened, Megan?" I ask.

"She then said for me to get Eleanor into the bathroom as soon as I could after she had consumed her drink. Then she kept a look out to wait until you or Josh went to the bar and let you know Eleanor needed help. When you went to the toilet, she went to speak to Josh and distracted him so she could steal your phone," Megan says almost in a whisper.

"So, Josh didn't leave it unattended?" I say in relief.

"I'd never have left it unattended, I looked after it but

Mia said she'd seen you in the toilet and you had asked for it. I thought you needed something from it," Josh says in surprise.

"I had told Mia earlier that James had always liked you so she alerted him to you needing help in the toilet and he rushed to help you as we all knew he would. Once he gave you a lift home, Mia told Josh that you had left with him and that tallied with what the doormen saw. I'm so sorry, Autumn, I should have been honest sooner," Megan says through her sobs.

"I'm going to tell Eleanor what happened, Megan, and she may want to press charges so this might not be the end of it. There could be serious repercussions for you both," I say.

"I know, Autumn, and I accept that. What we did was so wrong and I should have stood up to her and been stronger. I'm so sorry." Megan breaks down again and I say goodbye and put down the phone.

"I'm so sorry I didn't ask you what happened, Autumn. I feel we could have avoided all this if I'd just trusted you a little more. Mia has always known my weaknesses and it hurts to know she was so keen to exploit it. But yet I really wouldn't expect anything else," Josh says.

"I wish I'd said something to you too as it seems this has been able to carry on because we were both too pig-headed to talk," I say sadly.

"My feelings haven't changed for you, Autumn, and I know that perhaps we can't go back but I remain hopeful that we can and so would like to ask you on a date?" Josh says nervously.

I look at him, the uncertainty of my response etching itself across his face. I sigh as I look away and think of all that's happened and how we've both been guilty of making assumptions about the other and I wonder if we can go back to where we were.

"I can't promise you anything, Josh, but I can commit to a date and see what happens from there," I say at last.

"Thank you, Autumn, that's far more than I deserve." He kisses my hand and we both fall silent for a moment.

Later that evening, not long after Josh leaves, Eleanor and Keira come to visit and I fill them both in on what just happened.

"What a psycho bitch, it all makes sense now. What did I tell you about Megan? What did I say? Always knew we couldn't trust her. I'm going to call Derek now and I'm reporting it to the police." Eleanor rushes angrily out of the room, her phone in hand.

"So, what does that mean for you and Josh, Autumn? It's nice to know he wasn't just being cruel like we thought?" Keira asks inquisitively.

"I don't know, Keira, I'm not sure if I can dial it back to before all of this hurt and pain. I've agreed to go on a date with him but I'm making no promises," I say.

"That seems the best approach. If he's the one, you will know it so it won't ever pass you by." Keira reaches to hold my hand in hers.

After Eleanor finishes her call, she returns to my bedside and I feel a sense of relief that we finally know the truth about that strange night and all the questions that it raised and that this is sure to be the last I see or hear of Mia. I feel grateful that she will be out of our lives forever.

Chapter 33

30th June 2019 – Dublin

I sing along to the radio happily as I prepare the ingredients for the hummus I'm making, flinching slightly as the lemon juice stings a cut on my hand. I squeeze it into the tahini before whipping it up in my processor. Glancing over at the recipe for the next step, I see Eleanor is calling me.

"Hi, Eleanor, how are you? Any update?" I ask breathlessly.

"Absolutely, the police have just called to say that they are pressing charges against Mia, which was closely followed by Derek to say they are writing her out of the show with immediate effect," Eleanor says with a sigh of relief.

"So that really is it? We're finally all free of her. I can't tell you how much better it will be to go into work knowing I don't need to deal with her every single day." I sit down at the kitchen table with a cup of tea as I look out towards the sea.

"She's finished, she'll never work again in the industry and that's just what she deserves. Anyway, enough of her, what about your big date tonight with Josh?" Eleanor's voice drips with excitement.

"It's not a big date, it's a little date where we just talk and I see whether I could ever trust the guy again after what he did," I say, accidentally knocking my drink off the table. The mug falls to the ground with a crash and the warm liquid splashes my legs.

"Just remember, you were both as taken in by her as each other. That was the point, none of you talked and just silently seethed at each other and she won. So, don't get all high and mighty, Autumn, just see where it goes and if nothing changes, then you know." Eleanor's wisdom does annoy me even though I know she's right.

I say goodbye and replace my phone on the table as I walk into the utility room to get the dustpan and brush and clear up the remnants of my drink. As I mop up the brown liquid, I feel a knot twist in my stomach, thinking about the date tonight. Suddenly my thoughts are pierced by the shrill ping of my phone alerting me to a text message. My heart catches in my throat as I see it is from Josh. "Meet me tonight at the entrance of St Stephens Green at 7.00 p.m. See you there."

St Stephen's Green, Dublin

I disembark the tram and draw my breath for a second, knowing that when I turn the corner in front of me, I'll come face to face with Josh. In a way I didn't think possible, I feel a sense of dread as I walk the short distance to the entrance of St Stephen's Green.

As I round the corner, my heart leaps catching a glimpse of Josh nervously smoothing down his suit and making sure his tie is in its place before he looks up. His face breaks into a smile as he sees me.

"Hey Autumn, it's great to see you here." He leans in to give me a hug but is reluctant to come too close so it feels a little more awkward than I'm used to.

"I'm intrigued why I'm meeting you here. I thought I'd be meeting you at a restaurant," I say with a smile as Josh motions for me to follow him.

"Well, since you're only giving me the one chance, I thought it was all or nothing so I've planned something a little different that I hope you'll like."

We walk alongside the river. A family of ducks swim and play happily a short distance from us.

"I appreciate the effort, you know how much I love St Stephen's Green so I'm excited to see what you've planned," I say.

We walk towards the band stand and I see the faint flicker of a flame and realise that there's a table set up under it and a waiter standing close by.

"This is your seat, Autumn," Josh says. He pulls out a chair for me to sit down. Rays from the evening sun bounce off the meandering river, framed perfectly by the little stone bridge I've always loved so much.

"Josh, this is amazing. How is this even possible?" I ask.

The waiter hands us a menu and pours our wine into the glistening glasses on the luxurious table. I notice a single red rose in a white vase, contrasting beautifully with the crisp white linen and crystal-clear glassware.

He nods at the hotel across the road before saying, "One of my best friend's is the manager of the Shelbourne Hotel and let's say he owes me a favour so I called it in. I couldn't disappoint your expectation for a restaurant, now could I?"

I smile back at him, noting the family of ducks swimming past us and the little baby ducks diligently following their mum in an impossibly endearing way. The waiter returns with a cocktail for each of us, some entrees and some bread. Placing it on the table with a flourish, he says, "These come with compliments of the manager" before leaving us to ourselves.

"You want to feed the ducks, don't you?" Josh says. He offers me the bread basket. As if by magic, the little family waits patiently while we throw bread crumbs to each of them quickly before the seagulls and pigeons are aware there is food.

"Clearly, you can't come to the park and not feed the ducks, their little faces were so happy," I say. The nerves I felt earlier subside as we both tuck into the tiny entrees before us.

"I'm so sorry, Autumn. Truthfully, I did go out with Mia to hurt you but I only ended up hurting myself. To hear you say I had one chance was tough as it just shows how far we've fallen. I didn't think we'd get to a place where you might not want to spend time with me." Josh's eyes search mine for a reaction.

I sigh heavily and look across the river as I take a sip of my cocktail before I set it back down and look back at Josh, hesitating slightly before I reply.

"We both made mistakes, Josh. It was hurtful that you didn't give me the chance to explain but like you said, she knew how to play to your insecurities. She played us both. I'm not making any promises but I'm not closing myself off to anything either."

The waiter arrives with our main courses and sets them down in front of us as the orange glow of the dying sun baths the park in a dim but beautiful light. I look down to my plate and see the beautifully laid out guinea fowl with the rich smell of gorgonzola stuffed inside, sitting on a bed off wilted greens. The waiter takes our empty dishes and refills our glasses before leaving us to our dinner.

"That's very gracious of you, Autumn, as I know I couldn't blame you if you felt differently. So, let's raise a toast to seeing where this takes us."

I smile and raise my glass to Josh's and as we clink our glasses together, our eyes meet in the same intense way they always did and I feel my stomach take a huge somersault. I wonder why my head and my heart feel so at odds right now.

As the evening light dies out completely, we eat our desserts by candlelight with only the distant quacking of the family of ducks swimming happily around and our laughter filling the empty park. When we leave our table, Josh stops me for a moment, holding my gaze before saying, "Take this, Autumn, it'll be a memento of the night." He removes the single red rose from the vase and hands it to me. I take it with a smile and we go our separate ways. As I take the tram home, I wonder whether it will be my head or heart that will win the battle I feel within me right now and as much as I try, right now I just can't figure out which way it'll go.

Chapter 34

27th December 2019, Devon

Standing in the arrival hall, I excitedly await my boyfriend but grow a little impatient, looking once again at the board which states the plane landed forty minutes ago.

Caught up in my thoughts, I don't notice the stranger walking up to me until he stands in front of me with a smile. I step back slightly in surprise as he holds a single rose out to me and says kindly, "For you," before walking away. The surrounding people look at me in surprise as I blush and smile shyly. Then a little girl walks up to me with her parents behind her. She proudly produces another red rose with a smile as she says, "For you," before they too walk away with nothing more than those words. In fact, every passenger that comes through the arrival hall continues to present me with a single rose and the same simple words. But finally, this time when the door opens, I see him walking towards me with the biggest smile and a final rose. The crowd around me jostles to give him room to walk in front of me. Without saying a word, he lowers himself onto one knee as he presents the rose to me with a glistening diamond ring sitting delicately on top.

"Autumn Sutherland, since the day I first laid eyes

on you, I felt a special connection. Despite our ups and downs, I've never doubted that you're the person I want to spend the rest of my life with. In fact, it would be the greatest honour if you would agree to be my wife. Autumn, will you marry me?" He and the crowd of people around us wait with bated breath for my answer.

"Yes, I'd love to marry you, Josh," I say loudly so everyone can hear and a loud cheer erupts in the airport as Josh takes the ring from the top of the rose and places the ring on my finger.

"Thank you so much for everyone who took part in helping me pull off this amazing proposal, you're the best fellow passengers ever," Josh says to the assembled crowd as they all come to wish us the best before departing with their loved ones.

I look down at my ring in amazement, the prominent but delicate diamond and white gold band with little diamonds peppering the band around my finger.

"You did so well. This is a beautiful ring. I love it and it looks so good on me," I say as we reach the car for the journey back home.

"I'm glad you like it, Autumn, I wanted it to always remind you of how much I love you." He leans over to kiss me.

"Actually, I have a present for you too. I was going to wait to give it to you but I can't imagine any moment more perfect than this one, even if we are in a car park at the airport," I say with a smile as I usher him to open the glove compartment and take out a little bag with two little presents.

"Open this one first!" I say happily. I sit back as he unwraps the little box and tries to fathom what it is. His eyes widen as he reads the writing and it becomes clear.

"You're pregnant, I'm going to be a dad?" Josh says ecstatically.

"Yes, we're going to be parents. I had an inkling but waited to do a test so I could surprise you with the ultimate Christmas gift," I say as Josh moves to hug and kiss me one more time before we leave the airport and make our way home.

"So, how do you want to tell everyone, especially given Amelia?" Josh asks with concern.

"Well, we have Casey's party tonight and I'd like to tell people then, so I will need to call Amelia and Cian to tell them before that. I know she will be so happy for me but it's not long since she lost the baby and being told she can't have anymore has just devastated her. In that way, the timing is difficult." My heart lurches between wanting to include my friend but not wanting to feel like I'm being insensitive to her pain.

"I have no doubt she will be happy for us but it's going to hurt. There's just no way around it for her or Cian. It's been the roughest year for them." Josh puts his hand over mine as we drive back to my parents.

We are hardly through the door when my mum rushes out of the kitchen and throws her arms around Josh. In the year we've been together, Mum has looked at him as the son she never had.

"Josh, so good to see you again. Come on inside, I've made us all a nice lunch as it feels ages since I last saw you."

I slip upstairs, take off my ring, place it safely on my dressing table and drop off Josh's luggage before joining them back downstairs.

"Autumn, I was just saying to Josh that I have a feeling in my bones 2020 is going to be such a fantastic year. I'm just so excited about it," Mum enthuses as Dad raises his eyebrows and tucks into the warm goat cheese and chorizo tart my mum has made for us.

"I think you're right, Mum, this year I'm sure will be the best year of our lives and who knows what it will bring." Josh meets my gaze and we both smile knowingly.

Leaving everyone downstairs, I slip off to my room and video call Amelia in Dublin. She picks up and looks exhausted, her eyes puffy and vacant as she hugs her pillow close and tries to be her usual happy self.

"Hey Autumn, I'm so pleased to hear from you," Amelia says as her voice chokes.

"How are you, Amelia? You look unwell. Are you not sleeping?" I ask with real concern.

"I don't think I'll ever sleep again, Autumn. It's just so hard because every time I close my eyes, I dream of him, how it felt to be pregnant and each morning it's ripped from me all over again. To have him taken at six months is just cruel, we still don't know why." The tears drip down her face and she quickly tries to wipe them away.

"I just can't imagine what you're going through, Amelia, but you know I'm here for you whenever you need it." My heart breaks for my friend, knowing I can't make it better. I wonder if I should tell her but it feels deceitful not to.

"I'm just glad I got to see his face, touch his hands and hold him but the last six weeks have felt excruciating. I had a dream about us last night, we were at an antenatal class together and we were so happy. That did make me feel happier," she says with a faint smile.

"I'd have loved that to be true, Amelia. We've been through so much together. I'd have just loved to share this journey with you because I've actually just found out that I'm pregnant too and you are the first person I've told. I wanted you to hear it from me as I know it will be difficult and I know right now you need to focus on you and healing but the moment you are ready, you have a place slap bang in our lives, ok?" I say as a tear comes to my own eye.

"Are you really, Autumn? It was a premonition, I am so happy for you as you will be the best mum. It is hard to hear obviously but only because it's so raw but don't think I'll ever not be happy for you. I look forward to cuddles when I'm able to." Amelia's smile is genuine.

"I knew you would be but it just felt such horrible timing but I'd never want to keep it from you as that would be even worse. Josh proposed to me this morning too and so if you feel up to it, I'd love you to be my bridesmaid."

"I'd love that so much, Autumn. Cian and I have talked about marriage but we need to wait until we feel happy again but to have yours to look forward to, I know that will help. Maybe when you are back over, we can go for a walk in St Stephen's Green again like we did when we first met?"

"We absolutely can, honey, anything you want is fine by me. I'll leave you to get some sleep but if you need anything, let me know." I blow her a kiss goodbye.

"Thanks, Autumn, and congratulations times two, you deserve a lifetime of happiness and glad to see it starting to come in." Amelia blows back a kiss. We sign off and the room goes to silent.

Later that evening

Josh comes towards me with a champagne glass which he holds out towards me; the bubbles fizzle down to the bottom as I take a sip.

"Elderflower juice and sparkling water. The fizz will make it feel like you are drinking something alcoholic," Josh whispers in my ear as Casey and Darryl come to join us.

"So glad you could both make it. We've been so excited to see you as we haven't had a chance since the IFTAs. We've been in LA. Darryl was doing a new film with Scorsese but luckily it wrapped before Christmas as we wanted to be together for Theo's first Christmas. We'll have to get together soon so you can meet him properly," Casey says happily.

"I'd love that, Casey, and I'm so thrilled that things are really working out for you both, you are just the cutest couple," I say as Josh nods approvingly. Casey gazes lovingly at Darryl who returns her gaze and kisses her on the head.

"The best thing that ever happened to me was bumping into you all in Vegas. I was always the wild guy because I never met a girl who treated me as a person only a film star but Casey is the exact reverse. It was a risky move but I love it," he says.

Mum and Dad move over to join us and with everyone important to me nearby this seems the best time to tell everyone our news. I look at Josh and he smiles back at me as if reading my mind.

"Well, we do have a little bit of news for you all tonight

actually. You see, this morning when I went to collect Josh from the airport he proposed to me. Obviously, Casey, I want you as a bridesmaid," I say, flashing my ring finger as Mum and Casey take a look and Dad and Darryl shake Josh's hand.

"I'd love to, thank you so much, Autumn," Casey says with a big smile as she looks at the ring.

"There is also one other thing, it is a little early so you have to keep it to yourselves but we want to be able to tell you in person: Autumn is pregnant," Josh says as he places an arm around me.

"Autumn, that's the best news, you will love being a mum. It's the best thing, I mean excruciatingly exhausting but you won't mind." Casey pulls me into a hug.

"I can second that, Casey, I only wish we'd been able to have more but at least we were blessed with Autumn." Mum pulls me and Josh in for a hug.

"A blessing is an understatement for my girl, she's been the light of my life since the day she was born," Dad says proudly.

"Such a liar, Frank, you were dotty about her way before she was born, more like the minute he knew I was pregnant," Mum says as she plants a kiss on my dad's cheek.

"That's actually very true, she has me there." Dad gives me a big hug.

As the evening wears on, I feel incredibly lucky to be here in this moment and able to spend such a special evening with my nearest and dearest. The only person missing is Amelia and my heart breaks for the tragedy she has endured. I say a little prayer for her that she is able to overcome it in her own time.

Chapter 35

4th January 2020, St Stephen's Green, Dublin

As I wait by the entrance of St Stephen's Green for Amelia to arrive, my mind wanders back to the night of my date with Josh and how perfect it was even if I couldn't fully appreciate it at the time due to all the misgivings I had about us.

"Hey Autumn, it's great to see you." Amelia is in front of me, so painfully thin and tired-looking but with a big smile on her face.

"It's great to see you too. How are you feeling?" I ask as we start to walk around the meandering paths in the park, the trees bare and barren in the crisp winter air.

"I'm not great but I know you can see that. I just aim to get through each day and if I do then I'm happy," Amelia says.

We take a seat on the bench near the water.

"Oh Amelia, you're so clearly struggling and that's understandable but do you think Dublin is the right place for you at this time?" I ask sympathetically.

"What do you mean?" she asks.

"I think you need to spend some time at home to recuperate, get some counselling and be around your family, especially your mum who will take care of you as you can't expect yourself to be ok right now. I don't think Cian would mind."

"He's already suggested that actually but I didn't want to leave him to go through it by himself but I don't know, hearing it from you, I think you might be right. Would you keep an eye on Cian if I did, not obviously but just check in?" she asks.

"Of course, I can get Josh to arrange some time with him too in case he wanted to talk man to man. Besides, you'll be back in no time, happier, healthier and ready to make your wedding plans too." I rub her arm softly.

"OK, I'll go home for a bit. It would be great to see my mum and she did try to come over for a bit but work meant she couldn't stay long and she is worried. I do want to feel better, Autumn, I want to be able to remember him positively, not in this soul-crushing way that's just laden with grief. He deserves so much more than that." Tears well in her eyes.

"I know but it takes time so don't be harsh on yourself. You'll get there." I put my arm around her gently.

"Did you want to see a picture of him?" she asks, her eyes brightening for a moment.

"I'd love to," I say as she pulls her phone out and shows me the picture of her baby, his features perfectly formed, looking like he is just asleep. "He's beautiful, Amelia, look he has your nose and eyes but definitely Cian's jawline." I see the love in Amelia's eyes as she looks down at her baby.

"He really does, such a handsome boy if I don't mind saying so myself. The hearts he'd have broken if he'd had the chance. How is your pregnancy treating you?" She puts her phone away, a little brighter than before.

"He's gorgeous and at least you have a reminder of

what he looks like. He'll always be your boy," I say before I continue. "I have been feeling quite nauseous. I haven't been sick but I'm tired all the time."

"I was the same, it gets better in the second trimester though so hang in there. Do you have a preference around what you want?" Amelia asks.

"I don't but I do feel Josh wants a little girl. He hasn't said but I get the impression as he refers to the baby as her already and we haven't even had the first scan yet."

"It'll all become real when you do. When you hear that heartbeat like a train coming, that's when the baby becomes a real part of you and that's when I felt I became a mother." Amelia's hand subconsciously moves to her belly.

As we continue our walk around the park, it feels just like old times. Amelia seems to have perked up but it is clear she needs more help to overcome this than she has sought and to know she is going to return home to recuperate really makes me feel a lot better.

"Thank you so much, Autumn, for meeting with me. I can't tell you how much it has helped and when I'm back in Dublin, we can meet again and hopefully I'll be in a much better place then."

"I've no doubt about that but you need that TLC from your family. And get some counselling as this is a trauma and you need to come to terms with it in a healthy way. Then you can remember your little boy the way he deserves." I give her a big hug.

"Alfie, we decided to call him Alfie," she says with a smile as we break away.

"That's a perfect name for him, he looks just like an Alfie."

We say our goodbyes and I watch her go and I feel a tear spill across my cheek as her altered appearance and state shocks me to the core, the pain she has endured, robbing her of all her shine.

Chapter 36

Seaton Beach, Devon, August 2020.

Sitting on the beach on a blistering hot summer's day is not how I usually choose to spend my time by the sea but Josh is yet to be persuaded that it is better on a cold winter's day.

"I can't believe I can't beat you at this, you're nearly nine months pregnant and you can still skim stones better than me," he says with a competitive edge to his voice.

"I've spent a lifetime honing my craft. My father taught me so I learnt from the best. Still prefer a sandy beach? That's probably what's killing your game right now."

He pulls me closer for a kiss and places a protective hand on my bump. "Well, I suppose you've got to be able to beat me at something or it's unfair." His cheeky grin crinkles his nose.

"That's true, this is the one thing I beat you hands down on," I say.

He pulls me up from my sitting position on the stony beach and we walk towards the promenade to meet my parents for lunch.

"That's not the only thing, you're a better actor than me," he says, helping me navigate the big step onto the promenade from the beach. I sit on it and he helps pull me up the other side.

"That's not true at all, why would you say that?"

"Why wouldn't I say that? It's true and you have two IFTA's to your name. So, take the credit and accept the compliment."

"Thank you, I appreciate you saying that but from my perspective, you will always be the guy who took my breath away in the *Othello* audition and whose talent was undeniable. I felt out of place next to you but I take the compliment, I promise," I say as we approach Mum and Dad sitting on a bench near the promenade.

"Are you ready?" I ask as we all start to walk towards the exit towards the restaurant.

"Hello dear, how are you?" My head whips around and I see an elderly lady smiling back at me and for a moment, I can't place her. "Oh, Maggie, is that you?" I say with surprise. Dottie is obediently sitting by Maggie's side, her tail wagging in excitement as I pet her.

"Yes, it certainly is and look, I see you are pregnant, you look blooming, my dear. Now it seems this is just the start of your very own love story." She has a sparkle in her eyes. "I loved the shows you sent over to me too, what a talent you are. This town was way too small for you, so glad I met you that day. It has always stayed in my heart to meet a kindred spirit." She says with pride.

"It has always stayed with me too and I'm so happy to share the news that these shoes fit just perfectly," I say with a wink.

"They look like they do," she says with a smile as my mother, dad and Josh suddenly look at my feet with a perplexed look crossing their faces which makes us both laugh.

"Now, dear, my son bought me this new-fangled phone so pop in your number. When baby arrives, I can come and meet them." She hands me her phone and I tap in my number, noting the way her hands tremble, that she has become frailer since our first meeting.

"There it is, Maggie, I've called myself too from it so I have your number too and I'll let you know when we have the baby. It's been so nice to see you again. Without you, none of this would be possible." I give her a big hug.

"You just needed a kick up the backside and I was pleased to give it to you. Although, I did advocate waiting a bit longer if you remember," she says warmly.

"We did too, Maggie, but this one is headstrong and won't listen to a thing anyone says," Mum interjects with a smile.

"Well, I'm so glad it all worked out for the best and you are a very lucky young man. Be sure to look after this one, she is a very special girl and as precious as a jewel." She shakes Josh's hand as he agrees to do as she asks. "It was so nice to meet you both too, you've done a wonderful job with her, you must be so proud." My parents beam at the compliment and we all say goodbye and wish Maggie well.

"What a lovely old lady. She does look frail though, my love. Be sure to give her a call. She might be lonely," Mum says.

We leave the beach and make our way to the restaurant when suddenly a sharp pain grips my stomach and a rush of water pours down my legs, splashing across the floor, causing passers-by to look in concern.

"Your waters have broken, we need to get you to the hospital straight," Mum says as my dad and Josh rush off to get the car and I feel the pains intensify.

"But it's too early, the baby can't come yet, it's too early," I say in horror at the prospect of the baby being premature.

"Autumn, your practically full term now and it is fine to be a bit early. Everything is fully formed so you don't need to worry about that." She holds my hand as I feel another pain.

"But I didn't have any contractions. How can my waters have broken?" I say as Dad brings the car around and Josh and Mum help me in.

"You probably didn't realise what they were, it's not always easy to tell at first. It doesn't matter now. Here, sit on this newspaper so you don't spoil your Dad's car," Mum says, reverting to her clean freak ways.

Josh sits with me in the back as my mother calls ahead to the hospital and notifies them of my arrival. As soon as we arrive, Josh and I are whisked into the delivery suite where they find I am 7cm dilated already. In a little over two hours, I safely deliver our baby.

"Here you go, a beautiful baby girl," the nurse says as she places her on my chest and Josh and I look at her for the first time, the tears spilling from our eyes. Her little eyes look like slits, opening just slightly so we can see her pupils looking back at us.

"She's absolutely beautiful, Autumn, my two best girls and the light of my life." He takes her from me for a cuddle. Soon after, my parents meet their first granddaughter and although it wasn't planned quite this way, I feel happy that my little girl was born in the same hospital as me.

"What are you going to name her?" Mum asks

expectantly as she gently coos over her.

"We've decided on Aisling, it is Irish but not too hard for non-Irish people to pronounce or spell," I say as I take my daughter and hold her in my arms.

"That is a beautiful name, it's nice to have a name with an 'H' in it, don't ask me why it just looks classy," Mum says, continuing to coo at Aisling who sleeps quietly, ignoring all the fuss.

"Mum, it isn't spelt with an 'H', it is A-I-S," I say with a smile as I see Josh trying not to laugh.

"Well I still think it is a beautiful name for my beautiful granddaughter even without the 'H' in it," Mum says, distracted.

As Mum and Dad leave for the evening, I'm left with Josh as we rapidly learn how to take care of our baby girl and start our lives as a family of three.

"Just think, in only a couple of months, we'll be married, Autumn. Now Aisling is here safe and well, it's the thing I'm most looking forward to," Josh says affectionately.

"Me too. I can't wait to be your wife and with Aisling too, it just feels so perfect." I look over at Aisling sleeping in her cot and take a moment to rest before she wakes up.

Chapter 37

11 December 2020, Bridal Belle, Grafton Street, Dublin.

The material tightens as it's zipped up at the back and the buttons popped into place. A smile crosses my face as I look at the elegant tea length dress. It has a slight yellow hue with an overlay of delicately embroidered flowers and contrasting ribbon around the waist to add just the hint of warm wintery mauve. The veil is popped on with the crystal tiara and slipping on my heels, the look is complete. This is the dress that I will wear tomorrow to become the wife of Josh Bailey and I can't wait.

"What do you think?" The assistant asks as she fiddles with my tiara one last time.

"I think it's perfect and everything I'd hoped. I thought I wanted ivory but you were right about being slightly darker as it matches the wedding colours amazingly, it just ties everything together. I can't believe I'm actually getting married tomorrow." Nerves twist in my stomach.

"It looks fantastic on you and you'll make a beautiful bride. Josh is a very lucky man. Are you ready to show the others?" she asks, holding the curtain in anticipation.

"Absolutely." I smile as she pulls the curtain back and I walk out into the shop and stand in the middle of the room where my mother, Eleanor, Amelia, Casey and

Josh's mother all wait for me.

A silence descends. For a moment, no one says a thing but smiles appear on all their faces and they start to enthuse about what they see.

"Autumn, that's stunning, it's perfect, so you," Amelia says enthusiastically as my mother and Josh's mother take a photo.

"You're stunning, Autumn, Josh is going to be speechless when he sees you. Trust me, a mother knows these things," Josh's mum Mairead says as she claps her hands together in delight.

"You couldn't have chosen any better, my darling, it's the perfect dress for you. It's simple but not at all understated. It's stunning." Mum dabs a tissue to her eyes.

"I agree and love it, Autumn," Eleanor says.

I give a little twirl so they can see the back of it too.

"It's sensational, Autumn, I thought there was a chance we'd upstage you but no chance in that," Casey says cheekily, baby Theo in her lap.

As I take off my dress and it's packed away in its protective cover, I realise that this time tomorrow, I will be married. It feels so surreal and almost like a dream.

"Autumn love, do you want us to take Aisling for the night so you can rest up properly for tomorrow?" My mum asks kindly as I look over to my daughter sleeping soundly in Amelia's arms.

"Would you? That would be great, Mum. I can't tell you how nice it would be to have an evening to myself tonight," I say with a big smile as the lady in the shop drapes the wedding dress bag over my arm.

"I tell you what, I'll give you a lift home with your dress and we can pick up Aisling's stuff and I can drop you back to your hotel, Brenda?" Amelia offers.

"Are you sure, love? That's very kind of you, thank you so much." Mum puts her arm around Amelia and Aisling.

"You're so good to me, Amelia, what would I do without you?" I note the necklace she wears with Alfie's initial and feel proud of how far she has come in the past few months compared to when we met in St Stephen's Green.

"Well, what if I told you I'm fully intending on calling on your services when it's my wedding so it's only fair I help you out now," she says as she effortlessly transfers a sleeping Aisling to her pram.

"That's totally fine by me. Sure, after my wedding at least I'll have yours to look forward to," I say.

We leave the shop and drive to my house where I pack up Aisling's things and put the travel cot in Amelia's car, ready to take to Mum's hotel.

"Are you sure you don't want me to stay with you tonight, Autumn? Are you sure you want to be alone?" Amelia asks.

"Yes, I'm actually really looking forward to it. Come here tomorrow at 8.00 a.m. and let the wedding fun begin." I give her and my mum a big hug and lift a crying Aisling from her seat to soothe her cries and kiss her face before putting her back in her seat and waving them all goodbye.

Upon entering the house, I turn the TV on and see the news, which mentions our wedding day plans. The press are already camped outside Clontarf Castle which feels so bizarre. I listen to the report, a little bemused by it all.

"Clontarf Castle is the location for one of the most anticipated and talked about weddings Ireland has seen in a long time. *Phoenix Lives* lovebirds Josh Bailey and Autumn Sutherland will arrive here in only a few hours to say their vows and cement their relationship. But who can ever forget the other love of Josh's life, former co-star Mia O'Riordan, who only a few years ago looked poised to walk down the aisle to the same media frenzy witnessed now for Autumn?"

My heart lurches at the mention of Mia's name and as the camera pans, I see her face for the first time since she was sacked.

"So, Mia, as the one who got away, how does it feel to see your beau walk down the aisle with the woman who took your crown in the hearts and minds of the Irish public and media?" the reporter asks, unaware of the pain etching across Mia's face. I feel cross about how insensitive they are being.

"Who says that there will be a wedding at all and who says I will be the one who got away? Only a fool underestimates the underdog. When we fall, we rise stronger. Keep watching, you'll be pleased you did," Mia says with an eerie smile that makes the hairs stand up on my arms. Her eyes look glazed and cold as she stares down the camera lens. I turn it off and grab a glass of wine my phone suddenly rings and I see it's Josh.

"Hey Autumn, so are you all set for tomorrow?" Josh asks happily.

"Yes, I've picked up my dress, which looks fabulous. I just can't wait for you to see it. Mum has taken Aisling, so I have the whole evening to pamper myself and get a good night's sleep."

"Are you sure I can't come over and see you tonight? I'd love nothing more than to spend the evening before our wedding together. Superstitions are stupid anyway," Josh pleads.

"No, I'm a very traditional and don't want you seeing me before the big day. Besides, it'll make me miss you more. Did you happen to see the news tonight?" I ask.

"No, why, did I miss something?" Josh asks noting the change in my voice.

"They did a report of the wedding. They are literally camped out and who should they interview but Mia. I won't deny it did shock me, I wasn't expecting it," I say honestly.

"Oh, for God's sake, I should have known she'd have jumped at the chance. Look, don't let it worry you. It's all in the past now," Josh says reassuringly.

"I actually felt quite sorry for her but then she opened her mouth and was just like she always was so that's as far as my sympathy went. It just feels hard to know that she'll always be in the background," I say sadly.

"Not if you don't think about it. Anyway, are you going to be in all evening as I have something I'm sending over to you but it's a surprise," Josh says.

"Yes, I'm in for the night now so I look forward to receiving it, I'll text you when I have it."

"Hopefully it won't be too late, just waiting on my brother to call me so I can tell him he's running an errand."

"Well, I'll probably not be in bed before 11 p.m. so you've got time. I'm going to have a bath so I'll text you later." I say my goodbyes to Josh and go upstairs to start relaxing ahead of my wedding tomorrow.

Chapter 38

Mia's Perspective - 11 December 2020 – 10 p.m. – Dublin

I wait in the car on the darkened street, I see him through the window and for a while I watch him. Trying to gauge his mood, whether he's missing me as much as I suspect he does. I think back over the years we spent together, how he only went back to Autumn when I was no longer an option. And as I slick my red lipstick across my lips, spray his favourite perfume, I feel confident I can stop this marriage in its tracks. I look at myself one last time, a smile crossing my lips as I think about Autumn's face tomorrow when he stands her up at the altar, publicly humiliated and heartbroken.

Leaving the car, I saunter over to the familiar aspect and feel a surge of happiness as I ascend the steps of the smart Georgian house, knocking the door loudly and awaiting his answer.

"Thank goodness, I didn't think…" Josh stops as he sees me at the door, his mouth agape. My blonde hair shimmers in the moonlight, my skin-tight black dress showing every inch of where his hands have been so many times.

"Good evening, Josh, miss me?" I say with a smile as I walk into the house and take a seat on the sofa.

"Mia, what are you doing here? I thought it was my brother, I don't have time for this." He sounds impatient.

"Drop the attitude, Josh, I'm here to do you a favour," I say, my tone becoming agitated at his lack of respect for the sacrifice I am making to save him from the biggest mistake of his life.

"There isn't anything you can do for me, Mia, except leave and don't come back. I'm getting married tomorrow." He continues to hold the door open for me.

I laugh as I get up from the sofa, walk over to him and plant a kiss on his face, moving my hand downward but he pulls back angrily, pushing my hand away.

"Look, Josh, we both know you don't want to marry Autumn. I'm sorry if you thought I'd come back sooner for you but I'm here now, darling. We can both be the power couple we always were together." I bite the corner of my lip and raise my foot slowly up his leg.

"What are you talking about, Mia, did you hear I've had a baby with Autumn? Do you not understand that I chose her, not you?" The words sting as the anger boils deep within me. I swallow a couple of times as my throat begins to dry, words failing me for a moment, but I keep my calm on the exterior at least. My eyes fall to a big bouquet of red roses by the door.

"Who are the roses for?" I ask.

"Autumn, I'm sending them over with my brother before the wedding." He eyes me suspiciously and all of a sudden, an idea formulates in my mind.

"Ok Josh, I'll come clean with you. I wasn't sure you were serious about Autumn so I wanted to check. She deserves to be happy after everything." I walk to the door as if I'm about to leave. Before I cross the threshold, I stop and turn to him and say, "I just wish I had the chance to apologise. How I treated her is my biggest regret." I lower my head, a small tear trickling down my cheek.

"I appreciate that, Mia, but you must understand this is a really bad time with the wedding and everything."

"Then why don't I take the flowers? You don't have to wait for your brother and I can have the chance to make amends with Autumn so you can have a complete fresh start tomorrow," I say as his face softens and he looks to the flowers and back at me as I gently dab my eyes with a tissue.

"I don't know, Mia, I think it's best to wait for my brother."

"I understand, Josh, but just think of it from Autumn's perspective, how much more she would enjoy the day having the opportunity to resolve things once and for all." I start to feel this won't work but I keep my composure

"Fine, but if you are planning to take the roses and deprive Autumn of receiving them then I will make sure I blacklist your name with every media outlet in the whole of Ireland," Josh says sternly as he hands over the roses and writes her address on a piece of paper before giving it to me.

"I give you my word, Josh, these flowers will reach Autumn and I will not deprive her of this gift from you. I swear it on my life, Josh. It's the first day of the rest of your life and who knows what it'll bring."

I make my way to Autumn's house, punching her address into the sat nav.

I arrive less than twenty minutes later to the pretty beachfront house. I see the warm light illuminating the windows, emitting a calming orange glow that softens

everything it touches. In the upstairs window, I see
Autumn trying on her wedding dress and as I look down
at the roses in the footwell of my car, this seems the
perfect time to deliver them.

Walking up to the door, I knock loudly and quickly
hear the scurrying of Autumn's feet as she makes her way
to the door.

"Hi, Tom." She flings open the door, still in her
wedding dress. Her face drops when she sees me.

"Look, Autumn, I just want to apologise to you, bury
the hatchet between us so you can marry Josh tomorrow
with a completely clean slate," I say sincerely as I hold out
the roses towards her.

"What's with the flowers?" Autumn replies, her face
looking at me suspiciously much like Josh had earlier.

"They're not from me, they're from Josh. His brother
was meant to bring them round but he couldn't get hold
of him so I offered," I say warmly.

"He let you bring these round to me, the night before
my wedding?" she says angrily.

"I wouldn't say he let me as such, more I persuaded
him because it's really important to me to apologise. I
know how I've acted and it can't go any further than
tonight. It has to end here once and for all."

Autumn looks down at the roses with a smile that
makes my stomach churn. "Why were you at Josh's
anyway?"

"I wanted to apologise to him too, I did wrong by you
both and it was important for me to make amends. I can't
change what I've done but I can change the future."

I notice a slight smile creep across her lips.

"So, can I come inside? It's pretty cold out here and

I don't want you to get that dress dirty. Let's talk and resolve everything so you walk down the aisle with a clean slate and no baggage from your past." I place my hand gently across her arm to highlight my sincerity.

"Fine, you can make us a drink in the kitchen and I'll get out of this dress and we can talk. It can't be long though as I need to go to bed early to be fresh for tomorrow."

"Absolutely, you go up and change," I say as she rushes to change.

I close the door, locking it behind me as I take the roses into the kitchen and go through the kitchen cupboards to find what it is I'm looking for.

I silently ascend the stairs, peeping in to the front bedroom to see Autumn with her back to me in front of the mirror as she tries to unfasten her dress but it seems to have got stuck. I listen for a moment as she huffs and puffs before I enter the room and see her jump as she sees my reflection in the mirror.

"Do you need a hand, Autumn?" I say softly as she sighs heavily before she responds.

"Yes, please, my zip is stuck, I just wanted to try it on one last time before the wedding."

I step forward until I am directly behind her before I reply, "I'd love to but my hands are full." I pull a knife from behind my back and place the tip gently on her back. I see her face fall as she feels the point of the knife against her skin, the terror in her eyes making me smile.

"This was a trap, wasn't it? I should never have believed you." The tears threaten to spill down her face.

"No, that was just to get you to let me through the door. As I said on the doorstep, Autumn, I can't change the past but I can change the future and this has to end here tonight once and for all. Can you guess what the ending I have in mind is?" I press the knife a little harder against her skin, a trickle of blood escaping from her skin.

"You're insane, Mia, if you think you'd ever get away with this. I told Josh I would text him when I got the flowers and when he hasn't heard from me, he'll come looking for me. This will never work. How do you like jail?"

Her defiance aggravates me. I take the knife from her back and throw her onto the bed.

"You ruined my life, you took everything away from me because you were a jealous, conniving cow. Did you think you would get away with it? If Josh is likely to be here, I'd better make this quick." I lunge towards her.

She leaps onto the bed, crying out, "No!" as I step back laughing at the fear etching itself all over her face.

"Mia, let's stop this now. You're not a murderer, you're a good person who fell onto hard times and I can help you. Just don't do this," she pleads frantically.

"Am I though, Autumn? You know nothing about me. Well, let me tell you, Autumn, so you know exactly what you're dealing with here," I say as I think where to begin.

"Yes, tell me about your life. I'd be…"

I pull the knife to my lips to stop her talking as I resume.

"It won't surprise you I was a pretty child. Even as a baby, my father said I had a face that took his breath away. It was his dream that I would go into showbusiness and become a famous actress. This infuriated my mother and she kicked him out and refused to let him see me. When I turned thirteen, she told me I needed to start earning my keep to stay living under her roof and that's when the men starting coming around." I see Autumn's eyes widen with horror but she stays silent.

"When I told her I didn't like it, she slapped me and told me I was a disappointment and that if I didn't keep my mouth shut, she'd tell my father what a whore I was. I dreamt for years that my father would come to save me but he never did and that's when I realised I needed to save myself. When I turned sixteen, I left home and I've never been back. I got everything I wanted until you came along." I turn my eyes back on Autumn, the knife trained on her.

"Mia, I'm so sorry. I had no idea you were abused by your mother. The way you talked about your father, I thought you had a happy childhood," Autumn says sadly.

"My father is my hero but my mother took pleasure in cruelty and unfortunately for you, the apple didn't fall so far away from the tree so don't go thinking this is anything but a choice."

I sit next to Autumn, finding her fear rather exhilarating.

At that moment, Autumn grabs my hair and smashes my head against the wall. But as she grabs for the knife, I push it hard into her stomach. She looks at me in shock. Laying her down onto the bed, her laboured breathing starts to rattle, I go to the kitchen to retrieve the roses. Returning, I sit by Autumn's bed and gently stroke her hair, wiping a dribble of blood as it escapes her mouth.

"Don't worry, Autumn, I'll make sure you're still pretty for your wedding," I say before I inflict the final wound and her breathing stops. Carefully, I straighten her out, making sure her dress looks perfect before I place the roses in her hands. As I go to leave, I glance back one last time and think to myself that she really does look very beautiful tonight.

Chapter 39

Josh's Perspective – 12 December 2020 - The Wedding Day

I jolt awake, finding that I'd fallen asleep while waiting for Autumn to text me that she had received the roses. I click my phone to see no message and I feel suspicious that Mia did keep the roses from Autumn.

I go to my bedside cabinet and pull out a box. Luckily Mia had no idea the roses weren't the real gift and as I open it, I smile at the thought of Autumn's face when I awaken her on our wedding day with her "something new" for our nuptials. Quickly I get myself ready, check my watch and see it's 5.00 a.m. Before I know it, I'm out the door, on my way to wake Autumn up with a loving kiss.

Arriving at the house, I see that the lights are all on and smile that we are both up as early as each other on such a special day. But as I open the door, an eerie stillness hangs heavy around me and my heart begins to race. I quickly check all the rooms downstairs but find nothing untoward. I hesitate on the stair; my hands start to shake as I pray for Autumn to come breezing out of another room. This silence is deafening and a fear creeps over me as I ascend the stairs. I check in Aisling's room and true to Autumn's word, she is not there. Entering our room, I see her asleep on our bed and heave a sigh of relief as I go towards her.

"Autumn, you scared me, I…" But my words trail off as I get closer and see the grey pallor of her skin, her eyes fixed and staring. I touch her skin and it's like ice. I don't know why I didn't see it before, but in her hands are the roses I sent last night with Mia and suddenly everything falls clearly into place. That when I turned her down last night, she decided to take it out on the one person she could never win against, the only person I ever loved. I watch her for a moment lying there in her wedding dress and recall her excitement of me seeing her in it and I collapse onto the bed next to her, my head on her chest as I sob uncontrollably for the loss of my beloved Autumn. Holding her tightly in my arms, I kiss her face gently and realise I cannot live a single day without her, I think of Aisling and I pray she will one day forgive me for not being stronger.

"Autumn, I'm so sorry I couldn't save you. That the happiest day of our lives turned into our biggest tragedy but I promise I will avenge your death and our parting shall not be long my love. I will join you for our wedding night. I will never leave you." I give her one last kiss as I change my clothes and run to the car, driving the familiar roads until I'm at Mia's house. Ringing her bell, I take deep breaths, waiting for her to answer. She does so in her negligée, opening the door with a smile and opening her flimsy dressing gown to reveal how little she is wearing underneath.

"I was expecting you, see? I dressed for the occasion." She waits for my response, her eyes searching my face. I smile as I step towards her, placing my hand around her head as I kiss her passionately and I feel her melt in my arms as she throws her arms around me and sinks into the kiss.

"I knew you were lying last night, I knew you wanted me," she says with a breathless smile.

"Of course, you know me so well," I say with a wink, quickly adding, "I have a plan for us but we have to leave now." She scurries upstairs and I quietly slip into her bathroom and find where she keeps her drug stash. Slipping it into my pockets, I flush the toilet and wash my hands before meeting her downstairs as we leave Dublin behind. I look at the time and see it is 6.15 a.m. and breathe a sigh of relief that it should give us enough time to get mostly there before they start looking for us.

"Where are you taking me, Josh? It's all very exciting, like Bonnie and Clyde," Mia says with a smile as she leans over to stroke my face. I feel my insides flinch but I gently kiss her hand and gaze at her for a second before returning my eyes to the road.

"We'll need to stop off at some shops when we get to Cavan so that I can make you a nice dinner to celebrate our first night back together and then we can make up for lost time."

"That sounds nice, we can choose together." She rubs her hand down my leg.

"No, I have to go alone because if you were seen last night, they will be looking for you all over Ireland. We can't be discovered now, not when we're this close," I say genuinely as the leaden weight of determination rises within me to make sure Mia pays for what she did, not for me, but for Aisling as I fear she'll never be safe while Mia breathes.

"Ok my darling, I love how you're so protective over me, it's a side I've never seen before." Mia takes my hand in hers and I raise it to my lips for a gentle kiss.

"Of course, I'm protective, we've never found ourselves in a situation like this where you've needed my protection as much as you do now. But I've got you and you know you can trust me, right?" I say softly as I search her eyes deeply for any signs of doubt.

"I'd trust you with my life, Josh, I always have and I always will."

I smile with true sincerity and feel a surge of happiness that my plan seems to be working so far.

We arrive in Cavan in good time and I quickly park up at the nearest supermarket and look at the clock. It says 8.30 a.m. and my stomach churns knowing they must have found Autumn by now.

"Right, you stay here and I'm going in to get us what we need for dinner. We are so close, Mia. After dinner, we can book a sailing from Northern Ireland and then they will never be able to touch us, we'll be free." I feel reassured by the big smile that spreads across her face as she pulls me close for a big kiss.

"I'll reapply my makeup so I'm all gorgeous for when you return," she says as she pulls her bag onto her lap and I make my way into the supermarket, racking my brains for something to eat. I pick up a nice table cloth, candles, wine and dessert to play into the ruse of a celebratory meal together. Within fifteen minutes, I'm back at the car with the shopping and relieved to see Mia still sitting there and smiling at me when I get back in.

"What did you get?" she asks.

"It's a surprise, you don't want to spoil it, do you?" I

kiss her on the lips as her hands reach my face and we start the rest of the journey to Donegal to my holiday home.

"Oh Josh, it's so romantic we're going to Donegal again. Do you remember that amazing Valentine's we spent there? The hot tub sex was totally unforgettable." She bites her lower lip at the memory of it as she smiles at me, her eyes betraying the feelings she believes I am feeling right now.

"How could I forget, that was one of the best moments of my entire life and hopefully one we can re-enact tonight," I say.

Her face brightens into a happy smile. "I was hoping you would say that." She turns to look outside of her window at the changing landscape and the beautiful aspects flying past our window right now. My mind wanders to Autumn and how I would have loved to spend our holidays here together watching Aisling grow, crabbing in the summer and living the happy life I always dreamed we'd have. I throw the thought from my mind. I can't get upset, it'll blow everything. I have to be strong, just for a few more hours. I made a promise and I'm determined to keep it.

"Josh, you've always made me feel so safe, not since my daddy have I ever trusted anyone the way I trust you. Your loyalty is infinite. No matter what I do, you always love me." She speaks with sincerity and I find myself wondering if she feels any remorse for what she's done. But the calculated way she acted tells me that's it's unlikely she does.

"You can count on me, Mia, even more than your daddy and I'd never let your mother near you. I'll always protect you because I love you and I always have." I cup her hand in mine. Her eyes well with tears as we enter Donegal and find the secluded spot where my holiday home is located, with no other properties for miles around.

Later that evening

As I add some more logs to the fire, I feel the pipes and they are roasting hot to the touch. "Do you want me to run you a nice warm bath, Mia, while I finish cooking our dinner?" I ask, my heart racing as I see it is 6.45 p.m. and I know they must be looking for me now. A pang of guilt envelops me for what people must think and how it must look. While I've kept it in Mia's mind that they will be searching for her, at this stage they are likely to think it is me. It is true, I have no alibi other than Mia anyway.

"Yes, please darling, I can't believe how much you have pulled out the stops tonight and making your Gran's special lamb stew, you know that's my favourite when I'm not on my Macrobiotic diet." She kisses me and wraps her arms around me.

"Why do you think I chose it? I figured if there was ever a day you could forgo your macrobiotic diet, it was for our special celebration meal." I smile as I head into the bathroom and run the bath, feeling the pocket of my jeans to make sure that the drugs are still securely in my pocket and sigh with relief that they are. I add in the bubbles and a handful of petals from the flowers I bought earlier. I light tea candles all the way around the bath as I stop the taps and head back into the front room where Mia is reading her magazine.

"Come my darling, close your eyes." I lead her by the hand, turning off the bathroom light and when she opens her eyes she is delighted with what she sees.

"You put in petals! You know how much I love to be treated like an Egyptian goddess. This is amazing, thank you so much." She throws her arms around me and kisses me gently as I feel her pulse quicken.

"Will you undress me, darling?" she says as I kiss her and gently slip off her clothes until she is completely naked.

"I had better go and make sure the dinner doesn't burn, I'll come and get you when dinner is nearly ready. Take all the time and relax, ok darling?" I close the door behind me as she slips into the nice warm bath.

After listening at the door to make sure she's in the bath, I return to the kitchen and pull out a pen and paper from the bureau to write a letter explaining what has happened. The tears fill my eyes as I explain what I found when I went to surprise Autumn this morning with a gift for our wedding day. I also set out the arrangements we would like to be made for Aisling to ensure that she can have a happy and healthy life without us being able to be there for her. Slipping the letter into an envelope, I address it to my parents and put it back into the drawer of the bureau.

I jump as the timer for the cooker goes and I rush to see my stew perfectly done. I smile at how pleased my Gran would be and how perfect each dumpling is. I taste it to confirm it is ready and dish it onto our plates. Hesitating for a moment, checking that Mia is still in the bath, I slip the drugs onto each plate being sure to carefully mix it up to avoid detection. I feel a pang of fear as I realise each bite we take will lead us to our death and for a moment, I wonder how it is possible we could have ended up here. I look at my favourite picture of Aisling and Autumn one final time and find the strength to carry out my plan. Mia has to die and with that action, I am condemned in life as much as I am in death. I really have no choice and I feel a surge of rage rise inside me for the way Mia has torn my family apart.

"Mia, dinner is ready," I shout as I go to the bathroom to find her coming out with her towel wrapped around herself.

"Thanks, darling, I'll just slip into something more comfortable and be right out." She heads into the bedroom and emerges with her negligee and a new whiff of perfume.

I set the stew down on the table along with fresh bread and pour the wine. Mia takes a taste of the stew.

"Oh my God, Josh, this is even better than I remember, it's beautiful. Thank you so much darling, I'm starving." She eagerly tucks into the food. When it is all eaten, she sits back as she reaches for her wine.

"I'm glad you enjoyed it, Mia, because it'll be your last."

Her eyes grow wide as she looks at my stony face. I continue, "I have only ever loved Autumn and when I went to wake her this morning, I found her dead. I knew it was what you and I vowed to avenge her death. I brought you here to kill you, Mia."

Her face drops in horror. "How could you?" is all she can utter before she drops dead, her head falling onto her plate.

I leave my dinner and go to the bureau and place my

letter in a more prominent position. I see it is nearly 7.30
p.m. as I eat my final meal on the sofa before placing
the plate beside me. I lay down upon my bed and wait
peacefully to join my beloved on what should have been
our wedding day.

Chapter 40

11 December 2025, Devon

The sun burns brightly in the crisp cold air on the morning that marks the fifth anniversary of my murder. My little girl is happy and healthy and while she is too young to have any real memories of me or Josh, her guardians have our photo by her bedside.

Each morning, she bounds happily to wake up the only parents she has ever known. She is the centre of their world and that makes us truly happy.

"Mummy, Daddy, wake up, time for cuddles," she says as she bounds into the middle of them with her favourite elephant teddy we bought her as a baby.

"Aisling, it's 6.30 a.m., I'm sure it's Daddy's turn to get up with you this time?" Amelia says with a smile as she looks into the face of the little girl who healed her heart.

"For my little princess, anything, Daddy will make you the best breakfast in the world," Cian says as he scoops Aisling up in his arms and carries her down the stairs to the kitchen.

As Amelia pulls herself out of bed, a tear rolls down her face. She touches the friendship bracelet we bought all those years ago when we first met, opening the special little bag in which she keeps the other one ready to give

Aisling when she is old enough.

"Oh Autumn, how I wish you were still here. How can I ever repay you for giving me the family I could never have? Each day it's like you come back to me a little more." The tears cascade down her cheeks as the memory of that fateful day, five years ago, replays in her mind. The day she discovered my dead body lying in my wedding dress with the roses in my hand and the note Josh had sent with them. The anger she felt at that moment, the confusion when he went missing without a trace along with Mia. Those long hours were too much to bear, wondering if he could really have done something like this.

It was just after midnight on 13 December 2020 when officers forced their way into the holiday home of Josh, finding two more bodies. It seemed his name couldn't be any more blackened until the discovery of the letter which changed everything. It read:

"This is a true and faithful account of the events that led to the tragic death of my beloved Autumn and the subsequent deaths of myself and Mia. They are all linked but not in the way you think." The letter went on to describe the events as they happened but the part that has never left Amelia is the part that said this:

"With my death, our beloved Aisling is left an orphan at the very start of her life. I know I speak on behalf of Autumn when I say, it is our dearest wish for Aisling to have a family of her own, where she is cherished, adored and loved like one of their own. Therefore, it is our express wish for Amelia and Cian to have full custody of Aisling because in them we know that Aisling would never want for anything and she would complete their family in the same way she completed ours."

There has always been an element of guilt within Amelia that her biggest dream came from our greatest tragedy but life works in strange ways sometimes.

"Come on, Aisling, let's get your hair all pretty, shall we?" Once Aisling is ready, they leave the house and drive the short distance to where our ashes are buried. You see, upon our cremation, Josh's ashes were mixed with mine and split between the two families so that each had a plot to remember us by.

As we arrive, Aisling runs up to her grandparents who are waiting for her at the gates. Also there is Eleanor, Casey, Darryl, Theo, and their youngest, Jessica. Keira and George are talking to Maggie who is now in a wheelchair as her health continues to fail but each year she comes to mark the anniversary of our death.

Aisling has picked pink flowers, as this is currently her favourite colour, and she places them on our grave. As the others come forward, they also lay flowers on our grave, shedding tears at the memories we made over the years. They finish by saying a simple prayer. Aisling closes her eye but makes sure she peeps out of one to be sure she isn't missing anything.

"What now, Aisling?" Amelia asks cheerfully to disguise her cracking voice.

"The beach," Aisling says happily. She jumps up and down before running to hold Theo's hand and they skip down the path together.

Seaton Beach, a short drive later

As Maggie is taken out of the car and gently put into her wheelchair, she grips her basket for dear life. My closest family and friends continue to the beach. My father carries Maggie's chair while Cian carries Maggie to the shore line. Once there, Maggie offers each person a handful of red rose petals and just like the first time I met her on that cold beach on that icy but sunny winter's day, they all throw the petals into the ocean and watch, just like I did all those years ago, as the wind whips them around before dragging them out across the ocean. The sky on this day, the fifth anniversary of my death, is as clear as the day I met Maggie and the red petals streak the sky in just the same way. For a second, I feel that I am with them, and that there is no distance at all between us.

However, as we draw this story to a close, let me tell you what became of the other people you've come to know in this story. Eleanor became a Hollywood actress, leaving behind her beloved Dublin as Darryl had and finding fame in LA where she also found love and settled down with an American football star. They went on to have three children, two boys and a girl. Darryl and Casey also moved to LA and the families became close; it helped Casey and Eleanor not to feel so lonely, being so far from home. Stella and Melissa became business partners, launching their own successful consultancy business. With all the long hours they put in, they also fell in love and sealed their love with a civil partnership two years ago. James moved to America where he went on to open a successful Irish bar. As for Megan, she never recovered fully from the guilt she felt from her part in what Mia did. She continued to blame herself for my death and as a way to cope turned to drugs and alcohol. She died of an overdose last year. As for Maggie, she died a few months after the fifth anniversary of my death and reunited with her beloved husband. Keira and Conor married and, not long after my death, packed in their jobs to travel the world, realising how precious life is. As for my parents, they became great friends with Josh's parents and the families kept in close touch and make trips to see each other regularly.

Now as I said to you in the beginning, my death may have happened in a moment but it came about because of a decision I made three years previously. Stuck in a rut, I'd been desperate to escape the fears that bound me so I decided to take a gamble and place my bet. Did I lose? Absolutely not, I succeeded in every way I ever hoped to.

It is often said that everything must come to an end and while my story is a tragic one, we are not the sum total of our death. It's the life in the middle that makes it remarkable and sometimes life requires us to take a chance and throw that little white ball and see where it lands. Invariably one day we all lose the bet and trust me, when that day comes, you will want to make sure you made the most of every day and all the things you thought were important will pale into insignificance. Ultimately it is those we love that mean the most at the end and death can never change that. So, in this roulette game we call life, I hedged my bet and hit the jackpot in more ways than one.

END

Katie Ward

Acknowledgements

I would like to extend a special thank you to all the people who worked alongside me and whose support and expertise has helped make my dream a reality. These special people are:

Jessica Powers for providing editorial advice
Emma Haines for bringing alive my visions with her amazing illustrations

Ollie Eskriett for taking all the above elements and turning it into an incredible reality.

Paula Seal for sharing her experience and knowledge of her acting career.

You have all been amazing and I've really enjoyed working with you all on this novel.

Printed in Great Britain
by Amazon

68740920R00160